'Superior fiction, with depth, auther

TLS

'A storming triumph . . . wonderful fight scenes, deft literary touches
and salty dialogue'

'H   wing

HARRY SIDEBOTTOM

The BURNING ROAD

ZAFFRE

First published in the UK in 2021
This edition published in 2022 by
ZAFFRE
An imprint of Bonnier Books UK
4th Floor, Victoria House, Bloomsbury Square, London WC1B 4DA
Owned by Bonnier Books
Sveavägen 56, Stockholm, Sweden

A CIP catalogue record for this book is
available from the British Library.

Paperback ISBN: 978-1-78576-969-6
Hardback ISBN: 978-1-78576-967-2
Trade paperback ISBN: 978-1-78576-968-9

Also available as an ebook

1 3 5 7 9 10 8 6 4 2

Typeset by IDSUK (Data Connection) Ltd
Printed and bound in Great Britain by Clays Ltd, Elcograf S.p.A.

Zaffre is an imprint of Bonnier Books UK
www.bonnierbooks.co.uk

Harry Sidebottom was brought up in racing stables in Newmarket where his father was a trainer. He took his Doctorate in Ancient History at Oxford University and has taught at various universities including Oxford. His career as a novelist began with his *Warrior of Rome* series.

To Lisa, with love

SICILY A.

Drepanum

Panormus

I. Centuripæ
II. Eryx
III. Himera
IV. Tauromenium   VII. Selinus
V. Lilybæum   VIII. Cape Pachynus
VI. Parthenicum   IX. Hybla

Agrigentum

Selinus

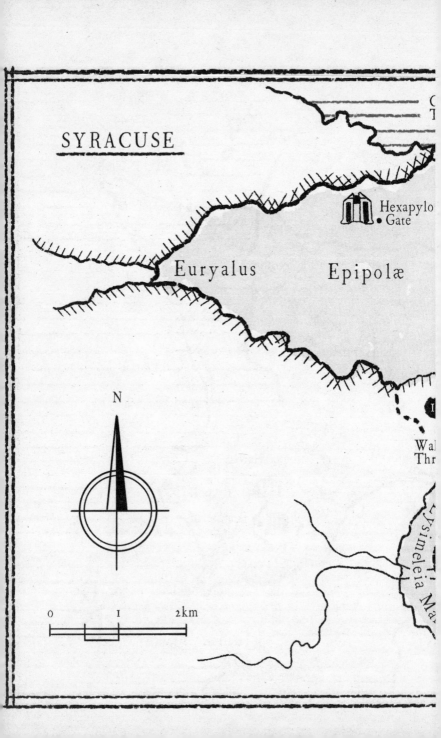

SYRACUSE

Euryalus

Epipolæ

Hexapylo
• Gate

I

Wal
Thr

Lysimeleia Ma

N

0   1   2km

Cove of
Trogilus

1. Neapolis
2. Achradina
3. Agora

Tower of
Galeagra

Tyche

Ampitheatre
Theatre

ll with
ree Gates

2

3

Lesser Harbour

Temple
of Apollo

Ortygia

Temple of
Athena

Spring of
Arethusa

Great Harbour

Plemmyrium

A man has as many enemies as he has slaves.
Roman proverb

(Seneca, *Letters*, 47.4)

Slavery is an institution of the common law of peoples by which a person is put into the ownership of someone else, contrary to the natural order.

The Digest of Justinian, 1.5

Men desire above all things to be free and say that freedom is the greatest of blessings, while slavery is the most shameful and wretched of states; and yet they have no knowledge of the essential nature of this slavery and this freedom of which they speak.

Dio Chrysostom, *Oration*, 14.1

PROLOGUE

REVENGE WAS SWEET. NOT COLD, but hot and red. The first taste had been good, but he wanted more – so very much more. Above all, he wanted freedom. And, now he had a sword in his hand, there was no numbering of those he would kill to win freedom.

Waiting in the warm darkness of the Sicilian night, Crocus thought of five long years of slavery. Five years since the Alamanni had been defeated at the battle outside Milan: five bitter years since he had been enslaved by the Romans. They had brought him to this island, chained with the other tribesmen in the stinking hold of a ship. At the docks, one by one, they had been forced to stand naked on the block. At first his owner, a man called Bicon, set him to labour in the fields. Endless days under a sun hotter than anything imagined in his homelands north of the Rhine. When he had tried to run, they had branded him, like a beast. F for *Fugitivus*, the Latin for 'runaway'. His forehead was still raw, reeking of burnt flesh, when they shaved his long hair – the pride of any northern warrior – and threw him into the mill.

Three years with the other slaves in the mill. Feet shackled, the scars of old beatings showing through their rags, round and round they trudged, turning the terrible weight of the millstone, doing the drudgery of a mule or donkey.

The dust ingrained in their skin, complexions sallow from confinement, their eyes were so inflamed they could barely see. Not all had survived those three years. Those who had died had been replaced. Four of the newcomers had been Alamanni shepherds accused of theft. Not one – Alamanni or otherwise – had been released.

Earlier that evening, retribution had come to the mill. In the confusion Crocus had strangled the first overseer with his chains. Taking the man's sword, he had cut down two more. Their bright red blood splattered across the white flour. The memory brought nothing but pleasure.

'Soter is waiting,' a voice said in the darkness. 'It is time to go.'

They went quietly up the steep path to the town of Eryx. There were forty of them: the dozen from the mill, some herdsmen from the surrounding hills, the rest freed from a nearby villa. Half were fellow Alamanni, the others down-trodden and broken slaves from the empire. The latter were *nothing*, men of no account. Yet all had some form of weapon, if only a rustic scythe or pitchfork.

Of course it would not have been possible without Soter, the *Saviour*. Crocus had not recognised him at first when Soter had been condemned to the mill. There were many men with long white hair who had lost an eye. It was when he talked in the darkness, in their brief hours of rest, that realisation had begun to dawn. Soter spoke in tongues, in all languages. He talked to each chained man in the language of his birth – in Latin and Greek, the incomprehensible jabber of the distant East, and to Crocus in the language of the forests of *Germania*. His pronunciation was strange to Crocus, like that of one who had long moved among foreigners. But the meaning of what he said was clear. He spoke dangerous and wonderful words of insurrection and courage, of dignity and honour. He painted a picture of a new dawn, of a golden age born in savagery and carnage, of the painful rebirth of freedom.

In the dead of night, shadowy figures came and whispered to Soter through the bars of the window: the herdsmen were coming; the slaves at the villa were ready; the time was close at hand. Soon those in the mill were ready to risk anything.

And then, in that squalid prison, Soter had worked wonders. He stood and, at the click of his fingers, his chains fell to the ground. He picked them up, and again they snapped closed round his wrists and ankles. When he prophesied, his breathing became hoarse, his voice seemed to come from far away, and in the darkness flames seemed to flicker from his mouth.

At those moments the slaves from the empire believed that the goddess of love came down from her temple in Eryx and possessed him. They thought he was a Syrian, and they called him *Epaphroditus*, the beloved of Aphrodite. But Crocus knew better. It had long pleased the Lord of the Gallows to wander disguised among mortal men. The Hooded One could take any shape or condition, no matter how lowly. One summer he had done the work of nine thralls to gain the mead of poetry. Crocus knew he was in the presence of Woden the Allfather, the king of the gods of the North.

At the top of the hill the gates of the town stood open. Soter was standing in their shadow. He led them through the empty streets. Behind shuttered windows the inhabitants slept, unsuspecting. The tall roof of the temple of Aphrodite loomed over their progress. Not one guard dog barked.

They arrived at the barracks. Inside slumbered the only soldiers on the whole island. A ceremonial troop selected from the noblest youths of Sicily to guard the temple of Aphrodite – the goddess who had betrayed them.

Crocus felt the old tension that cramped his muscles, and clutched at his chest, before battle. At Milan he had stepped forward from the ranks, and danced himself into a frenzy, had drawn down from the gods the ferocity of a wolf. Tonight there was no need. The Allfather himself was here with them.

The outer door was unlocked. In their complacency, the well-born youths had no thought of danger. The gatekeeper snored in his lodge. With a deft motion, as if offering sacrifice, Soter severed his throat.

Crocus followed Soter across the moon-washed courtyard. Outside the barracks, Soter paused, and spoke to his disciples.

'They are asleep and unarmed. Show no mercy. They have none for you.'

A low grumble of hatred showed the exhortation was unnecessary.

Crocus was first through the door. A long dormitory, at least fifty beds. Figures under blankets stirring at the noise of the intrusion. A door at the far end that led to the other dormitories. Crocus ran the length of the room. The first screams rang out behind him.

At the far end of the next chamber a couple of youths, alarmed by the outcry in the other room, were out of bed. They did not move when they saw Crocus coming. The surprise was too great. It was beyond comprehension. They were stock-still, not believing their senses, when Crocus cut them both down.

A staircase: the other two dormitories were on the floor above. Here the sleepers had been roused by the commotion. Half a dozen youths were snatching weapons from where they were piled in the centre of the chamber.

They turned to face Crocus and the warriors at his back. The corridor between the bunks was wide enough for two men shoulder to shoulder. Crocus feinted at the one to his right. As that youth leapt back, Crocus dropped to one knee, and cut open the left thigh of the other.

Rising, Crocus aimed a backhanded slash at the one recovering his balance. It missed. The blade Crocus had taken was not the long sword with which he had always fought, but some short Roman weapon. Another Alamann chopped the youth down.

Turning, Crocus batted away a feeble thrust, stepped inside his new opponent's guard, and punched the tip of the sword into his stomach. As the memory in his muscles took over, part of Crocus' mind noted this old-fashioned Roman sword was good for thrusting.

After that, it was just a massacre.

Back outside Crocus felt no fatigue, just pure elation.

Soter raised his bloodstained hands to the night sky.

'Tonight you struck the first blow for freedom. By dawn the city will be ours. In days the island will be in flames. In every town and village, in every farm and villa, the oppressed long to cast off their chains. We are not alone. The hour has come – vengeance and freedom!'

Vengeance and freedom!

CHAPTER ONE

AD 265, 8 November

A DARK LINE LOW ON THE HORIZON.

The merchantman was one day out of Ostia, the port of Rome, and bound for Sicily. Heeling slightly, with the light westerly wind steady on her beam, the vessel sailed sweetly, cresting the gentle swell in sunshine and spray.

The voyage had started well, but Ballista was worried by the strip of darkness behind the wind. It was five days before the Ides of November, only two days before the seas were closed for the winter. The *Fortuna Redux* had been the last ship leaving for Tauromenium. Now he was far from sure that her name would prove an omen of a fortunate return home.

Despite the lateness in the sailing season, the other passengers lounging around the deck appeared unconcerned. They were a disparate collection: a troupe of mime actors, looking to make a living in the towns of the island over the winter; an equestrian returning to his landed estates, accompanied by a few slaves; and a couple of more suspicious-looking characters, who had not volunteered their reasons for travelling. Moralists often condemned the bad company found on ships.

Ballista looked over at his son. The boy was near the prow, talking politely to the equestrian landowner. No, he was not a boy anymore. This was his fourteenth winter. Next year he would take the toga of manhood. Isangrim was already tall, broad shouldered, his frame filling out. He was fair haired, favouring his northern father, not the dark Italian good looks of his mother. There was more than a hint of moustache on his upper lip, golden down on his cheeks. Nodding attentively, Isangrim did not give the horizon a glance. It might well be that he knew nothing of the sea.

It struck Ballista, with a pang of conscience, that he knew very little about his eldest son. The Roman elite held that a good life balanced *negotium*, service to the state, with *otium*, cultured leisure. No doubt they were right. But a friend of the emperor, a trusted military commander, did not have the luxury of choice. For the last ten years Ballista had served abroad, on the frontiers and often beyond. At times, between campaigns, he had been with his family in the East. But, apart from a brief reunion in Rome this spring, he had not seen them for the last three years. Isangrim had been ten; now he was thirteen. That was a long three years. So much about him had changed.

Still, everything could be put right. At long last the emperor had granted Ballista's request to retire into private life. After all those years of service, Gallienus owed him that, yet with an emperor such things were never certain. When they were safe in the villa at Tauromenium, Ballista could get to know not just Isangrim, but his younger son, Dernhelm, as well. In the peaceful island – the house of the sun, as it was known to its inhabitants – he could rebuild his life with their mother. His marriage with Julia had been better than many. Once it had been very good. But they had been apart too long. Now everything could be made right.

Looking back out to the east at the distant storm clouds, Ballista was glad that he had sent word, before he had reached

Rome, for the rest of his *familia* to travel ahead. They would have arrived in Tauromenium a month past. Isangrim would have gone with them, had it not been necessary to negotiate his removal from the imperial school on the Palatine. It had taken all the influence Ballista possessed, and a certain amount of bluster, to secure the release of the boy. In his time, Ballista had attended the school himself. No one was more aware of its unspoken function. The emperor hoped to secure the never certain loyalty of important men: his own generals and governors within the empire, and client rulers beyond the frontier. Educating their sons in the palace helped cement that hope. There the boys could be watched, and were in his power. Afterwards, if their families remained free of suspicion, they might be promoted to high offices. The word *hostage* never needed to be uttered.

The storm was getting closer. The other passengers might be unaware, but Ballista was not the only one who had noticed. He had seen one of the deckhands put his thumb between his first two fingers, making the sign to avert evil. Not wanting the passengers alarmed, the captain had put an end to such behaviour with a quiet, sharp word. Ballista straightened up from leaning on the windward rail, and moved towards the stern. The pitch of the deck was easy, and he walked without trouble.

The captain was standing on the deck above the aft cabin, where the helmsman gripped the two steering oars. As Ballista climbed the steps, the captain, a short, powerful figure, greeted him with the deference due to a man who wore the gold ring of an equestrian – just one rung below a senator. Furthermore, Ballista was known to be a friend of the emperor. Yet the captain's eyes rested on the newcomer for just a moment before resuming their scanning of the ship and the sea and the sky. Only occasionally did he glance at the eastern horizon. Ballista admired his restraint in not drawing the attention of his passenger to the potential threat. For all his tact, it was evident that the captain did not welcome the intrusion of this barbarian-born imperial favourite.

'A storm coming?' Ballista spoke quietly, so his voice did not carry back down to the main deck. Out of politeness, he phrased his words as a question.

'Nothing of concern, *domine*.'

'I commanded warships in the East.'

Now the captain looked Ballista full in the face. He nodded, as one seaman to another.

'It will come on to blow in an hour or so. But the *Fortuna Redux* is a weatherly craft, my crew know their business, and we have plenty of sea room, all the way to Sardinia. As long as the wind does not shift into the north, we are well set.'

'She is heavily laden,' Ballista said.

The hold was full of amphorae of wine, carefully stowed and lashed down.

'Holds the sea better. She bounces around like a cork with no cargo, just her ballast.'

Ballista smiled to acknowledge the other's expertise.

'If you need an extra hand, I am at your command.'

'Thank you.'

Ballista turned to go.

'*Domine?*'

Ballista stopped.

'It might be best if you did not mention it to the rest of the passengers.'

'They are in good hands,' Ballista said. 'I would not dream of it.'

There was truth in the captain's words. The *Fortuna Redux* was a medium-sized vessel, about twenty-five feet across her beam, and less than a hundred from her prow to the rounded stern under her graceful sternpost, which was carved to resemble the head and neck of a goose. She was clinker-built, well founded, with a tall mainmast set centrally and a bowsprit jutting ahead. Her standing and running rigging was neat and cared for, and her crew had the almost languid efficiency of old hands. In rough weather, such a merchant round-ship was infinitely more seaworthy than a war galley. Given sea room, and well handled, she should swim in all but the worst of storms.

Ballista walked to the prow, and spoke a few words to the other equestrian. The landowner was civil, but reserved. His dignity was still offended by finding that he had to share the main cabin with Ballista and his son. No doubt, when he returned to his villa he would complain at length. What had the world come to that an emperor would award the gold ring of an equestrian to some petty chieftain born in the northern wilderness, would elevate him to the second rank in Roman society? It was a pretty pass when a barbarian considered himself too good to make his berth below the main deck with mime artists and other humble folk. Better if he bedded down with the baggage, or in the bilges.

Keeping such thoughts from his face, and duty done to formal manners, Ballista addressed his son.

'Isangrim.'

Hearing his name, there was a flash of anger in the boy's eyes.

'Although it is early' – in fact it was not past the fourth hour of daylight – 'we should eat.'

Too well brought up to remonstrate with his father in public, Isangrim bade farewell to the landowner, and followed.

The galley was situated below decks, just in front of the sternpost. Surprisingly roomy, it ran the width of the ship. Hatches admitted light, and provided ventilation. Every effort had been made to minimise the risk of fire. The hearth was a grid of iron bars set in clay, raised a couple of feet off a floor of tiles. The roof was also tiled. Nothing was more dangerous than fire on a wooden ship.

Ballista took a pitcher of water, and washed his hands. Then he found a skillet in one of the lockers. Prodding the hearth into life, he put some salt bacon on to fry.

'Would you find some of our bread? And some eggs?'

The utensils were shared. But passengers provided their own provisions.

Isangrim did as he was asked, but his expression was mulish.

'I still do not see why we did not bring some of the slaves to look after us. Even one of your barbarian bodyguards would have done.'

Ballista had sent the entire household ahead, leaving only two old retainers of Julia's family as caretakers of the house in Rome.

'You should be glad, the way Maximus and Tarchon cook. The other bodyguards, Rikiar and Grim, are even worse.'

Isangrim did not smile.

'A man needs to know how to cook.'

His son did not answer.

'Think of it like this,' Ballista continued. 'If a man cannot shift for himself, he becomes a slave to his own servants. It might be necessary in the field, if you do military service.'

'There is no chance of that, now you have taken me out of the Palatine school.' Isangrim sounded bitter.

'That is not true. When you are of age, if you wish, I will not stand in your way.'

'My prospects would have been better, if I had stayed.'

'We will see.'

Already this had become a bone of contention. They relapsed into silence.

As the bacon hissed and spat, Ballista noticed an increase in the roll of the ship. There was no point telling his son about the coming storm. He cracked the eggs into the pan. While they fried, he sliced open two rounds of yesterday's flatbread. When the food was cooked, Ballista broke the yolks of the eggs and slid them, with the bacon, into the pouches of bread. They ate standing up, in silence.

Returning to the deck, the aspect of the day had changed. The sun still shone, but fainter, and the first tattered clouds scudded across the sky. The wind was beginning to gust. The sail hung slack, then filled and cracked. The swell was higher, slapping against the side of the ship, lifting a mist of spray across the bulwarks. The other passengers, as if summoned by some unspoken covenant, had gathered around the mainmast. There they huddled – damp, penitent and anxious.

Ballista watched the captain take over the steering oars. Some orders were given, then the *Fortuna Redux* was brought on to a new course heading south-south-west. Without further commands, the deckhands squared the main yard a fraction, and hauled on the brails to trim the sail. The swell now on her quarter, she rode more comfortably, picking up speed.

The manoeuvre complete, the captain handed the oars back, and came down to address his human cargo.

'The wind is getting up. You might all be more comfortable in your berths.'

The two furtive travellers scuttled off. The mime actors, murmuring among themselves, trailed after.

'If you do not mind, I will stay on deck,' Ballista said.

'Of course.'

'I, too, will remain,' the equestrian announced. Clearly it was beneath his dignity to seek shelter while Ballista remained.

'If that is your decision.'

The captain looked as if he wished to say more – possibly something like *as long as you try not to fall overboard, and keep well out of the way* – but refrained.

Ballista turned to his son. 'You should go to the cabin. It is important to make sure none of the baggage shifts about or gets broken.'

Despite the face-saving instructions – Ballista stowed their belongings every morning – the boy went off with an ill grace. It could not be helped. Isangrim was no sailor, and he would be safer off the deck. At least for now.

Ballista went aft, and took up a position by the larboard of the two anchors either side of the stern. He braced a boot against one of the cork buoys of its coiled cable. There were another pair of anchors at the bow, and the sheet anchor – the *sacred* anchor, the last resort – was stored amidships. Whatever was to come, the *Fortuna Redux* was a reassuringly well-equipped vessel.

After a pause – to register that he moved of his own volition – the equestrian followed. It was a good spot. They had the rail to steady themselves, and would not get under the feet of the crew.

'You have made the crossing many times before?' Ballista, who had been watching the skiff, towed aft, bobbing in the wake, glanced over at the equestrian.

'And in far worse conditions.' For all his brave words, the man looked terrified.

A wall of darkness rolled inexorably towards them, trailing tendrils of rain.

'Put out the galley fire, extinguish all lamps, close the hatches and the cabin door.'

The voice of the captain rose above the singing of the rigging and the working of the hull, the hundreds of wooden planks and dowels grinding against each other. It would be unpleasant for Isangrim in the darkness of the lurching cabin, but far worse for those down in the hold.

The sun was swallowed and the first squall of rain slanted across the deck. Then the ship staggered as the storm hit. It was as if the *Fortuna Redux* had been punched by the fist of a giant. She heeled wildly, veered off course. Ballista caught the arm of the equestrian as he stumbled.

'Bring her round before the wind.'

Although the words of the captain were snatched away, the crew had been expecting them. His confidence was not misplaced. His men knew what they were about. With a lurch, the prow came round to the west.

'Haul the yard a third of the way down the mast. Brail up the centre of the sail.'

Once the wind was catching only the tips of the sail, and the pressure on the mast was lowered, the *Fortuna Redux* settled on her new track due west.

The rain, cold and heavy, raked the ship from sternpost to breakwater.

'I think I will retire, and get some rest.'

Without waiting for a reply, the equestrian set off. He had not gone three steps before the deck dropped from beneath his feet. Losing his balance, he began to half-run forward. Before he could fall, a crewman appeared out of nowhere and grabbed hold, before courteously escorting him away to the cabin.

At least he would be company for Isangrim.

Ballista looked out into the storm. In the new gloom of the day, great lines of waves were sweeping in, whitecaps curling on their crests. Yet now the *Fortuna Redux* was running before the storm, there was a regularity to her movements. Her stern lifted as she rode the front of a wave, then her prow, as she slid down the rear face. Again and again. Every third or fourth wave was taller, but the motion was the same.

Glancing up at the helm on the poop deck, Ballista saw the captain. His face shone with pleasure. Ballista realised that he was grinning himself – grinning like an idiot. Yes, there was an element of danger, but that was what made it so exhilarating. There was nothing quite like it.

They ran due west for the rest of the day, racing across the face of the waters, fleeing before the power of Eurus, god of the east wind. They were still running, reeling off the miles, when night fell.

The captain had dismissed half of his ten-man crew below. Having requested permission to leave the deck, Ballista went to the cabin. By the ambient light from the open door, he found a towel. Then, shutting the door, he stripped and dried himself in the pitch darkness. He felt his way quietly to his bedding, as if not to wake the equestrian or Isangrim, although he was certain they were not asleep. Settling down, he noted that the wind had backed a couple of degrees. Not too much to worry about yet. Not unless it backed all the way to the north. Then he was instantly asleep.

CHAPTER TWO

BALLISTA WOKE. NO TRANSITION BETWEEN SLEEP and full consciousness. It was still night. The *Fortuna Redux* was wallowing and rolling. The wind had dropped. Then the ship heeled horribly as the storm caught her again. Muffled orders were shouted aloft, bare feet thumped on the roof. Throwing off the blankets, Ballista carefully got to his feet, hands groping for his clothes.

'What is happening?' The equestrian sounded querulous with fear.

Ballista sensed Isangrim was awake, too.

'Stay here. I will go and find out.' He spoke to both of them.

Locating his clothes, Ballista struggled into his tunic. It was cold and damp, and clung to his body. His boots were also sodden. Shivering, he buckled his belt, then opened the door and went out, pulling it closed behind him.

The noise struck him like a slap. A cacophony of wind and water, shrieking rigging and squealing wood. He dragged the door shut and hung on to the handle, not trusting the purchase of his boots on the wildly tipping boards. Ahead in the blackness, out beyond the prow, the night was a chaos of white water. The wind had backed right round to the north, and raised a vicious cross sea. The ship twisted and reared and bucked like an unbroken horse.

'Bring the yard halfway down!' the captain roared from above by the helm.

All hands were on deck. They slipped and struggled across planks streaming with water. One lost his footing, went sliding across the deck until he collided with the starboard rail. He lay there for a moment, then doggedly crawled back to his allotted place. Inch by inch, they fought the recalcitrant winches and pulleys to lower the great spar of pine. It swayed and flexed, as if trying to tear itself free. Falling out of control, if its massive weight did not break the ship in half, it would overburden her superstructure, render her unmanageable. Dead in the water, the sea would do the rest.

'Belay there!' the captain bellowed.

The descent of the immense wooden beam was halted. The ropes made fast.

'Reef the sail to a couple of feet, just enough to give steerage way.'

Thank the gods, there was only the one mainsail. No need to go aloft. It was hard enough for the crew hauling the vertical brails from the slippery, plunging deck.

Once the following wind was catching the reduced canvas lower down the mast, the blades of the steering oars again bit the surface. Although still battered from rogue waves from first one flank then the other, the *Fortuna Redux* was under control. She began to plane the churning sea.

Holding on to the frame with one hand, Ballista reopened the door, and spoke into the dark cabin.

'The wind has changed direction, and the ship has altered course.' He spoke calmly, and wanted to add to Isangrim that there was nothing to worry about, but that would have been a lie. 'It might be rough, best stay inside.' Without waiting for a reply, he shut the door.

The steps up to the poop deck were slick and treacherous. Ballista took them cautiously. The captain, ashen-faced with lack of sleep, nodded a welcome.

'What latitude?'

The captain answered wordlessly by gesturing up at the overcast heavens. If the clouds had not parted during the night, and the stars had never become visible, there would have been no way of taking a reading, no way of fixing how far south they had travelled. As for longitude, it was always done by a dead reckoning. After the last day and night, it was anyone's guess how far they had been blown to the west. But it would not have been far enough for safety.

'How long until light?'

'Two, maybe three hours.'

They regarded each other. There was no need to speak. Ballista knew their thoughts were the same. *Will we strike the coast of Sicily before dawn?* Driven onto a lee shore in the darkness was the end for any ship, and most likely all aboard.

Clapping on to the rail, trying to roll with the agitated ship, Ballista gazed through the rain and spray. A cable was writhing in their wake, its pale cork floats winking in the gloom. The skiff was gone. It should have been lifted into the ship at the start of the blow. But recriminations were futile and unjustified. There was too much on any captain's mind in such circumstances. Ballista himself had not given it thought.

Yet there was a danger the trailing rope might foul the blades of the steering oars. With nothing to act as a rudder, the *Fortuna Redux* would turn beam on to the following sea, then she would be rolled over. Ballista set off down the steps. At their foot, he waited for the pitch of the deck, then crossed to the larboard rail. The air was full of water. Some waves half-breaking over the side. Clinging to the wales, he went hand over hand until he reached the stern. The cable was slimy, difficult to grip, reluctant to quit the embrace of the turbulent sea. Boots wedged against the bottom of the rail, his back against the sternpost, slowly Ballista dragged in the wretched stray rope inch by inch and coiled it around its stanchion. Finally it was done, and he tied it off. He rested, regathering his strength, embracing the gooseneck of the sternpost, like a slave seeking sanctuary, or the ruined votary of some debased cult.

Ballista pushed away the ill-omened thoughts. With infinite care – one false step and he would go sprawling, if the surging waves did not snatch him away – he retraced his route back to the helm.

The captain had the pumps double manned. The two men were staggering on the treadmill by the prow, their efforts turning the Archimedes screw hidden below the deck, pumping the water out of the bilges. It came out of the pipes in a fine flow, glimpsed for a moment, then lost in all the flying water of the storm. The work was exhausting. Already the first pair were being replaced.

'Thank you!' the captain bellowed in Ballista's ear. 'I should have seen to the rope, and the skiff beforehand.'

'You have enough concerns. You have kept us afloat.'

The man actually laughed. 'So far.'

The *Fortuna Redux* ploughed on to the south. The cross sea had died, but the gale had strengthened. It howled its mindless fury through the rigging, bending both mast and yard out of true. Mountainous waves bore down on her stern, their crests curling and breaking, their front slopes white avalanches of water. They lifted her stern high. In the depth of each trough her prow and bowsprit were plunged under, coming up streaming water. Blinding sheets of water flew across her deck. The scuppers were awash.

And through it all, through their fatigue and terror, the crew worked the ship in relays: manning the pumps; tightening the halyards; fighting the steering oars to keep her before the wind.

Ballista hung on to the railing, frozen hands like claws, blinking the rain out of his stinging eyes, his long, fair hair whipping around his face. He would have prayed, but there was no point. The gods of the Romans might answer them. Neptune, or the divine twins Castor and Pollux – they might be beseeched to bring aid to mariners, to calm the raging ocean. But not the hard gods of Ballista's childhood in the distant north. You may renounce them, but the gods of your youth never totally leave you. Even now Ballista felt Ran, the goddess of the sea, opening her pale eyes, spreading her drowning net. *Take me, spare the boy*, he thought. *Spare the boy.*

'Breakers! Dead ahead!'

At the helmsman's shout, the captain and Ballista leant forward, eyes straining to pierce the wild night.

At first, nothing but a jumble of darkness and water. Then there was something. A flash of white. Gone as soon as glimpsed. There it was again. This time quite distinct. A whole line of white water across their course. Impossible to judge the distance, but far too close. It stretched away out of sight on either side. In this tempest there was no chance of lying to, and no hope of steering around the coast of Sicily.

A dense curtain of rain hid the horrible sight.

'All hands!' the captain roared above the storm. 'First watch cast off the stern anchors, second watch ready with the brails!'

Ballista observed the men floundering to their duties. At the stern the foam of two splashes, dissipated instantly by the sea, and the cables were running out. The *Fortuna Redux* plunged on, no break in her progress. Then she tremored, slowed for a moment, as an anchor snagged.

'Ready with the brails!' the captain yelled.

But the anchor slipped, and the ship again forged ahead.

'Any moment now.'

With a terrible crack, and the screaming of a thousand tortured joints of wood, the *Fortuna Redux* juddered to a halt.

The impact forced Ballista and the captain down on their knees. Even as they toppled, the captain was shouting for the sail to be furled.

The mast itself was whipping fore and aft, threatening to spring free. The yard, vibrating with strain, was curved like a bow.

The men on the deck scrambled to their feet, and hauled on the brails with all their strength and weight. Inch by inch the sail rose.

'Put your backs into it! Before the mast comes down or it tears the anchor free!'

At last the sail was sheeted home. The gale now had nothing to catch aloft except the tightly furled canvas and the bare poles.

Ballista picked himself up with difficulty. Now the ship was stationary – held by one anchor or both? – her motion was far more violent. She tilted wildly, first stern then prow reaching up towards the sky.

'Break out the sacred anchor!' The captain turned to Ballista. 'All hands!'

Together they half-fell down the steps, and slithered amidships before the mast.

The sacred anchor was a monstrous thing. A lead collar held the wooden arms and shank together. The latter must have been eight feet long. The stock, also lead, projected at right angles to the arms, and was at least four feet. The gods alone knew how much it weighed.

'*Domine,*' one of the crewmen said to the captain, 'we will never be able to manage it on this pitching deck. If the sacred anchor is unlashed, it will punch through the bow or the stern, take us to the bottom with it.'

'No, we have no choice. It has to go overboard.' The captain seemed to be attempting to convince himself as much as the crew. 'We are on a lee shore, and the smaller anchors will not hold us long in this fierce blow.'

They all stood, soaked through and apprehensive.

The captain steeled himself to give the order.

'Everyone clap on. I will sever the bindings.'

There were nine of them. Every one of the ship's complement – except the captain and the helmsman – and Ballista. He took his stance holding one of the steel-tipped arms.

'Take her to the stern starboard of the helm.' From somewhere the captain had produced an axe. 'Ready?'

They mumbled an uncertain response.

'Brace!'

The axe swung. Already under immense strain, the rope bindings parted at the second strike.

'Hold!'

The anchor tried to slide aft, the steel tips of its arms gouging the woodwork. Grunting with effort, they got it under control before it ran the length of the deck and smashed into the cabin.

'Now lift!'

It was like trying to lift a wet, slippery sharp-edged boulder. The ship dived forward as a wave passed under her stern. The weight sent them staggering back towards the prow. One man was almost crushed against the capstan. Then the prow came up, and they tottered the other way.

'In time with the waves!'

Somehow they managed a few steps. But the next wave sent them sliding almost as far back again. Ballista's arms were already trembling with the effort, and his breath came in rasping gasps. His back was knotted with pain. For all their efforts, progress was agonisingly slow. Four or five short and laboured steps each time the stern dropped. A pace or two slithering back when it rose. Reeling like drunks, they gasped out their aching and uncertain journey towards the stern.

Then disaster. They had broken the back of the trek, were almost at the cabin. A cross wave took the ship on her quarter. Taken off guard, they careered sideways across the streaming deck. Their boots went out from under two of the crewmen. Losing their hold, they dropped the anchor. A high, agonised scream as the bar landed full on the legs of one of the sprawling sailors.

'Raise it up!' The captain grabbed the bar. 'Get the thing under control!'

Grunting with effort, they hefted the ghastly object.

The injured man was still screaming.

Unheeding, the rest left him. They got the anchor past the cabin. Desperate to put an end to this awful task, they began to rush, casual about their own safety.

'Steady, you bastards, steady!'

The captain unlatched, and hinged back, the gate in the rails. It was designed to let the sacred anchor pass. There was a groove below in the gunnels for its cable.

'Almost done. Don't get careless now.'

'For the gods' sake, get a move on,' a man panted next to Ballista.

'On the count of three – one, two, and throw!'

One last gut-wrenching effort, and the anchor was gone.

'Stand clear of the cable!'

The weary men, light-headed and stupid with relief, had been slow moving. Now they scrambled to get out of the way. The thick rope played out fast.

Ballista accompanied the captain to the wounded man. He was silent now, his eyes open, but unseeing. The white of the bone showed through his ruined legs. There was nothing to be done. The captain ordered him to be tied to a stanchion, out of the way. When they moved him, he started screaming again.

A lull in the rain showed the breakers. Perhaps a bowshot ahead. A hundred and fifty paces, no more than two hundred. The deep thunder of them was now audible above the storm. The fearful revelation seemed to drain all resolution from captain and crew.

The mast was creaking, sharp reports, each like a sapling breaking. Ballista put his hand on the backstay. It thrummed with tension, the note rising with each gust.

'We must chop down the mast.'

The captain shook his head. 'It would overturn us before we got it overboard.'

'We have to take that risk!' Ballista's voice was hoarse from shouting. 'While it stands, it will drag us from our anchorage.'

'The men do not have the heart for it anymore.' The captain spoke sadly in Ballista's ear. 'You can only ask so much.' Then he continued, more loudly. 'We are in the hands of the gods now. Get the other passengers up on deck.'

A crewman went below, and Ballista to the cabin.

The dark room smelt of vomit. The reek made Ballista's gorge rise. Isangrim and the equestrian were seated. The latter's tunic was stained. They were clinging on against the pitching of the ship.

'The captain wants everyone on deck.'

'What has happened?' Isangrim said. His voice was tight with control. Ballista felt a rush of admiration and love for the boy.

'We are anchored a bowshot offshore.'

'What shore?' the equestrian demanded.

'Sicily.'

'Then we are almost home.' The landowner beamed idiotically. 'The captain can beach the ship, and we are saved.'

'It is not that easy.'

'Nonsense.'

The equestrian bustled to his feet and lurched out of the door, calling for his slaves.

'How bad is it?' Isangrim said.

'Pretty bad,' Ballista replied.

The boy was already dressed. Ballista asked him if there were any small possessions that he wanted to keep with him.

Isangrim looked around, touched his bulla, the good luck amulet that hung around his neck, then said no.

Ballista checked the fittings on his belt: knife, coins and keys in a wallet, and a pouch containing flint and steel. He also gazed around the dark cabin. Odd not to take a sword, but that would be an encumbrance. At least he had sent his best sword home with the rest of the *familia*. There was nothing here that mattered – nothing except the boy.

Outside it was near dawn, but dark with the storm. The injured sailor was screaming again, harsh noises like an animal. If anything, the wind was gusting more strongly. Indistinct shapes stood around, apathetic or resigned, clinging to whatever handhold they could find. The apocalyptic scene evidently had silenced the false optimism of the equestrian. Amid the wild pitching of the tethered ship, Ballista felt a different movement. An almost imperceptible shifting.

'Come with me.'

He and Isangrim set off towards the stern. With each step the black water exploded into white foam around them, and Ballista was anxious for the boy. When eventually they got there, Isangrim clutched the gooseneck. Ballista, fighting for balance, cut two of the floats from the rope that had moored the skiff.

'Can you swim?'

'Yes,' Isangrim said.

'Well?'

'Quite well.'

'Take this. It will help.'

Ballista put one cork float down the neck of his own tunic, and tightened his belt. Then he held Isangrim steady as the boy did the same.

Isangrim peered over the stern into the teeth of the storm.

'Are we going to jump into that?'

'Only if we have to.'

As they made their tentative way back amidships, Ballista felt the ship once more shift forward. Only a little way, then again she juddered to a halt. In itself an insignificant movement, but enough for him to know that the stern anchors had pulled free. Now only the sacred anchor held the *Fortuna Redux* from her fate.

Back on the main deck, the bedraggled mime artists, male and female, were clinging to the mast. They chanted a prayer to some unlistening god. The equestrian had retreated to the cabin. Among the crew, all order had gone. They had broached the cargo. They huddled in twos and threes, in the lee of the cabin, and other parts that offered a modicum of shelter, guzzling from purloined amphorae. The wine was unmixed. Soon they would be insensible. That was their aim. Many of them would be unable to swim. The rest must have thought the ability would only prolong their suffering.

The captain stood forlorn up on the poop deck by the abandoned steering oars. In a warship, it was accepted that discipline collapsed if the vessel ran aground. Then orders meant nothing, and it was every man for himself. The *Fortuna Redux* was still afloat, but she was a merchantman. Her sailors had not sworn the military oath. They had greater freedom to give way to despair. Under the circumstances, it was hard to blame them.

Despite the storm, the light was gathering. Enough to see the breakers, about a hundred paces dead ahead. They were crashing with a malevolent and inhuman force on a shelving beach. Beyond loomed the dark shape of a cliff.

From the cabin came the sound of the equestrian berating his slaves, as if they were in some fashion responsible for the predicament.

'It is like the old joke!' Ballista shouted to Isangrim. 'A rich fool is caught in a storm. His slaves start lamenting, but he tells them to be happy. In his will they are all set free.'

The boy looked at his father as if he were insane.

The *Fortuna Redux* gave a great lurch forward. Inexorably she began to gather way. The force of the waves, and the pressure of the wind on the mast and spars and superstructure, had plucked the sacred anchor from the seabed. A hopeless keening rose from the mime artists.

Up above, the captain was wrestling with the steering oars, desperate to keep the ship from skewing across the sea. Better to run aground than to turn beam on and have her roll and be dashed to pieces in an instant.

No one went to help the captain. As their ship accelerated towards her doom, the crew remained lost in drunken despondency.

'Here!' Ballista and Isangrim were by the forestay. 'Latch on, and hold hard.'

Everyone standing went flying as the *Fortuna Redux* ran aground. The slippery rope was snatched from Ballista's hands. He went tumbling and sliding across the waterlogged deck. Isangrim was beside him. They both collided hard with the timbers of the forepeak.

'Get up, quick.' Ballista yanked the boy to his feet.

A deep grinding reverberated from beneath the hull. With every wave the *Fortuna Redux* was driven harder aground, about fifty paces from the breakers. She must have struck a crop of rock or an outlying sandbar. Now the remorseless sea would break her up, pound her into shattered lengths of useless timber.

The crew roused themselves into a parody of duty. With manic intensity, fuelled by the alcohol, they began to break up the flimsier fittings and hurl them overboard. Lockers, boards, the door of the cabin, even planks from the deck itself: anything that might float was tossed into the roiling sea.

'With me.'

Ballista ran to where the sailor whose legs were crushed was still lashed to a stanchion, forgotten by his messmates. He would die anyway, but somehow it was not right to leave him, bound and helpless, to drown. Ballista cut his bindings. The man, barely conscious, did not thank him.

Something heavy plunged onto the deck, not five paces from Ballista. A block from the standing rigging. As Ballista looked up, the rear stay snapped. Released from its unbearable strain, the thick rope whipped across the deck. It took a sailor full across the chest. One moment the man was there, the next he was gone into the tempest.

'Get down!'

Ballista tackled Isangrim to the deck. The mast was going by the board. The starboard shroud was snatched from its housing. Like the rear stay, the released energy sent it hissing through the air. Then the mast fell, landing across the larboard quarter. Its weight pushed the ship down on its beam end, the larboard rail underwater, the starboard up in the air. Even had the men been willing, there was no time to cut the mast free of the remaining entangling rigging. The ship would be gone before then.

'Starboard side!' Ballista yelled. 'Away from the mast!'

Together they climbed like monkeys, swarmed over the now almost horizontal rail.

No time for final, tender words.

'Jump!'

Ballista waited a heartbeat, to make sure the boy did not lose his nerve. Then he also jumped.

The water closed over him, black as Hades. He went down deep; his boots touched something firm. Then he was rising. But before he reached the glimmer of the surface, another wave sent him down again. Tumbling, no sense which way was up. His chest burning, tightening. Any moment he knew his body would force him to try to breathe. And there would be nothing but salt water, and he would drown.

Ballista broke the surface. He drew a shuddering breath, gazed around. There was debris everywhere. Then he saw the boy's head. He shouted, and something solid hit him with great force on the back of the head. He had just time to wonder if it was a part of the ship before the darkness welled up.

CHAPTER THREE

A CRUSHING PAIN ON HIS CHEST. Bearing down again and again; repeated and rhythmic and agonising.

Ballista retched.

Isangrim was pressing on his chest.

Rolling on his side, Ballista vomited. The salt water and bile was choking, burning his throat. He lay, gasping like a landed fish, then threw up again.

The boy sat back on his heels, relief lighting up his face.

'Are you all right?' Ballista's voice was little more than a croak.

'Fine.'

Isangrim looked surprised by the question. The young believe themselves immortal. Really bad things – death, disfigurement, drowning – happened to other people, to the old.

Ballista sat up. Gods below, his head hurt. Of course, something had hit him in the water. Gingerly he explored the back of his head. It was tender, the hair matted, but his hand did not come away covered in blood.

They were on the beach. The sun was out. A last few dark clouds racing overhead. The surf still pounded just paces away, but the storm had passed. There was wreckage strewn for a mile or more on the sand. Spars, planks, cordage, any number of amphorae, many intact: all that remained of the *Fortuna Redux*.

And there were bodies. Some still in the water, others scattered along the shore. A few of the latter were stirring. A couple away to the right were on their feet.

'Pass me one of those amphorae.' Ballista gestured.

Isangrim stood and retrieved it. Despite the ordeal, he moved with the vigour of youth.

Ballista's mouth was raw and dry. His knife was still on his belt, the wallet and pouch with the flint and steel, too. He unstoppered the amphora, sheathed the knife, and swilled out his mouth and spat. Then he drank a little of the strong, light wine. It caught in his throat; he spluttered, then drank a little more. It was sweet, a good Italian wine – maybe Alban or Sabine.

'Where are we?' Isangrim said.

Ballista looked around. At the back of the beach, about thirty paces away, was an unmade road. Beyond the country track was a terraced hillside of olive trees. Behind that rose a grey rock wall, its crest jagged and saw-toothed. The sun had risen over the cliff. The beach faced west.

'No idea.'

Ballista struggled to get up. His head was swimming, and he swayed slightly at another bout of nausea.

'Horsemen.'

Ballista followed Isangrim's gaze. A dozen or so riders coming down the road from the north. They rode at a canter, but with purpose. The leader was mounted on a magnificent chestnut. The horse would not have looked out of place in the Circus Maximus, or the stables of a nobleman. Yet its rider was clad in rough working clothes. The rest of the cavalcade were equally well mounted, and just as tattered in their own apparel. They were all armed. Swords on their hips.

'Run!'

Isangrim did not move. Ballista tugged at his son's arm.

'What is it?'

'No time. Just run!'

As they set off up the beach, the first horsemen wheeled down onto the sand. The two standing survivors did not have a chance to react. Perhaps they did not realise what was happening. Steel flashed in the sunshine. They were cut down where they stood.

Four riders had not turned off. They pressed on down the road, like sheepdogs aiming to cut off all the herd. They intended to let none of the shipwrecked travellers escape.

'Faster!'

The going was easy, the sand smooth and hard, battered down by the waves. Yet Ballista was struggling. He was short of breath, his head reeling, his limbs weak. The road seemed to get no closer.

Isangrim had pulled ahead, was at the top of the beach. He slowed, looking back at his father.

'Don't stop! Fast as you can!'

Isangrim turned and sprinted. Ballista laboured after him. When he reached the road, the foremost horseman was almost upon him – a looming and terrible presence in the corner of his eye. Ballista could hear the thunder of hooves, feel the drumming through the packed earth. Forcing his aching body, he ran across the road and into the trees.

The ground began to rise. It was soft and muddy after the storm. The olive trees were black with the rain. Ballista floundered upwards, swerving around the tree trunks, ducking under boughs. Great claggy clods of mud clung to his boots.

Behind he heard the horseman reining into the grove after him. Desperately Ballista drove himself up the slope. Ahead was a tall drystone terrace wall, Isangrim almost at its foot.

'Climb!'

Ballista slipped, went down on all fours. Clawing at the damp soil, he was up again in a moment, plunging uphill. Isangrim was scaling the wall, already near the top.

A glance back. The lead rider was less than a stone's throw behind. He was urging his mount on, but cautiously, wary of the bad footing and the overhanging branches.

At the terrace wall, Ballista almost gave up. He was a tall man, but the wall was high. Its stones were vertical, slick and crumbling. His strength was gone.

A triumphant yell from all too close over his shoulder, and Ballista was climbing. Fingers gouging at crevices, boots scrabbling, unheeding of ripped clothing, of torn nails and flesh, he inched upwards. Some toe- and footholds slipped. Once, he almost fell. This was taking too long. He could smell the hot, sweet smell of the horse. Every moment he expected the white agony as the sword bit into his exposed back.

He got an arm over the top, found a root on the upper terrace, swung himself over, and rolled away from the edge. Snorting, its harness jingling, the horse came to a halt. Turning, Ballista got to his feet, and drew his knife.

They looked into each other's faces. The wall was too high for the horse to jump. The rider was not a young man. Behind a fair beard, his face was dark, brown and leathery from long exposure to the elements. His hair hung to his shoulders in straight, dirty blond braids. On his forehead was a brand, the letter *F*, shockingly white against the tanned skin.

'Another time,' the horseman said. 'We will meet again.'

Ballista did not reply.

Not using the reins, the rider turned his mount with the pressure of his thighs and, sword held casually across the horns of his saddle, picked his path down through the trees. The way he handled both mount and weapon spoke of lengthy practice.

'What did he say?' Isangrim emerged from behind the bole of a gnarled, ancient olive.

Only then did it strike Ballista that the rider had not spoken in Latin or Greek, but the language of his own youth, the language of Germania beyond the Rhine.

'Nothing.'

'He said something.'

'Nothing of importance. Just a threat.'

The boy watched through the boughs of the trees.

Down on the beach the riders were busy in the pale sunshine. Dismounted, their horses efficiently hobbled, they went from one shipwrecked voyager to another. Methodically they cut the throats of those who showed any sign of life. Then they turned to plunder. No orders were given. It was as if they had done this, or its like, before. Some searched the corpses, others fished any objects that might be of value out of the surf. Those tasks completed, they gathered together the unbroken amphorae. The wine opened, they poured libations to the gods. Then they sat in a circle on the sand, toasted each other, and began to drink.

'Are you ready, Isangrim?'

Why did his father have to call him that? His mother, his friends, his teachers – everyone called him by his praenomen,

Marcus. He hated Isangrim, the ridiculous barbarian cognomen his father had given him.

'We need to move,' his father said.

'Where?'

'Anywhere but here.'

There was no going down to the road, so they had to climb the cliff. It was not that high, forty or fifty feet at most. Fallen boulders at its base made a slope, leaving no more than thirty feet of serious climbing. The rock face was limestone, fissured and ledged. But the surface was wet from last night's storm, and the stones looked loose and brittle. Marcus felt his heart sink. But he was not going to show any weakness in front of his father. The man might be almost a stranger, but he was still his father.

'We should get rid of the floats,' Ballista said.

Marcus had forgotten the cork buoy wedged inside his tunic. Following his father's lead, he stripped down to his breechclout. When they were almost naked, he noticed the extreme whiteness of his father's body. It was glimmeringly pale in the shade of the trees. All except for his face and neck, and forearms, which were tanned as dark as teak. The body was that of a man past the first run of youth, heavy around the middle, but still immensely powerful. The muscles and flesh of limbs and torso were seamed with a network of old scars.

It made Marcus very aware of his own body. He was also pale, but unmarked. He knew he was tall and well-built, his physique developed by hours of weapon training and hard work in the gymnasium on the Palatine. It was the body of a youth on the verge of manhood. Just the type that certain older men liked. It had drawn flattering but unwanted attention in the baths at Rome.

Struggling back into his clothes was unpleasant. Both trousers and tunic were sodden, stiff with salt and sand. Marcus shook them out, but it did little good. Lacing up his wet boots, he saw his father checking the fittings on his belt. Marcus did the same. Both knife and wallet were still in place. For all the good they would do. Although it was childish, Marcus touched the bulla that hung under his tunic. He was glad the storm had not taken the amulet.

His father stood and studied the cliff for a time. Then he led them off a little way to the right.

'How are you with heights?'

'Fine,' Marcus said.

His father grunted in reply. 'Follow me.'

At first they scrambled over the glacis of tumbled rocks. It demanded attention, but was not difficult. There were shrubs to help pull themselves up.

Ballista brought them to the base of the sheer face where a narrow chimney, opened by some old collapse, ran to the top. Inside the rocks were banded, offering hand and foot holds.

'Wait here,' Ballista said, 'but stand clear in case I dislodge any rocks. Watch where I put my hands and feet. When I am at the top, I will give you the word to start climbing.'

With no further ado, Ballista wriggled into the gap, and began his ascent. He had not gone far when something shifted under one of his boots, and the first shower of stones rattled down. Blinking the grit out of his eyes, Marcus hastily stepped to the side. After that, his father went more slowly.

In his youth, Ballista had won the mural crown for being the first man over an enemy wall. This, Marcus thought, would be as nothing to his father.

Soon Ballista was hauling himself over the edge. His legs, then his boots, vanished.

Marcus waited. If the stones could take the weight of his father, they could take his slighter frame. But what if they had been weakened by his father? Actually, he was scared of heights.

Ballista's head and shoulders reappeared, silhouetted against the bright sky.

'Up you come. Remember to use the same holds as me.'

Marcus was gripped with panic. In his anxiety, he had forgotten to pay any attention. He had no idea where his father had put his hands and feet. Too late now. He was not going to let himself down. Anyway, there was no choice. Slipping into the space, Marcus began to climb.

The rocks were slippery, friable under his fingertips, but he went carefully. At first it was easy enough. The fissure was not vertical, but ran at a slight angle. It was not much trickier than climbing a wet ladder. Then it went straight up. Marcus looked upwards. His father lying down, partly out over the drop. Not far, perhaps another twelve feet.

A stone gave way under Marcus' right hand. It went skittering down into the abyss. Wildly, he scrabbled for another grip. He felt one of his boots start to slip. Unsighted, face pressed against the rough limestone, his fingers groped for any crack or projection. The first he found came away in his hand. His own weight was trying to tear his left hand free. With a lurch of relief, he felt something solid to hand.

Spread-eagled in the fissure, he was safe for the moment. He glanced down. Jagged rocks that now seemed ridiculously far below. His muscles locked with fear. There was no way that he could move from this temporary refuge.

'Don't look down, Isangrim.'

That loathsome name again.

'Look at me.'

The boy looked up.

'It is not far.'

It was no great distance to his father's outstretched hand. But he could not move. His arms and legs were trembling from the strain. He shut his eyes.

'Just stay there. Keep calm.'

Something brushed the back of his right hand. Involuntarily, his eyes started open. A band of leather. His father's belt.

'Grab the belt. Wind it round your knuckles.'

It took all Marcus' willpower to release his hold on the rock. He snatched the belt, entwined his hand in it.

'Climb with your other hand. Keep a grip on the belt, and you will not fall.'

There was no way he could answer.

'Are you ready. It's just a few feet.'

Marcus' voice remained locked in his chest.

'I have got you, but you have to help.'

Marcus pulled on the belt, felt his father take the strain. Before he could think any more, before terror overwhelmed him, he set off. Half-climbing, half-dragged, he scrambled up the cliff. He felt the knee of his trousers tear, a stinging pain. Then a fist grab the scruff of his tunic, jerk him upwards. The grip released, then fastened on his belt. A mighty heave, and he was rolling over the edge.

They lay, side by side, panting.

Marcus went to stand up. His father put out a hand to restrain him.

'We are on the skyline. No need for the men on the beach to see us.'

Marcus looked back from where they had come. The sea was green and blue and purple under the sun. The men were still sitting in a circle on the beach. An amphora was going from hand to hand. An occasional snatch of song drifted up on the breeze. The same barbarian language the rider had spoken. They were a long way off, but still not far enough.

Together, Marcus and Ballista wormed backwards. When they were below the line of the ridge, they sat up. They were on a bare, slightly tilted shelf of rock. It ran for about thirty paces down to the treeline. At the reverse of the cliff the land sloped gently down to a broad, wooded valley. Further off, ranges of mountains notched the sky, ridge after ridge succeeding one another into the blue, misted centre of the island.

'How is your knee?'

Marcus pulled the torn material away. It smarted, but it was only a graze.

'Fine.'

'We will wash it when we find water.'

They sat for a moment, gathering their strength.

'If you are ready, we should go.'

They walked down into the trees. There were still autumn leaves clinging to the boughs of the oaks and chestnuts. It felt less exposed under their cover.

Ballista did not take them down to the valley bottom, where a road could be glimpsed through the trunks. Instead, he graded along the slope, heading roughly south-east. As they went it was necessary to duck under branches, avoid tripping over roots.

'We would make better time down there,' Marcus said.

Ballista stopped, head on one side, silent and thinking.

'There is no one on the road.'

'But there should be,' Ballista said. 'It is still early in the morning. Peasants should be going to their fields, herdsmen on their way to check the stock pens and winter pastures.'

Marcus peered through the trees. The landscape was deserted.

'That road must run around the ridge, back to the coastal path,' Ballista said.

There was a stab of unease in the pit of Marcus' stomach. 'Will those men chase us?'

'Probably not – they are drinking. But there may be others. Until we are clear, we will stay in the uplands. It is November. The shepherds will have driven their flocks down for the season. The mountains will be deserted.'

Except for bandits, Marcus thought. Everyone knew that outlaws denied fire and water lived in the mountains. They had nowhere else to go, whatever the season.

After a time the land lifted, and they walked through junipers and pines. Ballista went slowly, as if preoccupied or looking for something. Now and then he stopped. Once, he leant against a tree and threw up.

They came to a stream and drank like animals, lying on their stomachs, lapping from their cupped hands. Tentatively, for the water was icy cold, they washed their various cuts and scrapes.

'Do you know where we are?'

Ballista was wringing the water out of his long hair.

'By the look of the mountains, the north-west coast. Probably beyond Panormus.'

Marcus wanted to ask another question, but superstition held him back. To mention the men from the beach again might be to summon them.

They trudged onwards in silence. Marcus was tired, his knee hurt, and he was very hungry.

When the sun was well past its zenith, they saw an isolated shepherd's hut in a clearing by another small stream. Despite his assurances that the mountains were empty, Ballista got them into cover. For almost an hour they watched the hut and the sheep pen which stood next to it. Even then, Ballista scouted all around, before approaching, knife in hand, from the other direction.

The hut was deserted. The ashes in the hearth were stone cold. Ballista searched the tiny shelter thoroughly. There was little to be found: an iron pot and a millstone, both too heavy to bother to take down to the lowland pastures, and a couple of wooden bowls not worth the trouble. There was a terracotta grain bin set in the floor. As far as Marcus could see, it contained nothing but some husks and chaff. Nevertheless, Ballista sifted through them. His efforts produced half a handful of grains of wheat, which he set aside in one of the bowls.

Perhaps reassured by the illusory security of the rough log walls, Marcus found the courage to ask the question that he had not dared earlier.

'Who were they?'

'You saw the brand on the rider's forehead?'

'The letter *F*.'

'*Fugitivus* – the mark of a recaptured runaway. They were slaves.'

There was something else Marcus had to ask, something delicate.

'When he spoke, it was in *your* language.' It was impossible to keep the disdain out of his tone.

'Yes, by his accent he was one of the Alamanni.'

'One of the tribesmen enslaved by the emperor after the battle of Milan?'

'Several thousand of them were sent to Sicily as farm labourers or herdsmen on the imperial estates. Five years they have been on the island. Not long enough to forget they were once free warriors.'

A slave revolt was the great, unspoken fear of all landowners – of all freemen and women.

'What if they all rebel?' For generations, Marcus' mother's senatorial family had owned much land around Tauromenium in the east of the island. 'Other slaves will join them. It will be like Spartacus.'

'That was long ago,' Ballista said. 'There has been nothing like it since. The last servile war in Sicily was even earlier – four centuries or so. It will be a few desperate men, probably no more than we saw. Panormus and the other towns will call out the militia. They will soon be caught.'

Even though the sun still shone, there was a chill this high in the mountains. They went outside to gather wood for a fire. Marcus noticed that his father often paused, and scanned the woods, listening intently.

Ballista still had the flint and steel in the pouch on his belt, but the twigs were damp from the storm, and it took time to get them to catch. When the fire was going, not much of the smoke seemed to find its way out of the hole in the roof.

Once they were warm, Ballista used the pommel of his dagger to grind the grain on the millstone. With water from the rivulet, he fashioned rough pancakes, which he cooked in the pot.

'Where are we going to go?' Marcus asked.

'If we are where I think we are, tomorrow we will go south-west to Eryx.'

'To the temple of Venus?'

Ballista laughed, not unpleasantly. 'I was not thinking about the sacred prostitutes owned by the temple.'

Marcus blushed.

'The cities of Sicily maintain a guard of two hundred armed men there. They are the only troops on the island. Nowhere could be safer.'

The minute pancakes were tasteless and gritty, singed on the outside, partly raw in the middle. Marcus was so famished he ate his share.

As the sun dipped below the peaks in the west, they cut some boughs of pine to serve as a makeshift bed. Ballista announced that he would stand watch in the night. Although dog-tired, Marcus told his father to wake him to take the second watch. Ballista said that he would.

Even though he was exhausted, warm enough and not uncomfortable, Marcus could not get to sleep. The air in the hut was close and fuggy, the sweet scent of pine cloying. By the light of the flames he could see his father sitting by the door. Occasionally Ballista would get up and creep out. The rush of air and the flicker of the fire undid his attempts at stealth. He would be gone for a time, then slink back in, and resume his vigil.

This was all his father's fault. Marcus had been doing well at the school on the Palatine. Although still thirteen, he was no longer studying poetry under a grammaticus, but public oratory under a rhetor. He had been learning the skills necessary for a senatorial career. The rhetor had said that some of his practice speeches already showed exceptional promise. He should be safe in Rome, not hiding in this peasant hut, hunted and afraid, as if he himself were a runaway slave. This was all the fault of his father.

CHAPTER FOUR

BALLISTA WOKE SLOWLY – A GRADUAL and reluctant ascent into consciousness. The fire had burnt out, and a faint line of grey light showed under the door of the hut. Against his intentions, he must have fallen asleep. It was age – forty-three winters on Middle Earth. As a youth, standing watch all night had never troubled him. In the dead hours of darkness he had thought about waking Isangrim, but he did not have the heart. The boy had been sleeping peacefully. Ballista had sat, gazing at his son in the firelight. The delicate line of jaw and cheekbone, the flutter behind the closed eyelids, watching each precious breath. It had been almost like looking at a younger version of himself. Almost, but not quite, for there was also a hint of his mother about the boy. There was something miraculous about this youth, and a terrible pity that he was nearly a stranger to his father.

Getting to his feet as quietly as he could, he left the hut. It was an hour or more until sunrise. The time of the day the Romans called *conticinium*, when the cocks have stopped crowing, but men are still asleep. In the soft, grey light, he looked round. Yesterday he had scouted the clearing. He knew where to look, where a watcher might secrete himself. Small birds were singing. He glimpsed some sparrows, a couple of finches. There was nothing untoward. He sniffed the air. Fallen leaves and the lingering tang of woodsmoke. The fire had been a risk, but necessary. They had been cold and tired and hungry. Even in shelter, they had been in no condition to endure an autumn night in the mountains without heat. And a fire offered more than warmth; it gave a primeval comfort.

Ballista walked to the stream. Stiffly, he got down on his knees, then onto his belly. Every joint in his body ached. He splashed his face, washed the sleep out of his eyes, relishing the cold, sharp bite of the water. He drank, and felt the hollow emptiness in his stomach. Yesterday had been hard. The blow to the head that he had taken in the sea had left him light-headed and nauseous. The march inland had been a trial. He had tried to keep his weakness from the boy.

Too weary to rise, he lay and listened to the rill of the stream over the stones. A blackbird was singing, its notes clear and perfect. Today they would reach Eryx. They would be safe there, high on its hill, guarded by troops. Of course the latter were not real soldiers, just a barely trained militia. Yet they should be able to deal with a rabble of slaves. A doubt wormed into his mind. Five years of servitude would not rob any Alamanni warriors of their skill at arms. Maximus, his closest friend and bodyguard, had been a slave. It had not blunted Maximus' lethal efficiency in a fight. The militia were Sicilians, as soft and luxury-loving as any Greeks in the East, and now enervated by centuries of Roman peace.

Ballista set about arguing away his misgivings. The walls of Eryx stood on a precipice. Behind them, even women and children could defy an army. No more than a few dozen slaves would have risked everything. Alamanni or not, the majority would know an uprising was doomed. Retribution was inevitable: nails hammered through flesh and sinews, the lingering agony of crucifixion. Rome would show no mercy. There were good reasons that there had been nothing approaching a servile war for centuries. This was no more than an isolated outbreak of a handful of desperate men. Ballista believed everything that he had said to his son the day before was true. Still, he wished his four bodyguards were with him. Above all, he wished Maximus was with him. Together they had survived so much. With the Hibernian at his side, he had the confidence to confront any danger. They could have shared the responsibility of safeguarding the boy.

A pigeon clattered out of a tree down the slope. There were many doves at the temple of Venus at Eryx. The locals claimed that in the winter, when the goddess retired to the warmer climes of Africa, the birds accompanied her, crossing the wide sea to her sanctuary at Sicca. Long ago, Ballista had been to that dusty north African town. It had been high summer, and the sky had been full of doves. The ways of the gods were unknowable, but men will believe anything.

Two more pigeons took flight. Instantly Ballista was alert. Yet he got up slowly, betraying no alarm. He stretched languidly, looked around, acting like a man at ease. There was nothing in sight. The birds were some way downhill. But they were circling, evidently disturbed. Mastering an urge to run, Ballista walked back to the hut.

Isangrim was still sleeping. Ballista placed a finger gently behind the boy's ear. The boy woke with a start, was about to shout. Ballista placed his palm over Isangrim's mouth.

'Quiet! We may have company.'

Isangrim's eyes were wide with fear.

'It may be nothing.' Ballista tried to sound reassuring. 'But get up in case.'

The boy did as he was told.

'Stay here. I will go and look.'

Isangrim gripped his father's arm.

'Do not worry, I will not go far.'

Back in the clearing, Ballista tried to give the impression of a man with nothing on his mind, just placidly waiting for sunrise. The flight of the birds made him suspect that there was at least one man downslope to the north. Hoping it appeared natural, and yawning to disguise the keenness of his gaze, he scanned the forest to the east. The sky was a hard and bright blue, the scattered clouds underlit pink and gold. Not long until the sun crested the nearest rise, but for now the mountainside was shadowed, mist lingering under the trees. Although he could not be certain, once he thought he detected a movement. No escape east, then. Strolling the few steps to the stock pen, he looked south. The treeline was no great distance. Above it was hard, bare rock. No cover that he could see. It would have to be west. Turning, he wandered back towards the entrance of the shelter.

Hercules' hairy arse, this time there is no doubt.

A furtive figure, flitting through the trunks of the pines, about fifty paces away. There was nothing for it, but to head up the shoulder of the mountain. Pray they could outdistance any pursuit, or that there might be some cave in which they could hide.

'Quick!' Ballista called through the door. 'We have to run.'

Isangrim came out.

It was already too late. Five men in a line, well spaced like huntsmen, coming up the slope. Two more closing in from either side. Ballista looked round.

Allfather, even another couple moving down from the ridge.

'Get back inside,' Ballista said. 'I will deal with them.'

They were slaves all right. Rough working clothes, rough hair, unkempt black beards. Some had hunting spears, the rest crooks or cudgels: herdsmen or shepherds. Not Alamanni; their dark hair showed they had been born around the shores of the Mediterranean. Whatever their origins, they were men who lived on the margins, accustomed to violence in out-of-the-way places. It would take the cunning of Loki, the trickster god, to talk a way out of this. Even crafty Odysseus might have struggled to find the right words.

'That is far enough.' Ballista spoke in Latin, trying to sound as if he had an army at his back.

They halted, about ten paces away. Unsurprisingly, they did not look in the least cowed. Odds of almost six to one, and all Ballista and his son had were daggers.

'Well, well, two more runaway Alamanni.' The man spoke with dislike. Evidently even among rebellious slaves, ethnic animosities prevailed. 'One that speaks Latin, and his pretty boy.'

Ballista could sense Isangrim behind his shoulders. Ballista had a hand on the hilt of his knife. There would be time before they rushed him. Yet he doubted that he would be able to commit the terrible act.

'We have a couple of ropes.' The speaker laughed unpleasantly. 'Before we string him up, we will have some fun with your catamite.'

'Wait!'

Ballista held up his left hand, as if to physically ward them off. He needed time to force himself to strike. One quick blow – no degradation, no suffering. After Isangrim, he could turn the blade on himself, or fight until he was killed. Either way, *they* would not harm his son.

'And where did you steal that ring?'

Ballista had forgotten the equestrian's gold ring on the third finger of his left hand.

'Did you cut it from the hand of your murdered master?'

No point in further subterfuge.

'My name is Marcus Clodius Ballista, equestrian of Rome, companion of the emperor. The boy is my son, and you will not take either of us alive.'

The slaves looked at each other, suddenly uncertain.

'He might be telling the truth,' one said.

'Looks like a German to me,' said the slave who had issued the threats. 'Both of them do.'

'I was born beyond the Rhine,' Ballista said.

'We should wait,' the other slave said. 'Wait for the young *dominus*.'

A tiny spring of hope in Ballista's heart. Or was *dominus* only the title they had awarded to the leader of their band?

'Where is your master?'

'He will be here presently.'

They stood where they were, waiting in silence. The shepherds remained watchful and suspicious. Yet that was the nature of their profession. The threat of violence also remained, but its imminence had receded.

Soon the swish of branches and heavy footfalls announced the approach of the party of the *dominus*.

'You have caught some of the bastards?'

A heavy, florid young man in fine hunting clothes puffed into sight. Another half-dozen slaves followed him.

'Maybe, *domine*.'

'What do you mean, *maybe*?'

A thumb jerked. 'This one claims to be an equestrian.'

'I am Marcus Clodius Ballista, and this is my son.'

'Ridiculous, my father knows the family of his wife,' the young man exclaimed. 'The general has not been on the island for years.'

'It is ten years since I visited the estates of my wife.'

A look of shrewdness crossed the round face.

'And what is her name?'

'Julia Paulla, daughter of the late Gaius Julius Volcatius Gallicanus.'

'They could be slaves of the family,' said the herdsman who had advocated the rope.

The young man ignored the interruption. 'And where are her estates?'

'In the east, around Tauromenium,' Ballista said.

'Is it him?' The herdsman sounded as if he hoped the answer was no, and they could get on with the lynching.

'How in Hades should I know?' the young man snapped. 'I was a child the only time I saw Ballista.'

'Where did you see me?'

'At Syracuse, in the home of Flavius Vopiscus.' The crafty look reappeared. 'Where did you serve under the senator?'

'At the siege of Aquileia,' Ballista said. 'When the emperor Maximinus Thrax was killed.'

The attitude of the young *dominus* changed in an instant.

'Forgive my men. We were patrolling the boundaries of the estate. I am Quintus Caecilius Titianus, son of Publius. You must accept my father's hospitality. You will be quite safe at the villa.'

The estate was evidently extensive, and the route was long. They kept to the woods, walking in the shade through soft, blue-grey shrubs that smelled of thyme. The music of songbirds and cicadas rang in their ears.

Despite the sylvan scene, Marcus sensed the men were on edge. His father and Quintus seldom spoke, and the huntsmen were silent. Apparently they were not as far west as his father had thought, and many runaways had been sighted in these inland hills. Marcus thought the caution of his elders excessive. Surely no ragtag band of slaves would take on a group of twenty armed men? All slaves were cowards. They would seek easier targets. Whatever the reality of the threat, some hours later, when the party reached its goal, the general relief was palpable.

The Villa Caeciliana was typical of the main country residence of a rich man. The red tiled and white plastered house had two wings arranged in the shape of the letter U. A bathhouse stood close by. The residence of the family was separated from the barns, stables, slave quarters and other farm buildings by a low wall. Another wall surrounded the whole complex. The villa was built in a sheltered fold of the hills, dominated by a rocky outcrop topped by a huge oak. It was ringed by orchards, and a stream ran through the holding.

Marcus and his father were assigned two adjacent rooms on the first floor. A balcony connected all the bedrooms, and stairs at each end gave access down to the courtyard. After the last two days, the normal things of life – a bath, massage, clean clothes, servants at one's beck and call – seemed almost strange. They were welcome and reassuring, but somehow contingent and no longer quite certain.

The dining room was set for six. Ballista was on the main couch with the owner and his son. In an easy-going country way, Publius Caecilius' wife and daughter reclined on the second couch. Marcus was placed between them. The whole family were well upholstered. The daughter was about Marcus' age. She had a pleasant, although plain face. Modestly, the womenfolk had said little as the attendants washed their hands, and now, as the first course was served, everyone listened respectfully as the owner expounded the disaster that had fallen upon western Sicily.

'The root of the problem is the Alamanni. After their defeat at Milan, thousands of the . . .'

Marcus quailed inside at Caecilius' tact, as the host belatedly remembered Ballista's origins, and avoided the word *barbarians*.

'. . . captives were sent to the island. Most were put to work on imperial estates, but some were sold to private owners. There is always a danger when a large number of prisoners of war are held in one place. Not yet broken to slavery, they speak a language unknown to their owners. Conspiracy is easy. Foolishly, many of them were made herdsmen – free to roam about with weapons in their hands.'

Although his rescuers had given him bread and cheese that morning, Marcus was very hungry. He was trying very hard not to gobble the hard-boiled eggs and sausages. The salad and the mallow in pepper sauce, he hardly touched. To slow himself down, he sipped the watered wine and nibbled some bread.

'Although many of my friends would not agree, every slave uprising is caused by the brutality of the owners. In this case, a rich couple in Eryx. Bicon himself was the son of a slave, and his wife Selicia was a freedwoman. She behaved as you would expect in one of her sort, always slapping and biting her maids. When her hairdresser messed up her coiffure, she stabbed the girl with a pair of scissors. As for Bicon, he seldom waited for the whip, grabbed whatever was to hand, sometimes just used his fists. No self-control. A couple of years ago, it had to be hushed up when he struck their porter in the head with a sword. The blade was in its scabbard, but the edge bit through the leather and killed the slave. A cruel couple, lacking all humanity.'

Caecilius paused his exposition, and nodded to the servants to clear the tables and bring in the main course. At the sight of the haunch of venison and the roast chickens, Marcus' stomach felt like a bottomless pit. He watched hungrily as the carver wielded a long, razor-sharp knife with effortless precision.

'Some of Bicon's sheep went missing, in the hills near Segesta. He accused his Alamanni shepherds of selling them. They denied it, even under the lash. They may have been telling the truth. The hills are infested with rustlers. Bicon condemned them to the mills he has outside Eryx. It is a grim fate. Few survive long.'

Marcus was beginning to feel full. The venison was delicious. He helped himself to a little more.

'Even so, most likely nothing would have happened. The spark was provided by another of Bicon's slaves. A Syrian called Comazon, an actor and magician, he was employed to entertain his master's guests at table. Pampered and indulged by his owner, Comazon was given too much freedom. He set himself up as some form of priest to the slaves thereabouts. With all sorts of tricks and sleights of hand, he convinced them that the gods spoke to him. He began to prophesy, tell their futures. A few of the things he foretold came to pass. The rest were quickly forgotten. Playing on the simple nature of the Alamanni – somehow he had learnt their tongue – he got them to believe in him implicitly.'

Marcus had eaten himself to a standstill. The slave boy waiting silently at the foot of the couch washed and dried his hands.

'Then Comazon overstepped himself, and he was sent to the mills. Once there, he told the Alamanni that their god had promised them freedom and rule over the whole of Sicily if they took all the slaves on the island into their ranks and hailed him as their king. They rose up at night, seized Eryx, and massacred both the militia and the citizens. Bicon and Selicia they tortured to death in the Temple of Venus itself. So far the sacrilege has not been punished. The revolt has spread like wildfire, south to Lilybaeum, north-east to Parthenicum. Comazon now calls himself King Soter, the *Saviour*.'

At a gesture from Caecilius the remnants of the main meal were removed, and the nuts and fruit appeared.

Ballista put down his cup, and spoke thoughtfully.

'Alamanni means *All Men*. They have always welcomed outsiders.'

'The slaves are flocking to them,' Caecilius said. 'There are rumoured to be more than four thousand under arms.'

'Are you safe here?' Ballista asked.

For the first time, Marcus was aware of the silent figures serving the dinner. He thought of the man with the carving knife, then the slave-huntsman who had wanted to lynch him and his father.

'As safe as a man can be anywhere.' Caecilius smiled at his wine steward. The servant dipped his head in acknowledgment. 'The majority of the slaves on the estate are home-bred. Those that are bought in were babies abandoned on dung heaps and raised by dealers. They have known nothing but servitude. Only a fool purchases those captured in war. And other provenances are doubtful. All too often they claim to have been wrongly enslaved by brigands.'

Gazing around, Marcus detected no animosity from those dutifully waiting at the tables. Relieved, he took another drink. Lulled by the wine and food, and the perfume heavy in the air, he looked across at his father. Reclining in a spotless tunic, a wreath of roses on his brow, Marcus Clodius Ballista radiated the dignity of a Roman of equestrian rank. If only his father had not been away so long. Ambition was a double-edged weapon, so one of the tutors had said in the Palatine school. If in the service of Rome, prompted by a love of honour, it was a virtue. But if pursued for its own sake, *ambitio* was a vice. His father had held great commands, high offices of state. One so exalted that it had brought great danger to the whole family. That was never to be spoken of. Marcus' mother had warned, it was best not even remembered.

'You say the rebels have reached Lilybaeum and Par-thenicum,' Ballista said.

'Yes, they have divided their forces. Comazon is leading one horde towards Panormus and the north coast. The rest are moving along the southern coastal road to Selinus. The gods willing, they will pass by us in the interior.'

'Is it known where they are heading afterwards?' Ballista was sitting up.

'They have proclaimed that they will reunite in the east of the island, at Tauromenium or Syracuse.'

The drowsy complacency left Marcus. His mother was at Tauromenium, his brother, his home.

Caecilius actually laughed. 'Do not worry. They will not get that far. As soon as the news reaches the emperor, he will send troops. Ostia is only two days' sail.'

Marcus did not think his father looked at all reassured.

'Anyway,' Caecilius continued, 'tomorrow you will ride out of here, armed and equipped, on two of my best hunters. Well mounted, going via the interior, you will reach your family in Tauromenium long before any rabble of slaves travelling on foot along the coast roads.'

CHAPTER FIVE

BALLISTA LAY, SLEEPLESS IN THE DARK.

Do not worry. Ostia is only two days' sail.

Caecilius was a fool. Tonight was three days before the Ides of November, the very day the sailing season ended. Perhaps Caecilius was not a fool. Perhaps his confidence was an act, designed to allay any unrest among his own servants, a desperate ploy to keep the peace on his own remote estate.

No, Caecilius was a fool. Even if the seas were not closed, there were next to no troops in Rome. Leaving only a skeleton headquarters staff, the Praetorians, the Horse Guards, and the Second Parthian Legion had all marched off to the North. They were quartered in Milan with the emperor Gallienus, watching to see if the truce held with Postumus, the pretender across the Alps in Gaul. The only soldiers left in the capital were the Urban Cohorts and the Watch. They were useful enough when the Roman mob rioted, but they were not frontline troops, ready to stand in the line of battle. Even the former had hardly ever been deployed overseas.

Of course some vessels would still brave the winter storms. The news would reach Milan. But it would take time. Even when Gallienus knew of the uprising, the imperial response would not be immediate. Troops in winter quarters were not ready to take to the road at the drop of a handkerchief. Once mustered, it was a long way south to Ostia. The fleet at Ravenna was closer. Yet that would mean braving the Adriatic as well as the Middle Sea.

A cool breeze blew in from the courtyard. Ballista always slept with a window open. He abandoned calculating distances and times. The revolt ultimately was doomed. All slave insurrections were. The two great servile wars in Sicily; Spartacus himself in Italy: all had been crushed. Yet not before many thousands of freemen and women were massacred. The imperial forces would come, and they would put down the rebellion with exemplary severity – a welter of blood, stark crosses lining the roads. But it would not be soon. For now, Sicily was isolated. The inhabitants would have to face the chaos alone.

The rebels were heading for Tauromenium. Ballista thought of the villa, nestled below the theatre, its gardens looking out at distant Etna and the shimmering sea. He thought of his wife walking among the late flowering roses, his younger son running through the long corridors with their scent of polished cedar wood, of the old retainers going about their ordered existence. It was impossible to imagine the latter turning on the family. The danger did not lie with them. He was sure that Caecilius was right: well mounted, he would get to Tauromenium with Isangrim long before the rebels. But he had learnt on campaign that rumour outran the fleetest messenger. Not all slave-owning households were as beneficent as his own. If there was a rising in the town, his bodyguards would fight to the death to protect the family. Yet there were just three of them: Maximus, Tarchon and Rikiar. Four if you counted Grim, but the old Heathobard was almost crippled. Come to that, Rikiar was lame, too, and Tarchon was missing two fingers from his natural sword hand. Ballista pushed away images of a hopeless last stand.

Julia was a sensible and practical woman. She had money. The Straits of Messana were treacherous but narrow, Italy only a couple of miles away. Even in the depths of winter, for the right price, a boat and crew could always be procured. At the first hint of trouble, surely she would take Dernhelm to the mainland.

But she was proud. The daughter of a long line of senators did not run from an upstart servile throng. The villa had been in her family for generations. She would not willingly abandon her ancestral home.

Proud and sensible – they were two of her qualities he had admired from the start. There had been no question of love at the betrothal. Like all elite marriages in Rome, it had been arranged. Hers was a senatorial family in decline. He was a rising equestrian officer, in favour with the then emperor Gallus. It had been enough for her father to overlook his barbarian origins. No love at the beginning, but it had come. A Roman matron was expected to be modest and chaste. Julia had been neither. After the wedding night, a Roman husband should never again see his wife naked. Julia had liked to leave the light burning in their lovemaking. She had seemed to revel in its soft sheen on her olive skin, the play of shadows on their entwined bodies. And beyond the bedroom she had flouted convention. She had not just run his house – any wife would; her advice had guided him through the maze of imperial politics. Others, women as well as men, had raised their eyes at his reliance on her in public affairs. Ballista had not cared.

For a decade it had been the happiest of marriages, despite his prolonged absences on campaign. Then – was it five years ago? – when they were together in the East, something had changed. A distance had grown between them. Sometimes he thought it was his fault. Out of necessity he had taken the step that had placed his family in the gravest danger, the step that now could never be mentioned. The troops had acclaimed him emperor. After a few days, as soon as he could, he had renounced the purple. Gallienus had pardoned him, spared his wife and children. Perhaps Julia had never forgiven her husband for exposing their children to the perils of that awful eminence. Yet the distance between them had appeared before those terrible days. Now – lying alone in the dark of the night – he wondered if he had imagined the years of happiness. Certainly he had been content. Had he just assumed that Julia felt the same?

Noises from outside. Voices, low and urgent. Not on the balcony – further away, probably down in the courtyard. It was the dead of night. Caecilius had set watchmen at the gates, but no one should be about in the villa.

Ballista threw off the blanket, and rolled to his feet. He swayed, his head dizzy. The effects of the blow to the head had not altogether left him. The giddiness passed. He dressed quietly, pulling the baldric of the sword-belt Caecilius had given him for the journey over his head, buckling it to his own belt.

He peered out of the window, listening. The balcony was empty. Moonlight through the pillars slatted it with shadows. The courtyard was out of sight. There was nothing to be heard.

Even if he had not imagined the voices, they might signify nothing. A couple of domestic servants on some furtive but innocent assignation: a late-night drink; playing dice; visiting a girl. Yet these were unsettled times. Isangrim was asleep next door. Nothing should be left to chance.

Gently opening the door, he slipped out onto the balcony. Taking a position in the darkness behind the nearest pillar, he looked out. Half the courtyard was bathed in the bright light of the moon, the other in deep shadow. Nothing moved.

Ballista waited. The army had taught him patience in the long watches of the night. The villa slumbered, apparently at peace. By the height of the moon, it was at least three hours until dawn.

Another sound, too faint to identify. It seemed to come from the opposite wing, the kitchen range. There it was again. Hurried footsteps from inside the building. More than one man, trying – but failing – to move stealthily.

Something was wrong ... very wrong. Ballista went to Isangrim's door. It was not bolted. The boy was on his side, one arm thrown out. For a sickening moment, Ballista thought he was already dead.

Again, the boy started when Ballista placed a finger behind his ear. Again, Ballista had to clamp a hand over his mouth. At some point he would have to teach him field craft. Never make a sound when someone wakes you. It draws attention, increases the risk.

'Get dressed,' Ballista whispered.

Isangrim did as he was told, asked no questions. He, too, buckled on the sword he had been given. The boy was learning. War was a hard school. A servile uprising was worse. Nowhere was safe; no one could be trusted.

'We need to find out what is happening,' Ballista said. 'It might be nothing, but we need to be sure.'

They both crept out onto the balcony. Keeping to the shadows, they ducked down behind the rail. Now no one could be heard moving. Far off in the hills a dog howled. Afterwards the silence seemed yet deeper. If nothing happened, Isangrim would think his father a coward. Better that than have their throats cut in their beds.

Suddenly the peace was shattered. The crash of a door being kicked open, shouts and screams, things breaking. Lights flared in the main house.

'We should raise the alarm,' Isangrim said.

'No point,' Ballista said. 'There are six free people in the villa, perhaps ten times that number of slaves.'

Two men burst through the door of the main residence. On cue, as if at the theatre, a dozen or more slaves emerged from the opposite wing. They were carrying cleavers and other kitchen utensils. More came out of the house. They ringed the fugitives.

Publius Caecilius Titianus, owner of the Villa Caeciliana and miles of the surrounding lands, stood at bay. Only his wine steward stood with him.

'What harm have I done you?' His voice was plaintive and baffled, still more outraged than frightened.

They did not answer.

'Did I not raise you well, feed you, care for you? Have I ever punished any of you unjustly?'

The throng began to mutter. An elderly slave stepped forward, stripped off his tunic, turned his back. Even in the night, the scars shone white.

'That was your own fault!' the wine steward shouted. 'You stole food. You are a thief.'

'Because I was hungry.'

Another slave joined the old man. It was Caecilius' carver, the tools of his trade in his hands.

'Things are fine, for a master's pet like you. Night after night he shovels delicacies into his mouth, while I watch with my belly empty. *Carve that pheasant carefully.* Never any leftovers come my way, not even a gnawed wing. The dogs are fed before me.'

Others voiced similar complaints. They were talking to the wine steward, not Caecilius. They were using the present tense. Perhaps things had not gone too far. It could be that the deference induced by years of service might stay their hands. Perhaps the wine steward might yet defuse the situation.

Another group of slaves surged out of the house, and Ballista's flickering hopes were extinguished. The newcomers were led by the huntsman who had wanted to lynch Ballista and his son yesterday. The slaves dragged with them Caecilius' wife and daughter. The clothes of the women were dishevelled.

'We have to save them,' Isangrim whispered.

'No,' Ballista said.

There were two dozen slaves in the courtyard, all carrying some sort of weapon.

The sight of his womenfolk shocked Caecilius out of his silence.

'Where is my son?'

The huntsman smirked. 'You will be with him soon enough.'

'If you have harmed him . . .' Caecilius' threat trailed off.

The huntsman gestured to his followers to bring forward Caecilius' wife and daughter.

'Leave them alone!' Caecilius roared.

'You are not in a position to give any more orders. You are no *master*, nothing better than a pimp. You charge us to visit the quarters of the slave girls. Now you can watch us enjoy your womenfolk for free.'

With an inarticulate cry, unarmed as he was, Caecilius launched himself at his tormentor. The huntsman side-stepped his rush. As his master went by, he brought the blade in his fist slashing down into the back of Caecilius' thigh. The landowner went down, bellowing, clutching his leg.

'We have to intervene,' Isangrim said.

'There is nothing we can do.' Ballista took his son's arm. 'We have to go.'

For a moment Isangrim resisted, his eyes on the horrible scene below, then he let himself be led away.

They kept close to the wall, well away from the rail. Half-crouching, they moved in and out of the bands of moonlight and shadow. Even so, if one of the throng looked their way, they could not fail to be seen. Ballista found himself silently praying to the high god of his youth.

Woden, Allfather, hold your hands over your descendants.

For once, perhaps his divine ancestor was listening. They reached the head of the stairs away from the main house without alarm. Like thieves, they stole down the steps.

At the foot of the stairs, at the open side of the *U* formed by the wings of the villa, Ballista hesitated. The outer wall of the compound was but thirty paces to the left. They could slip from the villa unseen, but to get clear away they needed horses. The stables were beyond the inner wall ahead. The gate between the residence and the farm was open. No watchman was to be seen.

Their hesitation was their undoing. The Allfather had removed his protection.

'There!'

The shout came from behind them in the courtyard. Not all the slaves were engrossed in their bestial revenge.

'To the outer wall!' Ballista shouted at his son.

Fear gave their feet wings. Behind them came a baying, like hounds on a scent. They reached the wall together. It was higher than a tall man. Ballista gave Isangrim a leg-up.

'Get to the oak that overlooks the valley.'

From the top of the wall, Isangrim stared back at him, unmoving.

'Go now! I will lead them away, then join you.'

As his son dropped out of sight, Ballista swung round and drew his sword. The slaves were almost upon him. Without hesitation, Ballista attacked. Never expecting their quarry to turn and fight, the disconcerted slaves skidded to a halt. The leading man had time to get the cleaver in his hand up into some sort of guard. With the skill of long training, Ballista knocked it aside, then stabbed the tip of his own blade into the slave's stomach. The man grunted with surprise. With the flat of his left hand, Ballista pushed him away. The slave staggered backwards. As the pain hit, he screamed and fell, twisting, to the ground.

Ballista feinted a lunge at the next pursuer to his right. Leaping away, the slave collided with those behind. In the ensuing confusion, Ballista spun round, and raced back to the wall.

Timing his jump, Ballista got his free hand over the coping stones. He swung his body, and hooked a boot over. Now he was fleeing, the slaves would take no time to recover their nerve.

Landing outside the compound, Ballista was horrified to find Isangrim still there.

'I could not desert you,' the boy said.

'Go now! Hide up by the oak. I will lead them the wrong way, then find you.'

'But . . .'

'Now!'

Isangrim turned and ran into the trees.

Ballista sheathed his sword, and set off away from the route his son had taken. He could hear the slaves by the inner face of the wall. They were encouraging one another to have the courage to climb over. Their numbers meant it would not take long.

Going into the orchard, Ballista stopped about fifty paces out, making sure he could still be seen from the wall.

Soon enough he heard the scrabbling ascent, and the first heads, demonic in the blue light of the moon, appeared.

Ballista started to run, not too fast, making sure he made plenty of noise.

'Over there!'

Having seen him, they were tumbling down the near side of the wall. Now Ballista began to run in earnest.

The orchard was laid out in neat rows. Not ideal terrain for a fugitive. But there were still some leaves on the fruit trees, and the land soon started to rise. There was enough cover for a man who knew what he was doing. As a boy, following the custom of the North, Ballista had been fostered to the tribe of the Harii. They were famed night fighters. Even the Latin historian Tacitus had praised their abilities. As a man, covert missions for the empire had honed Ballista's skills. Ducking under low-hanging branches, watching for projecting roots, he went fast up the hillside.

After a time, Ballista paused. He could no longer see them, but could hear their lumbering pursuit. He thought he had gone far enough. Now it was time to hide.

The trees towards the upper slopes of the orchard were old and shaggy, overgrown with ivy. No doubt Caecilius had seldom bothered to walk this far. An ancient apple tree, half-wild, held out a thick branch, almost horizontal, just above head height. Bracing a boot on its trunk, Ballista swung up. He swarmed through the ivy to a higher bough. In the depth of the shadow, he flattened himself against the gnarled wood. Checking his scabbard was tucked between his body and the tree, and did not give away his outline, he covered the lower part of his face with the sleeve of his tunic. Stilling his breathing, he settled to wait.

The snapping of twigs and the swish of brush against branches announced the coming of the pursuit. In the quiet of the night, they were as loud as a herd of elephants. They were not moving that fast anymore. Now and then, one called out to his companions. These slaves were not all huntsmen. Even their voices betrayed their lack of confidence in the dark of the woods.

They came into view. Two at first, then a ragged line, bunching together for reassurance. There had been no time for them to get torches. The darkness obviously unsettled them. They had no wish to encounter the man who had so efficiently killed their companion, especially not out here in the wild. All together, they pulled up just short of the tree.

'We have lost them,' one said.

'Publipor will be furious if we go back without them,' one of the two at the front said.

A piece of ivy was tickling Ballista's nose. He willed himself to ignore it. Any movement would give him away.

'Then let Publipor come and hunt them.'

'You are right – he is a huntsman, not us. If he is as good as he claims, he can pick up their trail in the morning.'

'What does it matter? Where can they go, and who can they tell? The whole countryside has risen.'

'Let's go back.'

Without further debate, and with evident relief, they retraced their steps.

Ballista remained where he was long after the sounds of their departure had faded. For nine nights the Allfather had hung on the tree of knowledge. His descendant could manage another quarter of an hour.

For all his patience, Ballista could not remain concealed in the tree. Isangrim was out there on his own. It was improbable that the slaves would despatch another search party. Their chase had been spontaneous, disorganised and readily abandoned. They would not willingly give up their debauch to venture again into the darkness, where they knew at every step they might encounter a desperate man with a sword in his hand. By now the slaves would have broached their master's wine cellar. Most likely the majority would already be drunk. Isangrim should be safe for the time being, but he would be alone and frightened.

Carefully, Ballista climbed down from his hiding place. The final drop, he executed with the utmost caution. This was not the moment to risk a twisted ankle. On the ground, he stood for a time, listening intently. There was nothing untoward in the night. Then he stretched and rolled the stiffness out of his muscles and joints. He went about the task methodically, from ankles to neck, like a boxer preparing for a bout.

Tracking along to the outcrop was easy. The moon and stars visible through the remaining foliage guided Ballista east to the edge of the orchard. From there, he got a fix on the lone oak tree. He went slowly, frequently halting, straining his senses to pierce the veil of the dark. Once or twice the nocturnal breeze carried a faint shout or scream up from the villa. Terror or inebriated revelry, it was impossible to tell. Closer at hand the night was quiet.

The fruit trees ended at the foot of a slope leading up to the crag. The incline was rock-strewn bare of undergrowth. The cliff below the oak was sheer, honeycombed with fissures and caves. Isangrim must have secreted himself in one of the cavities.

Ballista stepped out into the pale wash of the moonlight, making no effort to mask his approach. Stones clicked and skittered under his boots. He walked with his arms held straight out on either side – the posture of a man on the cross. Halfway to the rock face, he stopped and lowered his arms. Isangrim was not his friend Maximus or one of his *familia* on campaign. The signal, that he was returning to the rendezvous and all was well, would be meaningless to Isangrim. Indeed, the unnatural posture, with its evocation of crucifixion, might be alarming. When this was all over, Ballista would teach his son the non-verbal language of the army, the gestures that could keep a man alive.

'Isangrim.' Ballista pitched his voice low. 'Isangrim.'

A scatter of pebbles, and the boy emerged from one of the openings in the cliff.

Ballista fought down an urge to run to his son and embrace him. Somehow he knew it would be unwelcome. Instead he walked, stretching out a hand. With a strange formality, Isangrim shook it. Ballista placed his other hand on the boy's shoulder.

'All good?'

'Yes.'

'Good.' Ballista squeezed his son's shoulder. 'Then you must wait here a little longer.'

'What?'

Ballista admired the boy's attempt to hide his fear.

'I have to go back to the villa. There is something that needs to be done.'

CHAPTER SIX

MARCUS WAS ALONE IN THE CAVE. He sat in the deep shadow by the entrance, close enough to see out. Ceaselessly he scanned the bare slope and the treeline at its foot. The breeze moved the branches. His eyes were tired, his body exhausted. Again and again he detected furtive movements down in the orchard. Nothing emerged into the moonlight.

The hilt of the unsheathed sword lay by his right hand. The things his father had given him were on his belt: the wallet of coins; the bag with the flint and steel. They showed that his father might not come back.

At first Marcus had thought that Ballista intended to do the right thing, was set on doing what they should have done before. Then his father had disabused him of that idea. Were all the stories of his heroics – first over the wall in Africa, defeating Goths and Persians – no more than tales that had grown in the telling? Of course, his father was barbarian-born. The tutors at the imperial school had argued that barbarians might be ferocious, but they lacked true courage. Lacking the rational part of a man, they could never possess Roman honour and virtue, which formed the true moral heart of courage.

It was easier to say the word, than live up to the ideal. Easy to hold forth on the subject, safe on the Palatine. Marcus remembered with shame his sickening relief back in the villa when his father had led him away from the scene of horror. He had been terrified. Did that make him a coward?

Not necessarily. Even the greatest heroes had been afraid. Hector had fled before the walls of Troy, trembling like a dove or fawn, in fear of Achilles. Pious Aeneas had admitted that in the sack of the city every breath of wind had frightened him, and how he had started at every sound. Yet Aeneas had steeled himself to return to Troy, and Hector had turned to face his killer.

Let me at least not die without a struggle, inglorious, but do some big thing first, that men to come shall know of it.

It was cold at night in the uplands. Marcus hugged himself to stop himself shivering. A coward dies a thousand times, a brave man once.

Despite his discomfort, despite his fear, he must have dozed. He was in the cave of the Cyclops. There was no one with him. One by one, the others had been seized by the monster. Their brains had been dashed out against the wall, their flesh eaten raw. Soon it would be his turn. He was huddled against the damp wall. The boulder blocked the entrance.

A noise woke him. Stones crunching under boots. Someone was coming. He grabbed for his sword.

Let me at least not die without a struggle.

Down through the trees, slowly and with care, nothing left to chance. Three hours until dawn – plenty of time. Leaving Isangrim had been hard. The boy's self-control had been tested to the limit when Ballista had handed over the money and the fire-making tools. His son had passed the test. It had been necessary. If something happened – if Ballista did not make it back – Isangrim would need both. In cold reality it was unlikely that a youth, a thirteen-year-old with a sheltered upbringing, would make it alone across the island amid the lawless brutality of a servile insurrection. But Isangrim was strong and brave. Best not to dwell on what might happen.

The parting had been hard, but unavoidable. To get away from the villa they needed horses. Ballista had heard the slaves say that in the morning the huntsman Publipor would get on their trail. On foot they stood little chance. Without horses, they were unlikely to reach Tauromenium and the rest of the family before the rebels. Ballista would not let himself think of that. Closing his mind to such an outcome, he ghosted down through the orchard.

As he got close, few sounds came from the villa. The occasional shout or burst of drunken laughter. It was a chill November night. A cold west wind was rising. The slaves would be indoors, gorging on produce from the larders, swilling fine wines from the cellars. All he had to do was avoid those stepping out to relieve themselves, or staggering from the warmth of one building to another.

A grisly sight greeted him at the entrance to the farmyard. The gates were open and unguarded. If all the countryside was in revolt, there was no need to set a watch. Above the gate, set on spears, were two severed heads. Publius Caecilius Titianus and his son Quintus, bloodied and inhuman, but recognisable in the moonlight. At least the women were not there. Most likely they were still alive, still suffering. If this was a Greek novel, then nothing too bad would happen to them. They would not be raped; the girl would keep her virginity.

In a Greek novel, the hero would rescue them. This was not a Greek novel, and Ballista had never seen himself as any sort of hero.

Slipping through the gate, Ballista got off the main path. He went to the right, by a steaming dung heap. If discovered, he might be able to again jump the outer wall and get back to Isangrim. Always ensure a line of retreat. Without horses, it would just be delaying the inevitable. But he and his eldest son would die together.

Beyond the reeking midden were the slave barracks, beyond them the barns, and closest to the cross wall and the house were the stables. The priorities of Caecilius were demonstrated in building materials and layout. The barracks were made of wattle and daub, and were thatched. The barns and stables were brick-built, with a tiled roof. The estate owner had lavished money on his supplies and horses, preferred their proximity to that of his servants. A choice that was hard to criticise, as things had turned out.

Somewhere out of sight a dog began barking. Others joined in, a fierce, full-throated yammering. Ballista eyed the outer wall. If the dogs were loose, it was all over. Why had he not thought of it before? He cursed his own lack of foresight. Any villa would have many hounds, for hunting, watching the flocks, guarding the yard. But if the dogs were roaming free, why had they not set them on him and Isangrim earlier? The howling died away. The dogs must be in kennels or chained up somewhere. The slaves who looked after them might have hated their master, but probably cared for the animals. They would have locked them away, not wanting them to run off, or come to harm, in the murderous uproar of the rising.

Ballista crossed the open space between the shade of the barracks and that of the barns. A rectangle of yellow light blazed out behind him; it brought a gust of voices. Ballista shrank down behind a buttress of the barn. Two figures emerged from the open door. One had his arm around the other's shoulder. Unsteadily, they walked straight towards him. Ballista did not move. At night, it was movement and noise that gave you away.

The couple stopped no more than three paces off. Separating, they fumbled with their clothes, then pissed against the wall of the barn. They must have been drinking for hours. There seemed no end to the splashing. Their urine stank of wine. Ballista readied himself. When their bladders were empty, if they lurched towards him, he would kill them. They were befuddled and unsuspecting. With luck, they might not get a chance to make a sound.

At last they finished. Sorting out trousers and tunics, they reeled back the way they had come. The door shut behind them. In the dark, Ballista exhaled quietly. He waited until his night vision had returned, then moved on.

This was taking too long, the delays mounting. But he could not afford to rush. Almost there.

The stables were arranged as a barn with doors at each end. Inside would be a walkway, with the stalls opening off on either side. At one end would be a tack room, at the other a feed shed. The trusted stable hands would sleep above in the rafters.

The nearer door was closed. Ballista put his ear to its boards.

Hades, a murmur of conversation.

Two voices, just audible.

'We never should have listened to Publipor. The master was not that bad.' An old man by the sound of it.

'He was a mean bastard.' A younger man talking. 'Feed your slaves, that is what Bulla told the Praetorian prefect.'

They lapsed into silence. Odd that slaves should remember the defiant words of a bandit executed far away in Rome half a century before. Perhaps the servile had their own myths, their own folk heroes.

'You know what they do when a master is murdered?' the older one said. 'They execute every slave in the household for not preventing the crime.'

'Only those under the same roof,' the other stable lad replied. 'We had no part in it, never went up to the house.'

'Tell that to the soldiers when they come.'

'The gods have told Soter that we will all be free.'

'And you believe that Syrian charlatan? You will be nailed to the next cross to me.'

Ballista had heard enough. The two stable hands were not going anywhere. He needed a distraction. A fire would draw everyone. The barracks were thatched. He touched his belt. The pouch containing flint and steel was not there. Of course, he had given it to Isangrim.

Allfather, nothing in life is ever easy.

Time was passing. He had to act soon. There was no point in delay.

Ballista pulled one of the double doors a little open. Drawing his sword, he went inside, shutting the door behind him. The two stable lads were in the tack room to his right. They were seated on stools either side of a low brazier at the foot of a ladder that led to their sleeping quarters. The air was warm, and smelt of horse and hay and leather. The homely scene was lit by a lamp.

The older man had an amphora in his hands. They both looked up, unalarmed until they saw the weapon.

'What—?'

'Don't say anything. No harm will come to you, if you do what I say.'

They stared at him, aghast.

'On your feet. Tack up the two best hunters in the string, the best stayers.'

'But—'

'They are not yours, and your master will hardly miss them.'

Ballista gestured with the blade, and they scrambled to their feet. The old man had dropped the amphora. It did not break, but tipped on its side, dark wine pouring from its neck.

'The tack.'

They grabbed the bridles and straps from the hooks, reached the saddles down from their trees. As they moved out into the walkway, Ballista kept close to their backs, between them and the door through which he had come.

The older lad opened the first stall, the younger the door two further along. They acted without consulting. Presumably they knew their horseflesh. Ballista stationed himself where he could keep an eye on both.

A sudden commotion in the tack room. A figure tumbled down the ladder.

The gods below, there had been another sleeping above.

The fugitive shouldered the door, and dashed out into the night. Ballista could hear his running feet, his wild shouts.

'Reins, get the bits in their mouths. Blankets and surcingles. Forget about the saddles.'

More voices shouting. Getting closer.

'That will do. Lead them out.'

As they did so, the double doors were flung wide.

'If it isn't our dear departed master's new friend, the great warrior.'

Publipor stood in the doorway, flanked by another man also dressed as a huntsman. Both were armed with swords. Outside, behind them in the gloom, was an undifferentiated mob.

'*Publius' boy*,' Ballista said. 'The man who wanted to lynch my son.'

'Pity he is not here.'

'I hoped to meet you again.' Ballista looked over his shoulder at the stable lads. 'Hold those horses, or I will kill both of you.'

Publipor guffawed. 'You think you will do better than Caecilius?'

'Much better.'

Ballista moved fast for a man of his size. Four quick, light steps, and a lunge. Publipor's companion was too slow. He tried to jump aside, but the edge of the blade caught him in the flank. It ripped a wide trench in his side. Doubled up, yelling with shock and pain, he stumbled back. The crowd recoiled away from him in the doorway, as if he were infected with the plague.

Publipor slashed at the back of Ballista's exposed right thigh. Ballista got his sword down in its path, and stepped back. The huntsman pressed forward, swinging blows to the head, first forehand then back. Ballista blocked both. The impacts jarred up into his shoulder. He had to finish this fast, before the rest joined the fight. But he needed an opening.

The horses were stamping, tugging at their leads.

Publipor thrust at Ballista's chest. Again Ballista turned the strike. His opponent's momentum drove them chest to chest. Publipor's breath stank of rich food and wine. Ballista twisted his body, used his shoulder and the power of his legs to shove the slave backwards.

Recovering his balance, Publipor roared at those outside for help. Then his eyes flicked over Ballista's shoulder to the stable boys.

'You two stab the bastard in the back!'

The momentary distraction was enough. Ballista aimed a thrust to the face. Publipor instinctively flinched and yanked his sword up to protect his head. Dropping to one knee, Ballista altered the angle of attack. The tip of his sword plunged deep into Publipor's stomach.

Heaving the mortally injured man away, Ballista recovered and sheathed his blade. Alarmed by the violence and the smell of blood, the horses were plunging and trying to rear. Every herd instinct warned them of danger, told them to run. A life-time of horsemanship kept the stable lads hanging on. The older was almost lifted off his feet. Ballista grabbed the mane of the nearest mount, and vaulted onto its back. As his weight came down, the beast sidestepped. Without thought, the younger lad let go of the reins. Gathering them, Ballista reached over and took those of the other horse from the old man.

Publipor was still alive, on the threshold, not moving, but bleeding profusely. The second huntsman was crouched just by the door, hands pressed to his wound, sobbing and swearing. The horses did not want to go near them. Ballista kicked his mount in the ribs. It dug in its feet, refusing to budge. An angry murmur was rising from the throng outside. Relinquishing the reins, Ballista drew his sword, brought the flat of the blade hard down on the horse's rump. It leapt forward so fast, the lead rein of the other was almost jerked from Ballista's other hand.

The crowd scattered as they thundered out of the barn. Ballista felt a fierce exultation. He went to turn his horse using the pressure of his thighs. The beast responded, but the blanket slipped. Through fear or design, the young stable lad had not fastened the surcingle. Ballista was losing his seat. He was going to fall.

A roar rose from the slaves. Once he was unhorsed, they were ready to tear him to pieces.

Dropping the sword, Ballista hauled himself halfway up the horse's neck. Letting go of the lead rein, he snatched away the blanket before it could deposit him on the ground. Settling himself bareback, legs clamped hard to the beast's flanks, he saw the second horse had bolted off towards the main house.

To Hades with it.

Ballista drove his mount down through the farm.

Even the hideous remains of Caecilius and his son could not quench the resurgence of a primeval joy as Ballista rode out of the gate into the night.

CHAPTER SEVEN

THE SLATE-GREY LIGHT OF PREDAWN found them riding east. They went through the hills along drovers' paths fringed by thickets of gorse and thistle, overlooked by stunted trees, both holm oak and juniper. They had ridden through the remaining hours of the night. The boy, his arms round his father's waist, was barely awake.

After escaping from the farm, Ballista had hacked the horse up through the orchard. There had been no immediate pursuit. Up at the cliff, Isangrim had been voluble with relief, the words tumbling out. Earlier he had heard footfalls. Crouching in the cave, he had thought it was a man. Then out into the clearing had stepped a stag with a huge spread of antlers. It was a sign. Diana's own beast. It had stopped, and looked straight at him where he was hidden, before leaving. The goddess had them in her protection. When the story was over, Ballista had hugged his son. He wished he shared the boy's faith.

With his son mounted behind him, Ballista had given the villa a wide berth. Once clear, he had pushed the animal as fast as the going and the darkness allowed. Killing the leader of the uprising at the villa might have two consequences. Either the rebellious slaves would be despondent, too disheartened to give chase, or they would be hot for revenge. If the latter, there were many other horses in Caecilius' stables, and other huntsmen to pick up the trail. Their mounts would not be burdened with two riders. Ballista knew they were far from safe yet.

By sunrise the land was dipping towards a wide valley. Here the scrub had been cleared, and the slopes were terraced. Each step was no more than a pace or two wide, the result of patient and back-breaking labour. Ballista reined in, and scanned the surroundings. There would be a settlement within walking distance, a rural estate or a village, but it could not be seen. He went on carefully, looking all around. Isangrim was asleep.

A road ran along the floor of the valley. Broad and paved, it had to be the one that crossed the island from Panormus to Agrigentum. Ballista had travelled it a couple of times many years before. From his point of vantage he could see for at least a mile in each direction. He did not recognise this stretch, but, more important, nothing moved on the road. Ballista nudged the horse down the incline.

Isangrim woke as they clattered out onto the road.

'Where are we?'

'Well away from the villa.'

Ballista turned south, and urged the horse to a slow canter. He kept to the middle of the road. The packed sand on either side would be kinder on the horse's hooves, but the stone slabs left no imprint.

The road followed the green lowland. The autumn rains had brought out the grass. At intervals were copses of chestnuts; good for foraging pigs, but no animals or swineherds were about. Off to the left rose bare, chalk-white cliffs. Their sides were furrowed and channelled, as if the rocks had once run like melted wax.

A gentle canter would eat up the miles, but the horse was already tired. Ballista brought it back to a walk.

'We should take the weight off its back, lead it for a bit,' Isangrim said.

Halting, Ballista looked back the way they had come. His heart lurched. A horseman in the distance. No more than a dark speck, but moving fast. Only one to be seen. Others could be following.

'There!' Isangrim had seen it too.

'Hold on!'

Ballista booted the horse back into motion. There was a stand of trees an arrow shot ahead. The horse did not want to run. Bareback, with his son clinging on, it was not easy to push the recalcitrant beast along with arms and legs. Ballista spoke to it encouragingly, clicked his tongue in his cheek.

They skidded to a standstill in the shade of the trees. Tumbling off its back, they led the horse deep into the grove. The thick trunks of the chestnuts provided reasonable cover.

'Give me the sword.'

Isangrim looked unhappy, but passed it over.

Soon they could hear the drumming of hooves. Just one horse, going at a gallop. Ballista talked quietly to their horse, bringing his face down to its nostrils, so that his breath mingled with the sweet exhalations of the animal. The big bay gelding ruckled quietly down its nose. Reassured by his companionship, it would not call out.

The traveller came into view. The flanks of his mount were foamed with sweat, great ropes of saliva streaming from its mouth. It had been ridden hard for a long way. As Ballista watched, the horse broke its stride. The animal was exhausted. Not for the first time, its rider spurred it savagely on. There were bloody weals on its sides left by the rowels.

The man rode as if the Furies were on his heels. This was a messenger bearing bad news, or a man fleeing for his life. If he had seen Ballista and Isangrim before they took cover, he did not care. Not once did he glance at the trees. His whole attention was on the road ahead. He did not look back. Whatever the malign cause of his headlong journey, for now he was sure that he had outrun the danger.

Before the rider vanished out of sight, Ballista judged his appearance. A tunic too dusty and travel-stained to reveal anything. But, although likewise matted with dirt, his hair and beard were short and neatly trimmed. If he was a slave, he was a favoured domestic – something like a secretary or bookkeeper.

The rattle of hooves faded. No one else came down the road.

'We will wait a little longer,' Ballista said. 'Hold his head, and keep an eye on the road.'

Facing its tail, Ballista picked up each of the horse's legs in turn, held them between his own thighs, and inspected and cleaned its feet. He removed a few small stones with his knife. Then, with his bare hands and wisps of dry grass, he rubbed the horse down as best he could. There was something calming about the mechanical repetition of the task. He paid especial attention to smoothing its coat along its back.

'How much longer?'

'Not long, but we need to be sure.'

Having seen to the horse, Ballista rootled about under the trees, gathering fallen chestnuts. He stuffed them into the wallets and pouches and the empty scabbard on Isangrim's belt.

Still the road was empty. More likely the man carried bad tidings than sought to escape some immediate threat. In the direction he had come there were no large towns until Panormus. Similarly there were none to the south until Agrigentum. Caecilius had said Soter and the main rebel force were headed to Panormus. Perhaps the rider brought news of their arrival. Ballista wondered if he would reach the south coast before the other band of slaves. It was improbable he would ever have the answer.

'That is long enough.'

They led the gelding out onto the road. Ballista gave his son a leg-up, and mounted behind him. The horse was somewhat rested, but they went at no more than an amble through the deceptively peaceful landscape.

After a time, the road snaked as it graded up into higher country. Ballista worried that the horse seemed to peck now and then, favouring its nearside foreleg. There was nothing to be done. He shook it into a brief canter, and it responded well enough.

Soon gaps appeared in the cliffs to the left. Green valleys ran away to the east. Ballista chose one with a tiny upland rivulet, and turned off the road. Where water runs, usually a man can follow. Sure enough, there was a track beside the stream.

Ballista's spirits lifted. They were heading in the right direction. These were the hills of Gemellus, outliers of the Nebrodes mountains. The peaks were high and wild, but down here the countryside was verdant. Rabbits scampered away through the undergrowth. The Sicilian autumn was fruitful. No man need starve in these hills.

As the sun neared its zenith, his good mood evaporated. The gelding was lame, no doubt whatsoever. They dismounted and walked. The animal did not want to place its near forelimb on the ground. Ballista felt the leg. It was hot. Ballista took the bit from its mouth, removed the reins, but left the halter. He spoke kindly to the horse, looked into its lustrous eyes, and turned it loose. Immediately it began to crop the grass.

'We have no baggage, and the mountains lie ahead.'

'Will the horse be all right?' Isangrim asked.

'He can forage for himself,' Ballista said.

Isangrim still looked concerned.

'Do not worry. He will be fine. Sooner or later someone will find him.'

Ballista ran his hand over the glossy withers. There was a brand – a C – that he had not noticed before. Whoever found the gelding would not be returning him to Caecilius.

Before they walked on, Ballista tied the reins over his shoulders. Good leather was always useful. Looking back, he saw the horse, head down, grazing.

Another hour and the stream turned towards the north. It would merge with other streams, at some point find a river, and eventually their combined waters would reach the coast and run into the sea. After Panormus, Soter and his followers would take the road along the north coast. Ballista did not share his thoughts with his son.

They trudged north – weary, hot and silent – until Ballista spotted a track branching off to the right. Trodden down by the passage of centuries of flocks, it ran up into the hills to the east.

'Are you ready to carry on?'

'I am hungry.'

'We can find food later,' Ballista said.

There were green places tucked into the folds of the uplands, but what dominated the view was shoulder after shoulder of bare white limestone escarpments. Each dotted with boulders, they receded, one after another, into the misted distance. At first glance it seemed impossible that any creature could live up here. Yet great predatory birds wheeled taut arcs above the peaks. Eagles and buzzards did not hunt where there was no prey. Along the trails were piles of stones. Tumbled from above, they were the relics of small avalanches caused by herds of goats in the summer. Once the eye knew where to look, small birds and shy animals moved in the oases of greenery.

A couple of hours of daylight remained when they saw the hut. Built of stone, with a shingle roof, it was in disrepair. One corner had largely collapsed. Ballista did not bother to wait and watch. During their long approach, it was obviously abandoned. Besides, there was much to do before darkness.

The door had gone, probably used for fuel by some previous vagrant drifting through these high places. Inside it smelt of mice and mouldering dust. The chimney still stood. The ashes in the hearth were stone-cold. There was nothing to salvage. Outside was a spring of sweet water. It ran in a tiny rivulet down to woods in a sheltered valley.

They drank, then together went down into the trees to gather firewood. Songbirds sang, and lizards and other shy creatures rustled away through the undergrowth. Ballista was very hungry. The boy must be starving. They had not eaten since the previous night. They dragged the wood back, laid the fire, but did not yet light it. Ballista fashioned the leathers of the reins into a sling, while Isangrim collected suitable rounded stones.

Back in the timber, the denizens of the first warren they found vanished underground before they got near. The rabbits of the second were less cautious. They sat on their haunches, noses twitching, suspicious but not alarmed. Ballista did not hurry. There would only be time for one shot.

Soon the rabbits returned to their feeding. Ballista selected a perfectly spherical stone, about the size of a hen's egg. As he whirled the sling around his head, his target looked up. Released, the missile thrummed through the air. The rabbit turned to retreat to safety. It was not the cleanest of strikes. The stone bowled the rabbit over. It screamed, and tried to hop away. One of its back legs was broken. Ballista went over, picked up the struggling bundle of fur, and ended its pain with a chop to the back of the neck.

They got the fire going and, while Isangrim tended it, Ballista skinned and jointed the rabbit. They used the sword and the two daggers as skewers. It was bad for the weapons. In time it would make the steel brittle. But needs must. They were too hungry to wait. The outside of the meat was burnt, the inside raw. They sucked everything off the bones, licked the grease off their fingers. When the flames had died, they fished the chestnuts out from the scabbard and pouches, and roasted them in the hot ashes.

It was dark. The smoke would have betrayed their presence to anyone in the surrounding hills. Tonight they would take it in turns to stand guard: three hours on, three off, through the twelve hours until light. The watcher would remain outside. The shelter commanded a good vantage point. The moon was not far off full. Unless it became overcast, no one could get close without being seen. Isangrim insisted he would take the first watch.

'Move about. It will keep you warm, help you stay awake.'

Isangrim said that he would.

Ballista gave him the sword. He wanted to say something to his son, some praise or reassurance, but the words would not come.

Going into the shelter, Ballista lay down by the residual warmth of the fireplace, and was instantly asleep.

In some corner of his mind, he heard the clink of stones as his son shifted his position, patrolled around the hut. But he was no longer in the hills of Gemellus, but far away in the North of his own childhood, far away by the cold Suebian Sea. He was in the great hall. His father was there, seated on his throne; his mother, too, behind her loom. All his brothers were around him, even the ones that were dead. *You and me, like snow drifting from one tree to another*, one of them said. There were two other figures, indistinct at the edge of the firelight. Kadlin, the first woman he had loved. And another standing beside her. With a terrible longing, he called to them.

'Wake up!' Isangrim was shaking his shoulder.

'What is it?'

'You were shouting in your sleep – barbarian names.'

'It was nothing – just a nightmare.'

'Are you sure?' Isangrim was looking at him oddly.

'Sure.'

'The gods send warnings in dreams.'

'Just a nightmare. How many hours have passed?'

'A couple.'

'I will take over the watch. Get some sleep yourself.'

Ballista took the sword. As he left, his son was still regarding him strangely – a look of infinite and sad compassion.

It was colder outside. No cloud cover, a mantle of stars. Methodically, Ballista scanned the treeline below. Nothing stirred. Treading softly, he walked all around the hut. In every direction, the rocky slopes were bare in the moonlight. Hugging himself against the chill, he moved into the shadow of the hut.

It was almost impossible that he would ever return to the North, almost impossible that he would ever see his family again. If he made that journey, few would welcome him. It was best not to think of them. By day he controlled his mind like a badly broken horse with a savage curb bit. But at night the beast was unbridled; free of the cruel steel in its tender mouth, it ran where it wanted.

In the morning they trudged on. The landscape ever changing, ever the same. Towards noon they came to a pass. A plume of smoke rose from the narrows. The cliffs were steep on either side. There was no way round.

Leaving the track, they crept closer, from boulder to boulder.

Six men near the fire. Spears and bow cases leaning against the rocks. Nets and stakes neatly rolled, backpacks stacked. The carcass of a roe deer. No horses. A hunting party on foot in the mountains. It was too far to make any judgements from their apparel, but their actions indicated the hierarchy among them. Two men were making an offering. It would be to Diana, patron deity of the chase. The others were standing at a respectful distance, right hands flat to their chests in a gesture of reverence. When due thanks for their success had been given, the two officiating sat at their ease. The rest got on with building up the fire and butchering the deer.

'We will go and talk to them.'

'Is it safe?'

'I think so,' Ballista said.

There was no commotion as the unexpected newcomers walked into the pass. The two in charge got up and waited at the edge of the little camp. They were dressed for the field in good quality cloaks and boots. The others, more roughly attired, did not pause from their tasks.

'Health and great joy,' Ballista said.

The two men replied in the same Attic Greek. Ballista relaxed a fraction. Only the elite spoke the dialect. It took expensive schooling to talk in the long-dead literary language of Demosthenes and Plato.

Before any questions were asked, Ballista recited some lines in the even older Ionic dialect.

'*Whose land have I lit on now?*

What are they here – violent, savage, lawless?

Or friendly to strangers, and god-fearing men?'

Both men smiled. 'Odysseus was naked when he appeared before the Phaeacians, not wearing a bloodstained tunic.'

'Let me explain.'

'And Odysseus told them a pack of lies.'

'My name is Marcus Clodius Ballista, and this is my son. We are on our way home to Tauromenium. Like Odysseus, we are castaways. Our ship was wrecked, up beyond Panormus. We were taken in by Publius Caecilius Titianus. The night before last, he was murdered by his household slaves.'

The two men looked at each other with consternation. Behind them, their slaves gave one another no more than a surreptitious glance.

'In the confusion, we escaped.'

'And the blood on your tunic?'

'That of one of Caecilius' slaves.'

The older man, who had said nothing so far, replied with a quotation.

Friend, you are hardly a wicked man, and no fool, I'd say –
It's Olympian Zeus himself who hands our fortunes out,
To each of us in turn, to the good and the bad,
However Zeus prefers . . .
He gave you pain, it seems . . .
But now, seeing you've reached our city and our land,
You'll never lack for clothing or any other gift.

He made a gesture of welcome.

'Not, of course, that you are anywhere near a city. My name is Lucius Aurelius Iuncinus of Messana, and this is my son. Our country estate lies south of here. Your name goes before you – the general who saved the sanctuary of Apollo at Didyma from the Goths, who defeated the Persian King of Kings at Soli. It is an honour to shake your hand.'

'You have been in the hills for some time?' Ballista asked.

'Since the Ides of October.'

Isangrim shot his father a questioning look. Ballista slightly shook his head.

'Come, accept what hospitality we can offer in this out-of-the-way place.' Aurelius called over his shoulder. 'Fides, break out clean tunics from the packs for our guests.'

As they washed and changed, Isangrim whispered, 'You have to tell them.'

'At the right time.' Ballista grinned. 'Just sometimes I should thank the schoolmasters on the Palatine for the beatings that made me learn so much of Homer by heart.'

Isangrim sighed at the attempt at levity.

Not long after, they all sat to eat. Except for the cook, the slaves were seated with their masters.

The venison was not quite ready, but there were olives and cheese. The hard, twice-baked bread had to be dipped in the wine to make it edible. Aware of his empty stomach, Ballista drank sparingly. He needed his wits about him. Before speaking, he checked where the hunting weapons were placed relative to those dining.

'Aurelius, I would speak to you alone.'

'There is nothing that cannot be said in front of all my *familia*.' Aurelius looked somewhat put out.

'Very well. The murder of Caecilius and his family was only a part of it. Other slaves attacked us as we came ashore. They massacred everyone else from the ship. Caecilius told us that there was a general rising of slaves across the west of the island.'

The servants of Aurelius looked, if anything, more shocked than their master.

'That will be all those Alamanni,' Aurelius said.

'Yes, whipped up by some Syrian wonder-worker. There are two groups of rebels. One advancing along the coast road in the north, the other in the south.'

Aurelius was calm. 'Well, we are in the centre of the island, and we have nothing to fear from my boys.'

The four slaves stammered that he should not think such a thing. They looked terrified.

'Those masters who say they have as many enemies as slaves are fools. If it is true, then their own vicious behaviour has made it so in their households. Every man has a spark of divine reason within himself. What we call slavery and freedom are no more than legal customs. True freedom and slavery lie within ourselves. Everything else is an irrelevance. Most rich men are slaves to their appetites – to lust and greed, to fear and hope, to ambition and wealth. Although the king of Persia sits on a golden throne, and all his subjects prostrate themselves in the dust before him, if he has a servile soul, he is no more than a slave. Likewise, the most abject prisoner labouring in the mines, shackled hand and foot, is a freeman, if he has a noble soul.'

Aurelius' face shone as he expounded his deeply held philosophic doctrine. Those of his slaves were rapt, but – to Ballista at least – inscrutable.

'All men are brothers, no matter their status in life. That is why we, who fate has favoured, have a duty to treat those below us with kindness. We must make sure that they are adequately fed and clothed. We must never cast them out when they are too sick or old to work. If punishment is necessary, it should be done with words, only when all else fails resorting to beatings. Better to praise and reward good service. Best of all, hold out the promise of manumission. And at no great length of time – after six years at the latest. These are the principles on which I have always run my *familia*, and that is why we have no reason to fear any in my household.'

The four unfree members of his *familia* present were nodding in complete agreement.

'Even the lowest member of my household has hope for the none too distant future, and in the meantime they can take comfort from the freedom they can find within themselves.'

Yes, yes, the slaves rushed to concur with every wise word of their master.

'So, my friend, we can eat and drink and enjoy ourselves this afternoon. Tonight we can sleep sound, and tomorrow my man here, Fides, can guide you on your way.'

CHAPTER EIGHT

SICILY WAS A TRIANGLE STRETCHED between three capes: Pelorias on the straits to Italy, Lilybaeum facing the winter sunset, and Pachynus, which looked towards Greece. Although Marcus had travelled the island as a child with his mother, visiting relatives or connections of her family, most of his knowledge of its geography came from books he had read in the schoolroom on the Palatine. He knew that the Nebrodes mountains ran, like a central spine, from northeast to south-west. There were two main routes through the uplands down from the north coast. One was the road from Panormus to Agrigentum, that he and his father had already crossed. The other – from Himera to Enna in the centre, and on to Catana on the east coast – was the one to which the slave of Aurelius was guiding them.

The country here was as wild as any through which they had passed. Remote wooded glens, alpine meadows with pools as still as glass, and open shoulders of bare rock. Ridge after ridge, each bristling like the back of a hog, marched into a blue infinity in the east. Marcus felt like a trespasser going through the rustling timber, and out on the open slopes it was easy to imagine every boulder on the skyline concealed some malign watcher.

Others might have found beauty in the isolated landscape. Marcus, like many of his class, just saw desolation. For him, the countryside was alien and dangerous. It was something you hurried through as fast as possible from one town to another, or to the safety of a landed estate owned by a wealthy family like your own.

Suddenly Marcus thought of his mother. Until the Palatine school, she had been a constant presence in his life, unlike his absent father. Of course, she had not been the only one. There had been his nurse, the rest of the household. It was the servants who had cosseted and spoilt him. His mother had the self-control of a traditional Roman matron, had insisted on the decorum fitting in a senatorial family. But Marcus remembered her scent, a waft of cinnamon and roses. He remembered her rare moments of spontaneous affection, like the sun on water, when she enfolded him in her arms and her dark hair fell across his face. Marcus felt like a child again, a child who wanted to be safe at home with his mother. And with that came a terrible dread. What if all that safety was gone? What if the rebels reached Tauromenium before them? Marcus struggled to push the awful thought away, tried to think like a man.

At least the weather was kind. Although there was a chill in the air, they moved through pale autumn sunshine, with gentle breezes and no sign of rain. And they were well equipped. Aurelius had been open-handed. He had provided not just new tunics and cloaks, but food and drink – cheese, dried beef, biscuit and wine – a drinking cup each and a pot for cooking, with packs to carry everything. Most importantly, he had given them two boar spears and a bow, with apologies that its quiver only contained six arrows; they had used many hunting. Marcus was gifted a sword. It was enshrined in the law of Rome that any free man had the right to be armed for the hunt or self-defence. Given the times, the latter eventuality was all too likely.

Such generosity was to be expected. The richer the individual, the greater the expectation of munificence. It was not entirely voluntary or altruistic. A reputation for meanness undermined status, threatened a man's standing in society. Gifts given to the people – oil for the baths, public dinners, gladiatorial shows, and the like – brought honour. Those to other members of the elite demanded reciprocity. From now on the family of Ballista was bound to that of Aurelius. In the future, favours would have to be returned. It was the way the world worked.

They crested yet another ridge, and descended into yet another forested valley. The repetition did not dull the apprehension. Under the trees, dense undergrowth cut vision to a few paces. Long black snakes slithered away without a sound, just glimpsed in the dappled sunlight, then gone. The noise of the cicadas, and of their boots crunching through drifts of dry leaves, meant an army could have approached them unheard, as well as unseen.

Marcus was relieved when they emerged onto another empty escarpment, until he noticed the sun. Fides seemed to be leading them not east, but north. Aurelius' slave was a man of few words. His silent reserve was unsettling. Marcus did not trust him. Back at the camp, all the slaves had been genuinely surprised by the news of the uprising. And they had all clamoured to express their loyalty. But what else would they say? Aurelius was an unusual owner. Most left their Stoic principles behind in the schoolroom or lecture hall. Few disagreed with the sentiment that they had as many enemies as they had slaves. Marcus had read that not that long ago – was it in the reign of the emperor Alexander Severus? – the senate had debated whether to order every slave to wear a distinctive costume. The proposed law had been vetoed, and with good reason. If the servile were made aware how they outnumbered the free, there would be no restraining them. Every citizen would have his throat cut. His wife and children would be raped, before their throats were cut as well. This slave Fides could easily be taking Marcus and his father to the rebels. The *good faith* implied by his name might prove no more than a misplaced hope.

Marcus looked over at his father. Spear in hand, pack on back, Ballista was striding along as if he did not have a care in the world. Everything about him radiated confidence in his place in the world – confidence to think his way around any hindrance, or cut through it with sharp steel. No Gordian knot would detain him long. But the other night Marcus had seen another man. His father had whimpered in his sleep. Trapped in the coils of a nightmare, he had shouted out in fear. Amid the incomprehensible barbarian names, there had been something else. Ballista had cried out in longing: *My son, my son.*

The unconscious moment of weakness, the unexpected tenderness, made him less remote, more human. Alexander the Great had said that only sex and sleep reminded him that he was mortal. The stern figure of his father, almost always absent on some distant campaign, had dominated Marcus' childhood. It was a daunting image that his mother had created. There was the martial virtue, and the unbending loyalty, both to be emulated. But there were the darker things hardly ever to be spoken: the dangerous ambition that had led him to take the purple, and the barbarian origins that caused the family such embarrassment. The latter had been mentioned often enough in the school on the Palatine. The sly deprecations of the masters, the cruel jibes of the other boys. At first, the fist fights with pupils, and the resulting beatings by the teachers, had left him in a permanent state of dread and resentment. As he had grown over the last year, and his capacity for retaliation had developed, there had been less trouble.

They bivouacked for the night in a small clearing in the pines. The splayed roots of a fallen tree made a windbreak. They gathered boughs to make bedding and a fire. Ballista announced the night would be divided into four watches. Fides would take the first and last, Ballista the second and Marcus the third. When he had sent the slave to fetch water from a stream downslope, Ballista told his son to wake him before turning in at the end of the third watch. He claimed that he wanted to see the dawn to judge the coming day's weather.

They ate their provisions round the campfire, largely in silence. Fides stood guard, patrolling beyond the firelight to preserve his night vision. Ballista said that he would sit up for a while. Tired beyond thought, Marcus bedded down.

Marcus woke in the middle of the night. Again his father touched him gently behind the ear. It was almost a caress. Marcus got up, brushing off the pine needles. The slave was rolled up in his cloak, on the far side of the smouldering fire, snoring loudly. Ballista lay down, and was instantly asleep.

The three hours crawled by, as the cold stars wheeled across the firmament. An owl hooted nearby, and was answered from far away. More than once there was the sound of movement through the trees. Although he told himself it was only animals, probably deer – like the stag back at the villa, beloved of the goddess – each time Marcus had to grit his teeth to stop them chattering. The ancient Spartans had a word for men like him. They were *tremblers*. Wiping the sweat off his palms, he gripped the shaft of his spear. Unless he was certain there was a threat, he would not wake the other two.

When he was sure his watch was over, he went back to the fire to wake Fides. The slave's eyes were open. It was unnerving. Without a word, Fides got up and went out.

Marcus took a drink. The wine did not settle him. His father was on his side, head cradled on an arm. Tonight his rest was undisturbed. In the ambient light he looked younger. Ballista had been little older than Marcus when he had come into the empire. It was the year in which the emperor Maximinus had been killed. That would put him in his fourth decade. Marcus knew his father's birthday. Every year his mother had made an offering to his genius the day before the Ides of February. But he did not know the year of his birth. It was one of many things that he did not know about his father.

Ballista was sleeping so peacefully, Marcus was reluctant to disturb him. One thing his mother had told him about his father was that before he was brought to Rome, Ballista had served on campaign with his own people, and had killed a man in battle. He had undergone the barbarian rite of passage to manhood at about Marcus' age.

Marcus decided to let his father sleep. He would remain awake, and watch for any treachery from their guide.

It was break of day, and Ballista was furious. He had sent Fides back down to get fresh water, so that he could discipline his son.

'All those Roman stories that you learn at school – do they mean nothing to you?'

Isangrim kept quiet.

'All those famous Roman commanders who executed their sons for disobeying orders? They were executed, despite fighting heroically, because they had left the line. Men like Aulus Postumius and Torquatus. A Roman youth obeys orders.'

Still Isangrim said nothing.

'In your Roman law, *patria potestas* gives a father complete control over his son. In the old days he could put his son to death without trial.'

'You were tired,' Isangrim said.

'We are both tired. You should have woken me up.'

'I will take the toga of manhood next spring. I have been trained in arms by the leading masters in Rome.'

'You are a child.'

Ballista sounded petulant even to himself. If anything, he was the one acting like a child. The anger caused by his worry was draining away.

'How old were you when you first fought in battle?' Isangrim asked.

'Older than you.'

'How much older?'

'A couple of years.'

Fides was making a great deal of noise coming up through the trees.

'You should trust me,' Isangrim said.

Ballista took his son's arms in his hands. 'You are right, and I am sorry. Thank you.'

After chewing some of the twice-baked bread and taking a swallow of watered wine, the three resumed their lonely odyssey.

This morning, Fides was more forthcoming. He pointed towards a flash of wings in the branches.

'A jackdaw, like in the fable.'

'Which one?'

'A man caught a jackdaw, tied a thread to its foot, and gave it to his child. But the bird could not resign itself to captivity, and the child was careless. When the bird flew away the thread got caught in a bush. On the point of death, the jackdaw lamented. Not being able to endure slavery to man, it had deprived itself of life.'

Obviously Fides had overheard Ballista's earlier conversation with his son. Ballista and the slave looked at each other, and both understood the moral of the story.

They halted at midday, ate some more of their rations, and rested.

'We will reach the road by mid-afternoon,' Fides said. 'The path is stony, but there is only one place that concerns me. We have to pass through a deserted village called Gorgion. It has a bad reputation.'

'Brigands?'

Fides nodded. 'It is an ideal lair. The road is visible from there, but Gorgion is difficult to approach, and in the cliffs are many caves in which to hide.'

'You have been there?'

'Yes, a couple of years ago, with the master. We saw no one, yet all the time we had a sense of being watched. We were a large hunting party. There are only three of us.'

'There is no way round?'

'Not that I know.'

'Then we must take care.'

Isangrim shot his father a look. Ballista was not sure that his son had drawn the intended message from the fable of the jackdaw – or, if he had, that it had allayed his suspicions. Indeed, words were one thing, actions quite another.

'How many years have you been with Aurelius?' Ballista said.

'Four and a half years.'

'You will be freed in eighteen months?'

'So the master has said.'

'Does Aurelius always grant manumission after six years?'

Fides paused, choosing his words. 'With those of us who serve faithfully in the house, yes. He has less contact with those who labour in the fields – sometimes they slip his mind.'

'Are they kept chained?'

Fides looked uncomfortable. 'Only the ones who shirk their work.'

'Iron bars do not make a prison. True freedom lies in a man's soul.'

'So the master says.' Fides gazed up at a buzzard circling on the updraughts of the hills. 'We have the same dreams as free men, but for us they have different meanings. Last summer, in Messana, I had a strange dream that I had been condemned to be crucified. For a few coppers I had it explained by a dream diviner in the market place. Had I been rich and free, it would have signified great harm, since those on the cross are stripped naked and lose their flesh. But for a slave it means freedom, since the dead are no longer subject to any man. There is comfort in that.'

Gorgion was like many abandoned settlements scattered across the hilltops of central Sicily. In the unsettled times before Rome conquered the island, people lived in such places for defence. After the establishment of Roman peace, their inhabitants drifted down to villas and villages in the more accessible valleys.

Gorgion sat on a saddle of land between two precipices. The cliffs reared up on either side. They were sheer, and pockmarked with the black mouths of caves. Fides was right – there was no way round. Although they could have been observed by any number of concealed watchers, there was nothing for it but to openly walk up the steep track to the village. Even so, they went spread out, in an arrowhead. Better not to bunch together, and make a better target. Like this, if something happened, they would not get in one another's way. Fides was leading, Ballista behind and to his right, Isangrim on the left. The slave and the youth each had his boar spear ready in both hands. Ballista had their one bow half-drawn, with an arrow nocked ready. His spear was hung over his shoulder by a loop. Looking at the caves, Ballista wished he had a shield and full armour. An arrow can punch through a mail coat, but wearing one increased one's confidence.

At the outskirts of the village, without anyone calling a halt, they paused. No words were necessary. Each was getting his courage up, eyes running over what lay ahead, scanning for the slightest hint of movement.

The houses huddled together in two rows flanking the narrow path through the hamlet. It was the perfect site for an ambush: complete cover overlooking a constricted space that left the victims nowhere to go. The dwellings of Gorgion had never been much more than hovels. Now they were in a state of long ruination. Doors and windows were gone, and the crumbling stones of their walls bulged and leaned ominously. The tiled roofs sagged. In many cases the timbers had given way, and most of the tiles had fallen; sometimes whole walls had collapsed. The latter had made piles of rubble, further narrowing the street.

But not all the dwellings were completely neglected. Ballista could see that the roofs of two in the middle of the village had been roughly patched. There was no telling how recently they had been repaired.

Ballista returned the bow to its case on his back, the arrow to the quiver. He unslung the spear from his shoulder. If men were waiting, this would be close work.

Fides looked over his shoulder. Ballista nodded. Again, wordlessly they set off. Ballista glanced at his son. Isangrim managed a tight smile in return.

They entered the confines of the settlement. Fides looking ahead, Ballista and Isangrim half-turned, walking crabwise, watching the openings of the houses on their flanks. No sounds, but the stones scrunching under their boots, their own hoarse breathing. There was no heat in the day, but Ballista's sides were running with sweat. Step after cautious step, senses strung tight like the strings of a lyre, they inched past the houses that had been repaired.

Nothing. They were at the far end. Behind them, nothing but mouldering ruins.

'What now?' Isangrim said.

'Check all the houses and the closest caves,' Ballista said. 'Then we can rest.'

They found the corpse in one of the caves. A young girl, perhaps not yet ten, one ankle shackled to the wall. She had been dead for some time; her dress was faded and ragged. There was little smell of putrefaction. In the dry air, her body was partly mummified. But animals had found her.

'Perhaps her family did not pay the ransom,' Fides said.

'Or the bandits were captured, and could not return,' Ballista said.

Isangrim went outside.

'We will at least free her spirit,' Ballista said.

'This is not a place to linger.'

'Help me break the chain.' Ballista's tone allowed no debate.

Both men worked in turns. It took some time pounding one link with rocks before it snapped. They did not bury her, but Ballista tipped three handfuls of earth on her head, and placed a small coin in her mouth. If the bandits returned, they would steal the coin. But that did not matter. Her spirit would have paid the ferryman, and crossed over the river to the dark meadows of Hades.

Outside, Isangrim was perched on a rock higher up, keeping watch.

'You can see the road from here.'

'Follow the track down,' Fides said. 'If you have no objection, I will leave you here. I need to get back to the estate.'

'No objection.' Ballista brought three high-denomination coins from his wallet. 'Our thanks, and give our regards to your master.'

Fides did not leave immediately.

'Every man has a master. The emperor is above the law. Every Roman is his slave. If true freedom lies in a man's soul, that may be more of a comfort to a senator than a slave.'

CHAPTER NINE

IT WAS AN EXTRAORDINARY PROCESSION. Ballista and Isangrim heard them coming down the road from Himera before they saw them. The sound of a flute, the clashing of cymbals and the beat of tambourines, mingling on the late afternoon air. There was no need to hide – the Phrygian music announced their nature.

They came around the shoulder of the hill. The effigy of the goddess nodded above her worshippers. She was seated on a throne carved with lions. A sceptre in one hand, a distaff in the other, on her head she wore a tall crown, like the walls of a city. Her robes were of many colours: white, sea-green, wine-dark. Splashes of paint mimicked emeralds, jacinth, and onyxes. A bauble of glass set in her headdress flashed in the sunshine. The goddess swayed, as if actually riding the donkey to which her image was tied.

Her attendants were more outlandish. There were six of them, clad in diaphanous eastern robes dyed saffron and purple, arms bare to the shoulders, with girdles around their waists. On their heads were Phrygian caps, like those of freed slaves, on their feet delicate yellow slippers. All were long-haired and beardless. Their faces were whitened, lips rouged, and their eyes darkened with kohl. Dangling earrings hung from their ears. As well as the musical instruments, they carried long swords, maces and whips.

At the front of the procession, the flautist – a strapping, bearded slave – was dressed and walked normally. Behind him, the eunuchs capered and minced.

'The blessings of the Great Mother Atargatis be upon you.'

The hedge-priest was older than his companions. His grey hair hung in long ringlets down his neck.

'Health and great joy to you,' Ballista said.

'I am Philebus, servant of the Syrian goddess.'

'My name is Marcus Clodius Ballista, and this is my son.'

The other Galli were cooing around Isangrim. The boy looked unhappy. It was unlucky on a journey to encounter a eunuch – only a monkey was worse.

'Where have you come from?' Ballista asked.

'We are on our way from Himera to Enna.'

'Are you not afraid to travel in such times?'

'The almighty goddess will protect us. But she warned us to leave Himera before the rebels arrived.'

'Have they already got so far?'

'They sacked Panormus some days ago. By now they will be in Himera.'

That was bad. The insurgents were moving faster along the north coast than Ballista had expected. Time was pressing, but he could still reach his family in Tauromenium before them. By all the gods, he must do so.

'There is a farm not far ahead. The owner is poor, but a god-fearing man. He has offered us hospitality before. We would welcome your company.'

Ballista and Isangrim walked behind the strange tinkling and drumming group.

'How can a man do such a thing to himself,' Isangrim said quietly.

'They dance themselves into a frenzy, then in their ecstasy use a blade or sharp stone. Oddly enough, most of them survive.'

'But why do it?'

'To free themselves from lust, although by repute they give way to the temptation more than an entire man. They are said to be more addicted to sex than the most wanton of women.'

'What deity would demand such a sacrifice?'

'In the East I heard many different stories. In Pessinus they say their self-mutilation honours Attis, who was emasculated by a goddess because she did not want him to marry a mortal woman. In Hierapolis they tell a tale about Combabus, who castrated himself to prove that he had not committed adultery with a queen.'

Isangrim's hand went instinctively to his groin.

'Don't worry, they do not try to force others to join their ranks. Although they are terrible beggars and thieves.'

Removing his hand, Isangrim gave a rueful grin.

'In Hierapolis, it is good luck if they throw their severed genitals into your house. Maximus lost a lot of money to me in that city. Outside the temple are two tall pillars shaped like phalluses. For some reason young men climb them, and sit on top for seven days. Maximus bet that one would fall off.'

'I want to see the world.'

'You will. All too soon for my peace of mind.'

Isangrim laughed. 'It can't get more much perilous than the last few days.'

Although it was not dusk when they reached the farm, the gates were shut, and behind them the dogs were loose. Either the owner was a cautious man, or local conditions were unsettled. Whichever, true to his reputation for piety, the farmer had his aged porter chain the dogs and open the gates as soon as the Galli made themselves known. The farmer himself was short, with broad shoulders. His face was seamed and leathery from exposure to the elements. He received the mendicant priests with warmth. Ballista and Isangrim were greeted politely, if with less enthusiasm.

There and then, in the small farmyard, the devotees of the Great Mother set about earning their night's lodgings. All the inhabitants – family and farm workers – came out to watch. The small crowd ringed the farmyard, keeping well back to leave an open space of bare earth. Torches were lit against the coming of the night. Ballista and Isangrim hung back in the gloom by the now closed gate.

The goddess was unstrapped from the donkey, and hoisted on the shoulders of two of the eunuchs. Philebus and the others began to dance to the playing of the flautist. At first their motions were stately. Soon they started to whirl and leap in the air, cymbals and tambourines beating out the rhythm. As the pace of the music increased, they bent forward, hair hanging down over their faces, then swung their heads in a furious circular motion, long locks flying.

Lost in the ritual, one stripped off his robes. With incoherent cries of lamentation, he called on the goddess, and lashed his own back with a whip. The leather thongs were knotted with vicious sharp stones. Soon his naked flesh was running with blood. Inspired to emulate such devotion, the others slashed their forearms with knives and swords.

'Barbaric,' Isangrim whispered.

'The goddess is Syrian,' Ballista replied. 'As Herodotus wrote, everywhere custom is king.'

As the daylight faded, even those carrying the statue began to move. They staggered this way and that, as if the goddess herself was impelling them. High above the onlookers, she advanced and retreated. Sometimes she drove her porters to circle the yard, forcing her other worshippers to jump aside or be trampled.

The frenzy built to a climax. A sign from Philebus, and it was over. The goddess was stationary. The dancers slumped to the ground. In the torchlight their heaving flanks were slick with blood and sweat. There were splashes of blood in the dirt.

'What did the movements of the goddess Artagatis prophesy?' The farmer's voice was quiet, awed by the savage spectacle.

Philebus drew himself up unsteadily. With a faraway look, he intoned the oracle:

'*Yoke the oxen, plough the land;*
High the golden grain will stand.'

'Why are you smiling?' Isangrim said quietly.

'They assume the farmer has never read Apuleius,' Ballista said. 'It is an old oracle, vague but favourable to any circumstances. For a journey, oxen are the least restless of beasts, and the good crop signifies a safe return. For the pursuit of bandits, their necks will go under the yoke, and their golden loot will be yours. There are any number of interpretations. It is designed to allay all concerns.'

The farmer did not share such cynicism. Evidently delighted with the divine message, he called out to his handful of slaves to heat water and prepare a meal.

The farmstead was small and shabby. There were tiles missing from the roof of the house. The stables were empty, and the outbuildings poorly maintained. There were no guest rooms, and no bathhouse. The guests would have to wash with pans of water carried to the hay barn, then later all bed down there together. At least the roof looked sound, and the hay would be warm.

Not wanting to wash with the Galli, Ballista and Isangrim sluiced off the dust of the road by the well in the yard. Drawn from a great depth, the water was ice-cold. They kept their few possessions to hand. The dogs, savage-looking things, strained at their chains, snarling and barking, until the old porter quieted them with a shout.

The farm did not have the wherewithal to afford domestic servants. There seemed to be only half a dozen farmhands. They both cooked and served the meal. There were no serving girls – in fact, no women at all. Yet rustic hospitality was not to be despised. There was flatbread, cheese and olives, and rough wine. A haunch of venison was butchered, and the steaks fried.

The living room of the farmhouse was cramped and bare of ornaments. Ballista and Philebus were placed with the master. The rest of the Galli occupied the other two couches. As a child, Isangrim was on a chair. Most likely it was the proximity of the eunuchs, not his seat, that made him appear so uncomfortable. Not that Ballista reclined at ease. The couches were hard and lumpy, stuffed with horsehair.

There were questions that Ballista wanted to ask the farmer, but he waited. Even at such a bucolic repast, the formalities of dining had to be observed. The farmer tipped a tiny libation to the gods, and said a prayer. Atargatis was invoked first.

The reverence of the host done, Philebus began to hold forth about his conversion to the Syrian goddess.

'Before I was called, far from my country, my possessions, my friends and parents, I was glory of the gymnasium. Mine were crowded doorways, flowers garlanded my chamber.'

As the hedge-priest painted a picture of the life he had left – the cosseted existence of youth from a good family – Ballista ate without speaking. Privately, Ballista suspected that Philebus might have emasculated himself to escape poverty and grinding drudgery. The eunuch was talking to the farmer in common Greek, as he had to Ballista. Although he was trying to sound poetic, nothing about his accent or phrasing suggested much education, or the ability to converse in Attic Greek.

'Dull delay departed from my mind. With hurrying feet, I followed the company of the goddess, where the hollow cymbals clash and the tambourines echo through the dark forests.'

Ballista's mind wandered. Rome had ruled Sicily for five hundred years. Latin was the everyday language of the coastal cities. Across the island, anyone with pretensions to elite status had to claim to be bilingual. Yet here in the centre, everyone – farmers and shepherds, small town merchants – all spoke Greek. In the backwoods, it was said, even older languages survived: Sicel and Elymi and Sicani – incomprehensible tongues of primitive peoples, ancient before the Greeks arrived.

'Now I pass my life under the high summits, with the hind that haunts the woodland, with the wild boar that ranges the forest.'

What would be left when Rome fell? Ballista did not believe that Jupiter had granted the Romans empire without boundaries or end. Again and again, the legions had marched into the forests of Germania. Every time they had failed. It was the same story in the East, beyond the Euphrates. All the great empires of the past had fallen: Egyptian, Assyrian, Mede, Persian, and Macedonian. The imperium of the Romans would be no different. What would be left after the passing of Rome?

Finally the monologue of Philebus drew to a close. Fulsome like a river in flood, it had been well rehearsed. Not the first time the talk had been delivered. Perhaps the lengthy diatribe was designed to distract the host from the prodigious quantities of his food and drink being consumed by the other acolytes. At last the farmer was free to talk to his other guest.

'Where are you going?' A blunt question, as you would expect of a rustic.

'To Tauromenium,' Ballista said.

'You have business there?'

'My family.'

The farmer nodded, curiosity satisfied.

'You live alone?' Ballista asked.

'A fever took my wife and son, three years ago.'

'May the earth lie lightly on them.'

The farmer looked fondly at the Galli helping themselves to his provisions. The main course finished, they were guzzling apples and nuts.

'The goddess Atargatis has been a solace.'

Evidently at some material cost, Ballista thought. Fearing Philebus would interject with more eulogies on a peripatetic life of religious observance, Ballista quickly moved the conversation to the mundane.

'Your stables are empty?'

'An imperial procurator bought both my horses a few days ago. He was in charge of an estate of the emperor up near Panormus. Like you, he was heading east.'

A look of sly avarice crossed the farmer's face. Doubtless the procurator had paid a high price.

'Do any of your neighbours have horses they might sell?'

'All gone east, too.'

'But the rebels are staying on the coast road.'

'Bad news travels fast. The slaves have risen at the Villa Geminiana, a big estate two days' walk south-west of here.'

Ballista dropped his voice. 'Then are you safe?'

The farmer made a self-deprecating gesture. 'I am not a rich man. I labour in the fields alongside my boys, eat the same food, sleep on a straw mattress just like them. On market days we visit the same brothel. I have nothing they do not.'

Except freedom, Ballista thought. *Never underestimate that.*

Drink taken, and their bellies full, the younger Galli were getting boisterous. Some of them were eyeing the brawny farm workers. Others broke into shrill, high-pitched song.

'*Come away, Galli, come away,*
Together to the mountains,
Across the savage sea.
Come away, Galli,
To cheer the Lady's heart.'

Ballista turned to his host.

'Our thanks for your hospitality. We have far to go, and will leave early in the morning. It is time we went to our beds.'

The cosmos was ruled by a single divine intelligence. So Marcus' philosophy tutor on the Palatine held. It was the key tenet of Stoicism. All the gods were aspects of that one cosmic *logos*. A spark of that celestial reason was in the heart of every man. It made mankind kin to the gods. It meant all men were brothers. In which case, why did Marcus feel such revulsion in the presence of the priests of the Syrian goddess?

The Galli had woken him when they tipsily entered the barn. Now they were snoring, but Marcus was finding it hard to get back to sleep. The hay was scratchy, and the air suffused with the fumes of stale wine. At least his father was sleeping between him and the eunuchs.

Marcus turned on his other side, tried to get comfortable. But his mind ran on, down drowsy, ill-defined paths.

By definition, god was good. If all men shared in the divine reason, why did so many choose to be bad? Why was the path to virtue difficult, and that to vice easy? Why did virtue live in solitude on a remote mountain peak?

Marcus was dreaming. A hand was stroking his penis. If a slave dreamt he was aroused by his master, it signified that he would be bound and whipped, as that was the way he would be extended by his owner. If a freeman . . .

'Hush, little dove.'

The young eunuch clamped his hand over Marcus' mouth. He stank of cheap perfume and wine. Marcus tried to push him off. The weight of the priest was pinning him down.

'No need to be alarmed.'

The other hand again groped for Marcus' groin.

The palm was covering his nose as well as his mouth. Marcus struggled to breathe. With all his force, he sank his teeth into the palm.

'You little bitch!' The eunuch raised his fist.

Marcus jabbed his fingers straight into the priest's eyes.

The eunuch reared back, yelping, clutching at his face.

Marcus clenched his fist. Before he could throw a punch, the priest was hauled off him. Ballista had the man by the throat. With his free hand, he hit him – two, three times, powerful jabs. Marcus heard the crunch of broken bones. It sounded like breaking the carcass of a chicken.

The barn was full of strident cries. Ballista threw the eunuch away. Colliding with the wall, the priest slid to the ground.

Marcus scrambled to his feet.

'My face, my face,' the injured man repeated in a falsetto of pain and horror. 'He has ruined my face.'

'Nothing but a misunderstanding.' Philebus was in the middle of the barn, arms spread wide.

Ballista rounded on the head priest. The others cowered, but Philebus stood his ground. He smiled, tried to make light of it.

'Isn't that just the sort of accident that would happen to honest men like ourselves?'

Ballista moved forward. From nowhere, his sword was in his hand.

'It is sacrilege to threaten ministers of religion with death.'

'Your gods are not mine.'

Philebus was not without courage. This was not the first time his calling would have put him in a bad place.

'The farmer is a devotee of the goddess. He has six strong labourers. The noise will have woken them. Men and boys just disappear in the country.'

Ballista stood very still. A muscle twitched in his sword arm. Marcus could see his father was fighting to maintain the self-control that the implied threat had nearly snapped. One false word or move, and the barn would become a slaughterhouse.

Outside, the dogs were barking.

'You have beaten the youth who importuned your son,' Philebus said. 'I will punish him further. But it would be best if you left, before things get worse.'

Without taking his eyes from the hedge-priest, Ballista picked up and buckled his sword-belt.

'Get our things.'

As Marcus gathered their meagre baggage, Ballista pulled on his boots and cloak.

In the yard, the farmer was shouting at the porter to quieten the dogs.

'You had better pray that you never see me again,' Ballista said.

Philebus nodded. 'We are all in the hands of the gods.'

CHAPTER TEN

'I DID NOT NEED YOUR HELP.'

The sun was coming up. They had walked in silence for several hours. Even before he finally spoke, Ballista could tell that Isangrim was angry. Ballista himself was torn between concern for his son and a white-hot fury directed at himself – a fury mingled with self-contempt.

I should have killed the eunuch, killed every one of the filthy creatures.

'It was nothing.'

It was nothing. Among Ballista's people it would not have been nothing. Among the tribes of Germania, a man who attempted to violate a youth or another man was less than nothing. Such ones would be bound, led out into the marshes, and drowned. Heavy wooden boards would press them down, deep out of sight, out of mind. They would be gone, as if they had never existed. Never spoken of again, they would be banished from all recollection.

'No worse than some men in the gymnasium. I could have dealt with the eunuch as easily as them.'

Ballista did not trust himself to speak. After all these years – more than half a lifetime in the imperium – Roman attitudes to sex still confused and troubled him. In the army, sex with another soldier was punishable by death. Romans often claimed

sex between males was an imported Greek vice. Philosophers –
Greek as well as Roman – branded it as unnatural. Yet almost
any Roman man was happy to fuck anyone, male or female.
However, if they were the one penetrated, even just the once,
they would be tainted for life. To let yourself be penetrated made
you less than a man. No, it was not just the morality of Ballista's
own youth. What sort of a Roman father was he, if he could not
protect his son from such a fate?

'At times everyone needs help,' Ballista said.

'I am not a child anymore.'

Ballista did not reply.

'I can take care of myself. You have to accept that I am
a man.'

Ballista looked at his son: tall and broad-shouldered, intelligent and confident, but not yet hardened by the adversities
of adult life. His anger ebbed away, leaving only a terrible
tenderness.

'Even a man can need help. A long time ago, in Persia,
something similar was going to happen to me.' Ballista had
never spoken to anyone about the incident. In all these
years, not even Maximus, or those closest to him. 'There was
nothing I could do. Someone saved me. I was not angry, but
am grateful to this day. If he is ever in any sort of trouble, I
will repay the debt.'

'Even if you had to journey to Persia?'

'A debt is a debt.' Ballista smiled. 'It only takes a few months
to get there.'

They walked in silence for a time.

'I want to travel the world,' Isangrim said.

'So you have mentioned.'

The tension between them had almost gone. It might return, but Ballista had to ask the question.

'What did the eunuch . . .?'

'He tried to grab my cock while I was sleeping. When I woke, I did not appreciate his attentions.'

'Are you all right?'

'Much better than him.'

'Good.'

They went on in a more companionable silence.

The road here tracked around outcrops of the mountains. Some were bare shoulders of rock, their crests like fingers clawing into the sky. Others were wooded slopes, where yellow flowers bloomed under the trees. The twists limited the view ahead.

'Are you hungry?' Isangrim asked.

Ballista was, but he made a non-committal noise. There was next to nothing left of the provisions given to them by the hunters.

'Last night, while the Galli were gorging themselves, I hid some bread and cheese in my tunic.'

'You are getting resourceful,' Ballista said. 'On campaign, always eat whenever there is food, carry off as much of the rest as you can. You might do well on active service.'

They walked on for the best part of another hour, until a timbered slope came down to the roadway and offered them shelter. They sat in the shade and ate.

'How far is it to Enna?'

'Not far,' Ballista said. 'Less than a long day's walk. We should reach there before dusk.'

'We will get to Tauromenium before the rebel army?'

'Unless the gods are cruel.'

Isangrim did not look reassured.

'Your mother is a sensible woman. If there is trouble, she will leave.'

'Where?'

'If I were her, I would find a boat to get me to Italy. Failing that, I would go to Syracuse.'

'Will they be safe there?'

'The walls of Syracuse still stand. It is the seat of the governor. If anywhere on the island is safe, it is Syracuse.'

'But Sicily is an unarmed province. The governor has no troops.'

'The governor will raise a militia. He will not lack help. My old commander Flavius Vopiscus lives there.'

'What if the slaves rise in Syracuse itself?'

Ballista did not want to think about that.

'They will not. Anyway, Maximus and our other bodyguards will not let any harm come to her and Dernhelm.'

Ballista stopped talking. He knew he was clutching at straws.

They finished the last of the food, and went back down onto the road.

Grading around the next hill, the view opened up. Ridge after ridge was etched against the sky. Beyond the nearest, a broad smudge of dust hung in the air.

'Follow me, back into the woods.'

Under the oaks the ferns and thorn-bushes offered scant cover. There was a break in the trees about fifty paces upslope. It was a dry run-off from the heights, roughly parallel to the road. They threw themselves down, the boar spears on the ground next to them. The natural ditch was shallow, and far too near the road, but there was nothing better further up.

Looking down through the trees, the road was empty and peaceful in the weak sunshine. The haze of dust was out of sight.

'How do you know they are hostile?' Isangrim eased the pack on his back.

'I don't, just that there are a lot of them. An isolated and dense cloud like that is raised by a column of men on foot. If they were mounted and moving faster, it would be taller and thinner.'

Birds sang in the branches above their heads as they waited. The thorn-bushes smelt like musk. The column must be moving slowly. Eventually they heard the tramp of feet and the rumble of a wagon. The men emerged into sight. At least thirty of them. They carried pitchforks and flails, even hoes and rakes – any agricultural implements that could be used as weapons. They were hooded in shabby cloaks, but some had added incongruous items of finery. One had a toga draped around his shoulders like a blanket. They were watchful, their cowled heads turning from side to side. But they advanced in no order. Behind them came a wagon pulled by four oxen. In its bed was a teetering ziggurat of useless plunder: a statue, a table, other furniture, rolls of expensive carpets, even a painting. Tethered by their necks to the rear of the wagon were three women and two youths. They were barefoot, and their clothes in tatters.

Just when it was opposite, the wagon squealed and juddered to a halt.

'Hades,' Ballista whispered.

Typical lazy slaves – not yet midday, and, of all places, they had to halt here. Slowly, keeping below the rim of the ditch, Ballista got the bow from its case.

Most of the men milled around the wagon. They got down bundles of food, amphorae of wine. A couple went to the rear of the wagon.

'Don't watch,' Ballista said very quietly.

They pushed one of the women and one of the boys down on all fours. They mounted them there on the road, in full view, like animals. One or two of their companions called out crude jokes or obscene encouragement. The majority sat and ate and drank, ignoring the rape, as if it was already too commonplace to warrant any attention.

'Hades,' Ballista muttered again.

One of the rapists had stood up, and was strolling directly into the wood. Rolling onto his side, Ballista drew and notched an arrow. Inwardly he cursed the perverted shreds of decency that let a slave couple openly like a beast in the fields, but called for seclusion to relieve himself.

The thin undergrowth provided scant privacy. The slave was coming straight to the dry watercourse. Ballista let him approach to about ten paces, then raised himself on one knee, drew the bow, and aimed at the man's chest. Holding up his trousers, watching where he placed his feet, the slave took another couple of steps before he saw Ballista. The man stopped, eyes wide with surprise.

'No noise,' Ballista said.

The slave started to turn his head.

'Don't look back.'

The man stood still, as if turned to stone.

'Just look at me.'

'What do you want?'

'Don't talk.'

'You brigands?'

'No concern of yours.'

'We got food, our own slaves now. Why don't you come down and join us.' The man's eyes slid to Isangrim.

'Don't look at him.'

The slave licked his lips.

'Not at him, just look at me.'

The slave returned his gaze to Ballista. 'You would both be welcome.'

'Walk towards me, nice and slow.'

'So you can murder me out of sight?'

'If you don't, I will shoot you where you stand.'

'And the others will kill you.'

'You won't know anything about that. Come here.'

'At least I have lived a few days as a free man. Cut my master's throat, fucked his woman and his children.'

The slave started to turn, took a deep breath to shout. Ballista loosed the bowstring. The arrow caught the slave in the side, punched deep through his ribs.

'Up into the hills,' Ballista said.

As they scrambled over the rim of the ditch, they heard the outcry down on the road.

Not looking back, they pounded up the slope. They swerved around thorn-bushes, ducked under branches.

'Drop the spear!' Ballista shouted. 'It will slow you down.'

Bow in hand, he had left his in the watercourse.

The packs thumping on their backs, straps digging into their shoulders, they fled like draught horses that had slipped their traces and bolted, but were still encumbered with harness. The sounds of pursuit were close behind; there was no time to stop and unburden themselves.

The land began to rise more sharply, and the trees were thinning out. Ballista's chest was burning, his breath coming in tearing gasps. He was getting too old for this.

They came out of the treeline onto a slope of coarse grass dotted with boulders. Some way ahead loomed a sheer wall of limestone. To the right, the land seemed to drop away.

'Straight up,' Ballista gasped.

He was not sure that Isangrim had heard him, but the boy was pulling ahead. Willpower and sheer desperation kept Ballista moving. Get to the cliff and either find a way up, or set their backs to it and make a stand.

A chorus of yells signalled that the pursuers had cleared the trees and sighted their quarry. Ballista ducked behind a low free-standing rock. Shouting at Isangrim's back to keep going, he looked back. A ragged throng of slaves were about fifty paces away, closely bunched, but coming up fast. Ballista did not know if the slaves had bows, but he had one. Time to slow their headlong chase.

Sucking in great lungfuls of air, Ballista took another arrow. Only four more were left in the quiver. Must make each one count. Trying to still his breathing, he drew the bow and selected his target. A big brute, out in front, brandishing a billhook. Ballista aimed, exhaled, did not rush the shot.

The arrow thrummed through the air. The man saw it coming, threw himself to one side. The arrow sped by to lose itself harmlessly among the trees. Yet its effect was immediate. The dense mass of slaves scattered across the slope, every man diving for safety in the shelter of a boulder.

Ballista turned and ran after his son. It would not hold them long, but every step – every moment – would help.

There was a jumble of fallen boulders and loose scree at the foot of the cliff. A precipice to the right, as if a deity had chopped away the ground with an axe. No climbing down there. Coming up with his son, Ballista scanned the cliff ahead for any line of ascent. There was none. Not even a mountain goat could have found a path to the crest.

Ballista took a stance, half screened by an outcrop.

The slaves were still following, but moving more cautiously. Widely spread out, individuals dashed from the lee of one rock to another. Even so, they would soon be close enough to make a concerted rush. This time Ballista could not miss.

The tall slave with the billhook was still near the front. Perhaps the dead man had been his friend. Perhaps he had recently acquired a taste for killing. Ballista tracked him patiently. There was about twenty paces to the next boulder. No cover, and a steep incline. The big man set off. This time Ballista did not miss.

As the mortally injured slave tumbled down the slope, the others went to ground.

Ballista took stock. The cliff at their backs could not be scaled. So, too, the precipice which dropped down to the east. No way out – but equally, no lines of approach. The only directions from which the slaves could attack were head on, or work round to the west. The former would be suicidal for the leading men. Ballista had to stop the latter outflanking move. But he had only three arrows left, and more than six hours of daylight remained.

The wind was picking up, dark clouds drifting in from the east, outliers of a storm building over Enna and the Nebrodes mountains. Once the sun was obscured, the day turned cold. Worse, the overcast conditions made accurate shooting more difficult. Ballista worried that when the rain started to fall his bowstring would get damp and lose its tension.

The nearest slaves were crouched behind scattered rocks just forty paces away. They could be heard calling to one another. A few voices tried to encourage them not to delay, but advance all together and overwhelm the fugitives: *There are only two of them, and one is no more than a boy*. One repeatedly suggested that they fall back to the treeline, wait until darkness, then make a rush. Most advocated flanking their prey to the west, then charging from two directions. Although the latter seemed to win general approval, there was a reluctance to make the initial move and be the one exposed to danger.

The first big, fat drops of rain were falling when two men got their courage up. They sprinted from one boulder to another. One was wearing a looted bright saffron tunic. As he made the bound to his third rock, Ballista shot him.

It was not a clean kill. The arrowhead embedded itself in his thigh. The man was down in the open, screaming. A simple shot, but Ballista did not finish him. Only two arrows left. There was a lot of blood. Almost certainly he would bleed to death. And the screaming was good.

It was raining heavily by the time his companion dared go to his aid. The other slave grabbed his arms, and started to drag him towards a boulder. It caused a renewed outbreak of screaming. Two arrows left. Ballista did not shoot him either. Besides, he was hunched over, keeping his bow dry under his cloak.

The screaming did its work. The lone voice suggesting retreating to the woods won much support: *Deal with them when it's dark*. In a series of unco-ordinated bounds, the slaves fell back to the treeline. The one with the arrow through his thigh was left where he was. His screams soon got fainter, then ceased altogether.

Only two arrows left in the quiver. But, thank the gods, the slaves did not know that.

The rain fell, with the briefest of lulls, all through the afternoon. Water sluiced down the rock face, and ran in rivulets to the woods. Ballista had secured the bow in its waterproof case. He could retrieve it in a moment, but was worried about its condition. Both father and son were soaked to the skin, both shivering in the downpour.

It had to be assumed that the slaves were still watching from the timber, but they did not show themselves. The closest oaks were no more than a hundred paces away. Although most of the leaves had fallen, and there was little undergrowth, it was impossible to see beyond the treeline through the curtains of rain. The storm would shorten the hours of daylight. Dusk was the crux. It might give Ballista and Isangrim a chance to slip away to the west. But equally, it would give the slaves a chance to rush the slope in relative safety. Even were the quiver full, it would be hard to hit a moving target in the gloom.

Blinking the rain from his eyes, Ballista never let his gaze leave the sodden trees. It was like a new punishment in

Tartarus, where the souls of the impious were condemned. Instead of ceaselessly pushing a boulder up a cliff, you endlessly watched a dark wood, because a moment of inattention might cost your life.

As the light began to fade, well before true evening, Ballista led Isangrim from their damp refuge. Best make the first move, before the slaves came howling up the hill. Progress through the fallen rocks at the base of the cliff was slow, and not without its risks. The boulders were sharp-edged and slippery. The loose scree was loud underfoot. But the drumming rain should cover any noise, and their scrambling headway probably kept them out of sight.

Ballista soon lost all sense of time and distance. The world narrowed to just the next awkward, slimy and sharp obstacle to be negotiated. Certainly, they had been crawling through this wilderness for what seemed like an age. Yet he could not judge how much ground they had made. He had heard nothing from the place they had left, but there was nothing to hear except the beating rain.

Now it was fully dark, and they were both tiring. Their movements were becoming clumsy with fatigue and cold. One slip and either might break an arm or leg. They had to get out of this stony hell. They had to stop, find some sort of shelter.

'That is far enough!' Ballista had to shout in his son's ear to make himself heard over the storm. 'We will go down into the trees!'

Even though it was pitch-dark, it felt terribly exposed walking out onto the open slope. Anything could be lurking in the dark line of the timber. They both drew their swords. Walking on the balls of their feet, every sense taut, they edged into the treeline.

There was nothing but the black outlines of the trunks of the trees, the branches overhead in the cascading rain, the fresh mud underfoot. No animal or bird would be out on a night like this. They would be snug and dry in burrows and nests. Ballista envied them. Only a desperate man, or those with evil intentions, would be venturing abroad.

Cautiously they went deeper into the wood. In this storm there would be nowhere dry to lie up. But they needed to find somewhere out of sight, preferably somewhere with a modicum of shelter. A huge oak lay across their path. It must have come down in the autumn gales. There were still leaves on its widely spread branches, which fanned out across the ground. They crawled under the makeshift cover. The earth was damp, and water dripped through the leaves. They lay back to back to share what body heat remained. Heads resting on their packs, they dragged the blankets over themselves. It was a tawdry and uncomfortable lodging, but they were out of the wind and direct downpour. And they were hidden. On this foul night, anyone could walk right past without seeing them.

Ballista slept for hours. When he woke, the rain had stopped and the sun was up. The floor of the forest steamed in the sunshine. Stiff and aching, he dragged himself out from under the branches. Isangrim was already awake. The boy was sitting on the fallen bough, methodically looking all around.

'Anything?' Ballista said.

'Nothing.'

Ballista went off to ease his bladder. When he returned, Isangrim was rifling through both packs. There was still a little watered wine, but all he could find to eat was a few overlooked slivers of air-dried beef. Ballista said he was not hungry. Isangrim smiled, and handed over half of the tiny scraps.

They both chewed very slowly, savouring every last drop of the juices.

'There will be things to eat in this wood,' Ballista said. 'But we should not wander too far.'

Isangrim nodded. 'And we should get moving. As soon as we reach Enna, we can hire some horses.'

'We should wait for a few hours.'

'But we need to get to Enna.'

Isangrim did not need to add that the sooner in Enna, the quicker they could be on the road to Tauromenium.

'Think about yesterday,' Ballista said. 'The slaves stopped to eat well before midday. For the first time in their lives they are masters of their own time. If they did not move on yesterday afternoon, they will not leave early this morning.'

There was nothing to reply to the logic.

The wind that had taken the storm away to the west stirred the treetops. Although the sun was warm, it was a cold breeze coming down from the Nebrodes. Ballista and Isangrim made short patrols through the timber, more to keep warm than in expectation of trouble. The slaves were unlikely to scour the woods. Ballista found some edible mushrooms. They peeled them and ate them raw. They were both very hungry. Ballista was proud that Isangrim did not complain.

When it was about the third hour of daylight, they began to move down towards the road. It was still on the forest floor, but the wind gusted through the upper branches. The branches squealed as they rubbed against each other. Sometimes they sounded like men crying in pain.

CHAPTER ELEVEN

THERE WERE MEN ON THE ROAD. One was standing; the others were dead.

Marcus watched with his father from back in the timber, off to the west. The survivor was searching the bodies. When he found something worth keeping, he stashed it in the panniers of the two donkeys. Now and then he stopped, and regarded the woods with his head on one side, as if considering some important issue. His debate concluded, each time he returned his attention to the dead.

Despite their gaudy clothing, until he saw the idol of the goddess, lying abandoned on its side by the far verge, Marcus did not recognise the eunuch priests. Their blood was fresh. They had not been dead long. He felt a surge of exultation. The assault at the farm had shaken him more than he cared to admit. He had not wanted to show any weakness to his father. If the stranger had killed them, he had done Marcus a favour.

Ballista was deep in thought. He spent less time observing the site of the massacre than studying the woods and the road.

'He is looking for someone in the woods,' Ballista said. 'But I do not think he is waiting for them.'

'Then he is alone?'

'Only one way to be sure. Let's go and talk to him.'

They went down onto the road, making no attempt at concealment. Ballista walked a couple of paces ahead. The man turned and watched them approach. Both adults moved normally, but Marcus noted that their hands remained close to the hilts of their swords.

Ballista halted just out of reach of a blade.

'Health and great joy.'

The man returned the formal greeting. His accent was from the marketplace, not the schools and gymnasium.

'I am Marcus Clodius Ballista, and this is my son.'

The stranger did not answer instantly, as if weighing up this information, and wondering whether to divulge his own identity. There was an unusual stillness about him.

'I am Falx of Catana, the fugitive-hunter.'

Marcus followed Ballista's gaze to the five corpses strewn across the road. That of the chief priest was much hacked about. There were several wounds to the forearms, indicating that he had defended himself. The other four Galli had been despatched with more economy: a cut to a leg to bring them down, then a single blow to the back of the head, or they had had their throats cut. All the visible injuries had been caused by a heavy and sharp blade.

'They were not runaway slaves,' Ballista said.

'No, they were thieves.' The eyes of the *fugitivarius* contained no hint of compassion, or even interest. They were clear and brown, as blank as pebbles in a stream. 'They stole a golden chalice from the temple of the Syrian goddess. I have been tracking them from Himera. The rebellious slaves found them first.'

Ballista made no comment on this, but asked if the fugitive-hunter had any food he could sell. There was no question of gift-giving with such a man. Falx produced some twice-baked bread, a hunk of cheese and a flask of watered wine from a saddlebag. Ballista gave him some coins. They did not haggle. The exchange was conducted in silence.

Marcus and his father went and sat a little way up the bank. As they ate, the *fugitivarius* resumed going through the possessions of the dead.

'Where are you heading?' Ballista called over.

'Home to Catana. You?'

'To Tauromenium.'

'Safer we travel as far as Enna together,' Falx said.

When father and son had finished eating, they got up. The fugitive-hunter gathered the lead reins of the donkeys. Both were too heavily laden for a rider.

Marcus gazed at the slashed corpse of the young eunuch who had assaulted him. Despite everything, he felt a certain pity.

'Should we bury them?'

For the first time, the *fugitivarius* looked straight at Marcus. It was an unnerving experience. Marcus had to force himself not to shrink away.

'No point,' Falx said. 'They would have ended up on a cross. No one puts a coin in the mouth of the crucified.'

Without further discussion, they set off down the road to the east. The fugitive-hunter led the way. Marcus and Ballista followed at a distance, behind the donkeys, as if their fellow traveller carried some contagion.

'Why would the slaves have killed them?' Marcus spoke quietly.

'The eunuchs' slave is missing,' Ballista said. 'He might have encouraged the rebels to murder them.'

'Then why not loot the bodies, and why leave their donkey?'

'That would be strange,' Ballista said.

'Only five bodies. One of the eunuchs got away.'

Ballista nodded. 'That might be who our new companion was looking for in the woods.'

They went through a land washed clean by the night's storm. Broad pastures and sylvan glades; rugged mountains above: a peaceful bucolic landscape, where in poetry rustic swains would play their pipes for virginal shepherdesses – a world away from murderous slaves and remorseless solitary killers.

'The *fugitivarii* are no better than those they hunt,' Marcus said. 'Everyone knows they are vicious and corrupt. For a few coins they let any slave escape, and they are the worst of all thieves. In their audacity they break into any man's property. Why does the law allow them to search the estates of senators, or even the emperor himself?'

'Someone has to,' Ballista said.

'Why not soldiers?'

'There are never enough troops in the provinces to guard the roads. Now, more than ever, they are needed on the frontiers.' Ballista smiled. 'Besides, soldiers are not gentle creatures. There is nothing they enjoy more than beating and robbing civilians. It is one of their keenest pleasures.'

'Then why not the Watch from the towns?'

'They are little better. They lack discipline. The town councillors employ them for their own ends. Often they arrest and torture the innocent, execute them without trial.'

They trudged on for a time. Marcus broke the silence.

'Do you think the eunuchs stole the chalice?'

'Probably.'

'Did he murder them?'

'They were killed with a sword,' Ballista said. 'The slaves yesterday were armed with implements like pitchforks.'

'Will he try to kill us?'

'We have swords.'

'So did the priests.'

'We know how to use ours.'

'We are in bad company.'

'Only until Enna.'

As they went on, the countryside on the right opened up into broad pastureland, but on the left the mountains approached closer to the road. A steep grassy slope ran up to a sheer grey cliff. The grass was embedded with big, pale boulders.

Falx was striding out some fifty paces ahead. Marcus was glad his father made no attempt to keep up. There was something deeply unsettling about the cold-eyed fugitive-hunter. It was as if the unquiet shades of those he had killed were hovering just out of sight.

A dreadful foreboding crept up on Marcus. What if his mother fell into the hands of such a man? A fugitive-hunter and a rebellious slave were just two sides of the same coin. Neither had compassion nor remorse. What if merely travelling with Falx brought blood pollution down on Marcus and his father? They had eaten and drunk his provisions. What if the gods punished them for the impiety? Back outside the villa of Caecilius, when he had seen the stag, Marcus had felt secure in the protection of Diana. Now he was unsure. The goddess might have turned against them. All the gods could be cruel. Time and again in myth, divine anger fell not only on the transgressors but their innocent families. What if Marcus and his father were bringing retribution on their *familia* in Tauromenium?

A strange groaning sound from above broke his thoughts. Looking up, Marcus saw a huge chunk of rock slowly lean out from the summit of the cliff. It hung for a moment, at an impossible angle, then toppled into the void. Mesmerised, Marcus stood and watched it plummet. It crashed onto the top of the slope. A massive cloud of dust blossomed, and then a wall of noise hit Marcus. His father was shouting. Marcus could not make out the words.

Jagged rocks hurtled out of the spreading pall of dust. The great slab had shattered into a thousand pieces. They bounced down the slope. Although some were the size of a man, they looked deceptively harmless, almost playful. White against the green grass, spinning and leaping. They sounded like rain on a tiled roof. Then, as they got nearer, they seemed to pick up speed. And there was nothing harmless about them.

Marcus turned to run away, out into the pasture. His father caught his arm. Ballista was still shouting. He began to drag Marcus back towards the maelstrom accelerating down the slope.

'Follow me!'

Was his father mad?

'Quick!'

Marcus sprinted with his father. The leading rock hit the road off to their left. Wicked splinters scythed through the air. Another was heading straight at them. They swerved out of its path. Marcus felt the wind of its passing.

'Here!'

Ballista grabbed Marcus and shoved him down into the shelter of a massive boulder, a relic of some previous avalanche lying by the verge. Marcus felt the breath knocked out of him as his father landed on top of him. Now the rock fall clattered all around like hail, but infinitely louder. The very ground seemed to vibrate. The dust was choking, impossible to see through. Marcus heard his father grunt with pain.

And then it was over. The roaring cacophony was replaced by a deathly silence. Marcus could neither see nor hear. He wondered if he had been deafened. He felt the weight of his father lift off him. A hand pulled him to his feet.

Marcus tried to wipe the dust out of his eyes. His vision was blurred, but his hearing was returning.

'Are you hurt?'

'No,' Marcus said. 'Are you?'

'It is nothing, a graze.'

Ballista was peering upslope, checking the danger had passed. 'We would never have outrun it. Finding shelter was our only chance.'

As the dust dissipated, Marcus saw Falx and the donkeys standing in the road. Away from the course of the avalanche, they were completely unharmed.

'Thought that was the end of you,' the fugitive-hunter said as they approached.

He handed Ballista a flask of water. Ballista tipped some into his palm, bathed his eyes, splashed some over his face, rinsed his mouth, and handed it to his son. Marcus did the same.

'You were lucky,' Falx said dispassionately.

Without further comment, he gathered up the reins and set off with the donkeys.

Father and son each took a drink, let the fugitive-hunter move some way down the road, then followed.

'Did he lead us into that?'

Ballista did not reply instantly.

'An accomplice might have dislodged the rocks.'

Ballista stopped, gazed up the slope and at the cliff.

'Possibly, but it would be an uncertain sort of ambush. The rocks could go anywhere. And how could Falx have had a chance to warn an accomplice? He has not been out of our sight. Anyway, falls are not uncommon here. The old boulders strewn across the slope show that. The autumn rains will have weakened the rock face.'

They walked on in silence through the long day. Marcus did not want to talk. He was lost in gloomy thought. If Falx had not arranged the landslide, was the cause natural? So Ballista claimed. But his father was no more pious than his Epicurean mother. Marcus suspected the hand of a deity.

They were getting near Enna, when, with a thunder of hooves, the horsemen burst round the shoulder of the hill. There was no time to react.

'Stand still,' Ballista said. 'Keep your hands away from your weapons.'

The horses were mettlesome and well bred. They plunged and arched their necks as they surrounded the travellers. The riders were young. They were armed and accoutred with no thought of the expense.

'Name, race, free or slave?' The lead rider rapped out the questions as if in court. Most likely he had observed his father presiding over many trials as a local magistrate.

The *fugitivarius* waited for Ballista to speak. In such circumstances, even a man of his sort deferred to the social hierarchy.

'My name is Marcus Clodius Ballista, *vir egregius*, of Tauromenium, and this is my son.'

The rider looked dubious, manifestly unconvinced that the dirty and bedraggled figure, with its long hair, could genuinely claim the elevated title of an equestrian.

'The family is known to mine.' Another horseman, even younger, edged forward, then spoke to Ballista. 'Which of your wife's cousins lives in Rome?'

'Decimus Julius Volcatius Gallicanus.'

'And what does he do there?'

Ballista smiled, and quoted some verse:
'*Grey time moves silently, and creeping on*
Steals the voices of articulate humans.'

The younger rider smiled back, then turned to his companions.

'This must be the *vir egregius* Ballista. Decimus gave a recital I attended in Syracuse, two years ago.'

'Then who is this?' The slightly older rider gestured at the fugitive-hunter.

The younger rider answered. 'I know him – Falx the *fugitivarius* from Catana. Not long ago he recovered two of my father's slaves who were hiding on an estate near Centuripae.'

'Then you may proceed.'

The younger evidently thought this too brusque.

'Refugees are flooding into the town. There are reports that slaves have risen in the interior. The magistrates have ordered us *ephebes* to patrol the approach roads. Our apologies for detaining a man of your rank.'

'Think nothing of it,' Ballista said. 'You have your duties to perform.'

Marcus wished he was mounted with them. It would be glorious to be hunting down the rebels, rather than skulking from them. The *ephebes* were little older than him, but entrusted with the tasks of men. It made sense to employ them. The rich youths enrolled in the gymnasium received some military instruction.

Rounding the hill, they entered a wide valley full of people. It was the olive harvest; nets were spread, the branches beaten, baskets of the fallen fruit carried to the presses. In the lower fields, teams of oxen were ploughing. Men were sowing wheat and barley. Small children ran, shrieking to scare the birds. After the solitude and dangers of the last days – after just surviving the avalanche – the bustling routines of normal agricultural life on a peaceful November day somehow appeared strange, if not bizarre.

Marcus raised his eyes, and there was Enna. A steep wooded slope, tinged with the russet and gold of autumn. Above, a vertical wall of pale rock. At the summit, tightly packed white houses. On a massive outcrop, jutting out over the valley, like the prow of a ship, was the Temple of Demeter.

They had reached Enna, the navel of Sicily, the impregnable city, the sanctuary where the devout believed that the gods still walked.

Ballista thought about opening his eyes, then did not bother. The luxury of clean sheets and a soft mattress – a real bed at last – held him motionless. Although he could tell that the sun had risen, the room was still dark. The window was shuttered, but the day must be overcast. Another half an hour would do no harm.

It had been a long climb up to Enna. The road zigzagging through the woods. The air smelling of leaf mould and rosemary. The valley below shaded for the night by the time they emerged in the late evening sunshine which still illuminated the top. The polite youth on the horse, the one that liked Decimus' poor poetry, had been right. The town was crowded with the displaced. It had been hard to find any lodgings. At the third inn, it had taken a hefty bribe to secure a room for them to share. It was small, high up under the rafters. But it was clean, and the one bed was large and comfortable. They had left their meagre possessions and had gone out, wearing their sword-belts. The baths were still open. A few more coins, and their clothes were in lockers, and they wallowed in the waters of the warm room, eating pistachios and roasted broad beans, sipping cooled wine. After a massage, tired and hungry, they had returned to their quarters. The innkeeper had produced a large meal: hard-boiled eggs and sausages, suckling pig and artichoke hearts, apples and a cheese made with sheep's and goat's milk.

Isangrim had gone straight to sleep. It had taken Ballista longer. Enna was wedged on a plateau. There were sheer drops all round. The paths up were few, narrow and winding, easy to defend. Enna was often said to be impregnable. It was not true. Philip, the father of Alexander the Great, had said that he could take any town into which he could get a mule with a sack on its back. Enna had fallen many times – to Dionysius of Syracuse, to the Carthaginians, and twice to the Romans – every time by treachery. It was at Enna that the slaves had risen and massacred the townsfolk at the start of the first great servile war in the days of the Republic. Before he could sleep, Ballista had needed to reassure himself that the like would not happen again. Surely it was unlikely. This revolt was caused by the Alamanni. A concentration of too many first generation barbarian slaves, incited by some Syrian wonder-worker. Those joining were unfree field hands. Urban slaves had little in common with those in the country. With luck, the uprising would have no appeal to the domestic servants of Enna.

Eventually, lulled by such reasoning, Ballista had slept.

Ballista stretched languorously. The graze on his back from the rock fall was not too sore. His body was rested. He could do with a woman. For many years in the past he had been faithful to his wife. Fellow soldiers had commented on his strange eccentricity. Their jokes had not unduly troubled him. It was not some odd and overdeveloped morality. Somehow the idea had grown in his mind that, were he to have sex with another woman, he would die in combat. Many front-line troops created their own superstitions and private rituals to try to improve their chances of survival. Ballista himself had a routine he followed before battle. In the East, Ballista had twice been unfaithful. He had not died. Yet those around him had, and his oldest companion had been killed. In many ways, Ballista blamed himself. Since then he had drifted back into his unconventional practice of abstinence. Anyway, now was not the time to break the habit. There was nothing reprehensible about visiting a brothel, but no father, not even a Roman, would take his son to one.

Today they would hire or buy a pair of horses. By evening, they could be at the town of Centuripae; the following day on the east coast at Catana. Having spent the night there, a long ride north, and they would be at home in Tauromenium late on the third day. And what then? It would be best to take the advice that he hoped Julia would have already adopted. Assuming the family had departed, they would follow them, either south to Syracuse, or find a boat and cross to the mainland. If the family was still in the town, they could all leave together. A passage to Italy would be safest. Ballista loved the villa, but the protection of the *familia* was far more urgent. Besides, all too often in the past he had been forced to play the hero. It had taken years to earn imperial permission to retire from duty. Let someone else, some officer keen for martial glory and advancement, fight the rebellious slaves.

Ballista opened his eyes. The light filtering around the shutters had a dim, subaqueous look. Isangrim was awake. The boy lay on his back, staring up at the beams. Ballista wondered what he was thinking about. The boy had stood up well to their trials. Thank the gods, they seemed nearly to be at an end.

'We should get up and eat,' Ballista said.

Although it was towards the end of the second hour of daylight, the public room of the inn was almost full of people still taking breakfast. There was no pressing business to which even well-heeled refugees had to attend, and the dreary weather did not encourage sightseeing. Ballista and Isangrim found places at a table in the corner. The innkeeper brought them bread, cheese and hard-boiled eggs. Some of the other customers tried to make conversation, always about the insurgency. Ballista answered courteously, but briefly. He had no desire to talk about their experiences. Isangrim copied his reticence.

Having eaten, they left the guests to their desultory and anxious speculations. Ballista paid the innkeeper, and obtained directions.

Outside, the town was blanketed in a thick fog. Enna was built on a high plateau. Often the clouds did not lift. Today you could barely see across the narrow street. They walked up towards the main marketplace. It was damp. Beads of moisture instantly appeared on their cloaks. Eddying breezes shifted the banks of mist. They coiled like spectres through the porches and balconies of the houses.

The theatre loomed up out of the murk. Once it had been the scene of a real tragedy. During the wars against the Carthaginians, a Roman general had suspected the loyalty of the people of Enna. By some duplicity he had lured them to the theatre. Once they were trapped inside, he had set the soldiers loose on them. They had all been massacred. Of course, the inhabitants of the town now had Roman citizenship, yet Ballista wondered if, watching in comfort as the actors strutted on the stage, they ever reflected on the fate of their predecessors.

The fog had lifted a little in the agora. It was thronged. Neither the astrologers and dream diviners and other charlatans, or those selling more tangible goods around the edge, had any customers. Yet none of these diverse merchants seemed downhearted. Instead they all were infected with the general air of hushed excitement in the crowd. The town magistrates stood on the steps of the temple at the far end of the marketplace. Something was exhibited on a trestle table below them. Ballista and Isangrim worked through to see.

It was a dead baby. The tiny corpse was horribly misshapen. The chubby little arms and legs were perfect. There was nothing wrong with the torso or the diminutive male genitalia. But it had three heads. Two were well formed; the eyes of one open, the other shut. The third was a deformed lump of bone and gristle.

It was an evil prodigy, as bad as a child born with the head of a dog or both sets of genitals. The crowd was listening to the opinions of various magistrates. The issue was not what should be done. Everyone knew that. If such an aberration was not stillborn, it would be weighted down and drowned in a river, or burnt alive. As this one was already dead, it would be cremated, and its ashes scattered to the winds in some deserted place. The debate concerned what message the gods had sent by such a monstrosity.

In his conclusion, the orator winding up argued that it portended the slave uprising on the island. The creature had three heads, and Sicily had three promontories. As the insurrection had already happened, the crowd were unimpressed by this reasoning.

The next speaker took his place. All the magistrates were dressed alike in tunic and cloak. Each kept the folds of his himation decorously draped over his right arm. It was the conventional dress and pose of a member of the Greek elite, but inferences could be drawn from their subtle differences in appearance and gesture. The cloak of the last speaker was homespun, and his movements slow. It was intended to present to the world an image of antique virtue, of rigid control of the passions, and a wife spinning yarn in a traditional home. The clothes of the new orator were smooth and expensive. Before he spoke, he touched an amulet half-hidden at his throat. When he looked at the prodigy, he clenched his thumb between two fingers. Had he not been so well-bred, he would have averted evil by spitting on his own chest. At its own evaluation, the self-presentation proclaimed a man of refinement and piety. Ballista judged him vain and superstitious.

Unsurprisingly, the explanation moved on a divine plane. The miscreation had three heads, as did the giant Typhon imprisoned beneath mount Etna by Zeus. It was a warning from the king of the gods that the slave revolt could be overcome only with courage. Again this failed to catch the imagination of the public.

A third speaker took his place.

'This one may be more interesting,' Ballista said. 'He sees himself as a philosopher.'

'How can you tell?' Isangrim asked.

'A man rich enough to be a magistrate can afford a good barber. His hair and beard are long and badly cut. He wants people to think that he does not care for appearances, but only for things of the mind. And he has a papyrus roll in his hand. It is tightly tied up. He has no intention of reading. It is no more than a symbol. No doubt any statue of him will look just the same.'

A dramatic pause as the orator frowned, head bowed as if in profound thought.

Ballista nudged Isangrim.

'This does not portend evil for Sicily' – another pause – 'but for the whole world!'

The crowd liked this better: something cataclysmic, but not threatening them alone.

'The empire has three rulers – our Lord Gallienus in Milan, the usurper Postumus in Gaul, and Odenaethus, king of Palmyra in the East.'

A murmur went through the crowd. This was close to treason. Odenaethus claimed to rule as a loyal deputy of Gallienus.

'All three are mortal, but one of them will soon wither and die!'

His gnomic prediction uttered, the speaker withdrew.

This set the crowd buzzing. Which one would die? Was it outright treason? Had he predicted the death of the emperor?

'Clever,' Ballista said. 'A sword hangs over the head of every ruler. Whichever dies first, his prediction will be held to have come true.'

'What if he is denounced?' Isangrim said.

'Then he will say that, as a loyal subject of Gallienus, he has foreseen the imminent death of Postumus.'

Yet another magistrate was going to speak. After this, he would have a struggle getting the attention of his audience.

'Come on,' Ballista said. 'We need to buy the things for our journey home. There is no time to waste.'

CHAPTER TWELVE

THE LIVESTOCK MARKET WAS NOT FAR from the main agora. The fog was lifting, as were Ballista's spirits. The prodigy meant nothing to him. All animals gave birth to deformed offspring. It was no different with humans. It was no sign from the gods, nothing but a natural mischance.

They had got almost everything they needed from the agora. Under their old cloaks, father and son were wearing new tunics, and on their heads were new broad-brimmed travelling hats. They had spare boots in their packs. The latter were bulging with provisions: bread and biscuit, bacon and cheese, onions, fresh and dried apples, and flasks of wine. Enough rations for three days, as the army always required a soldier to carry. Their blankets were rolled, and tied on top. A fletcher had even sold them a quiver full of arrows. All they needed now were a pair of horses and their tack.

It was a good job that he had left Rome with a wallet full of high-denomination coins. If you had money, you could spend your way out of most difficulties. The wallet was quite a bit lighter. Two nights' lodgings still needed to be paid. It would be necessary to haggle. But every horse trader expected that.

The livestock market smelt and sounded like they did any-where in the world. The odour of animals and their dung mingled with that of unwashed men. The bleating of sheep and the grunting of pigs and the occasional bellow of cattle competed with the hoarse shouts of the stockmen. The pens were full. There was no shortage of animals for sacrifice or food on the hoof in Enna.

The corral at the far end was empty. There was not a horse in sight. Ballista went over to where a group of men were sitting around watching a game of *latrunculi*. None of them looked up. The board was scratched into a flagstone. Ballista waited until one of the players had moved a piece representing a brigand.

'We want to hire or buy a pair of riding horses, complete with saddles and tack,' Ballista said.

'I wish you luck.' The player did not take his eyes off the board.

'We have money.'

'Makes no difference.'

'Why?'

Now the trader looked at Ballista. 'You could be as rich as Croesus, and none of us could sell you a broken-down pony.'

'What has happened?'

They all looked at the newcomers. There was none of the usual cunning inscrutability of their trade on their weathered faces. They were angry and bitter.

'No horses to sell.' The player spat in disgust. 'All been requisitioned by the magistrates. *Requisitioned* for a fraction of their true price.'

'That is right,' the other player said. 'All taken so that the well-born youths in the *ephebes* can ride around playing at soldiers.'

'If the rich treated their slaves properly, there would have been no trouble.' The new speaker was a foxy-faced spectator.

'We have been robbed. The magistrates are no better than brigands themselves.'

'That is enough of that sort of talk, Titus.' The aedile had approached unnoticed. Clad in a gleaming toga, he was one of the young officials in charge of the markets. 'In an emergency it is necessary for individuals to make sacrifices for the good of the town. You have all been reimbursed for the horseflesh taken. Reimbursed at the proper rate, not what you would have tried to cheat out of a customer.'

The horse traders met this with a stony and hostile silence.

'If we discover that any of you have kept stock back, hidden horses away anywhere, you will feel the full weight of the law. All of you had better bear that in mind.'

After uttering his threat, the official went on his way. His toga billowed like a ship under sail.

'Bastard,' someone muttered. 'His younger brother is out there, lording it over any wayfarers he finds, mounted on my best stallion.'

'Are there really no animals tucked away?' Ballista asked. 'Our need is urgent, and we will pay well.'

'You heard the aedile.' The player returned his attention to the board. 'All taken. The stable is bare.'

Ballista turned and walked away, Isangrim following.

'What do we do now?' Isangrim said.

'Look at some of the pigs over there, and wait.'

The pigs were plump and scrubbed for their trip to market. Ballista liked pigs. They were intelligent creatures, and sociable.

'They are in fine condition.'

It was the spectator with the vulpine face. The approach had taken less time than Ballista had thought.

'Clever animals pigs – resourceful,' Ballista said. 'A man once told me he had been shipwrecked in the Hollows of Euboea. The vessel struck a reef. None of the crew could swim. They tied a rope to a pig and threw it overboard. The pig swam through the breakers, took the line to shore.'

'Might be able to find you some mounts.' The dealer spoke quietly, his eyes alert for the return of the aedile, probing the loiterers for one who might be an informant. 'A hack for you, and a pony for the boy.' He named a price.

Ballista snorted. 'We want to ride them in the usual way, not take them into the bedroom.'

'You are not going to get horses anywhere else in town.'

'In the army I got used to walking,' Ballista said.

The man could probably tell that Ballista was a veteran. There was something about the way ex-soldiers held themselves and moved. Still, there was no harm in making it clear to the trader that he was dealing with a man trained in violence.

After offer and counter-offer, they settled on a price – just under half of what had originally been asked. It was still far too high, nearly enough to buy a racehorse, not a couple of nags.

'Where do we collect them?'

'You know the grove of Persephone?'

'No.'

'It is at the foot of the north-east track down, just where the road to Centuripae starts. I will meet you there.'

'Best we come with you.'

'No, someone would see you. Give me the money, and I will bring them to the grove in two hours.'

Ballista fished out about a quarter of the price they had agreed.

'You get the rest when we see the horses.'

'Give me half. I am the one running all the risks.'

'Do I look like a man from Abdera or Kyme?'

The inhabitants of both places were bywords for stupidity. Any imbecile in a joke came from one or the other.

'No, sir, you look like a gentleman.'

The trader smiled, an unconvincing effort at amiable innocence.

They moved together to a portico, where they were not overlooked. The horse dealer spat on his right palm. Ballista did the same. They shook hands. Ballista handed over the money.

'Two hours, in the grove.'

The trader turned and slipped away.

'Do you think he will show up?' Isangrim said.

'In their parks, some Roman senators have a swineherd dressed as Orpheus. The wild pigs are trained to come running when he sings.'

Isangrim looked dubious.

'We will find out in a couple of hours. In the meantime, let's go and see what makes Enna famous.'

The sanctuary of Demeter was on the final outcrop of the plateau. On its outer wall were pinned small pieces of papyrus. Ballista stopped and read one.

Ploughman, about twenty years old, broad-shouldered, light-skinned, sluggish in his movements, scars on back. Hilarus by name. Anyone who gives information, or returns him to Plotinus will receive a reward.

Like the others, with careful parsimony, the notice was written against the grain on the back of a reused scrap of papyrus. There were at least two dozen of them. The outwardly tranquil town of Enna was a surprisingly good environment for a fugitive-hunter like Falx of Catana.

In front of the temple itself stood two huge statues: Demeter and Triptolemus. The myth was known throughout the world. Out tending his herd, in the fields below Enna, Triptolemus had seen the earth gape open. With a heavy thud of hooves, a chariot drawn by black horses had dashed down into the chasm. The face of the charioteer could not be seen, but his right arm held a shrieking girl. Having witnessed the abduction of Persephone by Hades, Lord of the Underworld, Triptolemus told her mother Demeter. As a reward, the goddess had given Triptolemus seed corn, a wooden plough, and a chariot drawn by serpents, in which he travelled the earth bringing mankind the art of agriculture.

'Some say the abduction was at Eleusis,' Ballista said.

'Or in Crete or Arcadia or other places,' Isangrim replied.

'This is as good a place as any,' Ballista said. 'Look.'

The sun had burnt off the mist. From where they stood they could see for miles. The green fields and meadows below, and ridge after ridge marching to the horizon. And there, in the distance, no more than perhaps forty miles as a god might fly, or a man in a chariot drawn by magical serpents, was Etna. And they knew that at the foot of the far slopes of Etna was their home at Tauromenium.

A foreboding, like the dark vision of a prophet, overcame Ballista. He was in the house in Tauromenium, walking down the long corridor from the main door. It was dark. The shutters were drawn. In the gloom he could see the corpses at the far end. Tarchon, Rikiar and Grim the Heathobard were piled together. Their dead flesh was pallid and waxy. Maximus was a little apart. The body of his friend lay over that of his younger son. Dark blood pooled from under Dernhelm. Beyond was the corpse of a woman. It was Julia.

For the first time, Ballista plumbed the full depth of his fear. If he lost Julia, he lost everything: his wife, his young son, his friends. And he would lose his home. He knew that he would never set foot in either the house in Tauromenium or the one in Rome again. Like one of the shades of the unburied, he would wander the face of the earth, consumed by envy and hatred for the rest of mankind.

But he would still have Isangrim. How could he face the boy if he failed to save his mother? Whatever happened, he must save his family, or die trying. If he failed, there would be no life worth living.

The grove of Persephone was easy to find. It was just where the horse dealer had said: at the foot of the north-east path, where the road departed for Centuripae. It was the only stand of trees for miles in the patchwork of open fields on the floor of the valley. Its sanctity must have preserved its oaks from the encroaching agriculture.

'He is not coming, is he?' Marcus said.

Ballista scanned the countryside. There were many men working in the fields.

'It would be impossible to bring horses here unobserved.'

'What will we do?'

'Walk.'

'About him?'

'We commissioned a crime. It would be unwise to denounce him to the authorities.'

'We do nothing?'

Ballista shrugged. 'Even if we could find him, we are strangers in this town, and he will have friends. It is only money, and time is pressing.'

In the shade of the grove, a party of travellers had assembled with a cart and some pack animals. A respectable-looking man came over and, with a certain deference to the gold ring on Ballista's finger, introduced himself as Aulus Calpurnius Apthonetus.

'Where are you bound?' Aulus asked.

'To the coast,' Ballista replied.

'If you permit, we would welcome your company as far as Centuripae. In these uncertain times, two more armed men would be welcome.'

Marcus felt himself swell with pride at being classified with his father.

'We are in a hurry,' Ballista said.

'My wife and daughter will ride in the cart, the mules are rested. We will not delay you. There is safety in numbers.'

'Then it would be our pleasure.'

No sooner had his father spoken the words than Marcus felt something rise like a shard of glass in his chest. From where he had been checking their load, Falx walked out round the two donkeys. The fugitive-hunter greeted them in a flat voice. As before, his eyes showed no emotion, as if pleasure and sorrow and all other emotions were strangers to him.

They walked through fields and pastures dotted with bright scarlet poppies, where the air smelt of sweet asphodel and rosemary and thyme. Ahead were green rolling hills, whose crests were topped with lines of pale bare rock like whitecaps on a wave.

'Why did you let *him* accompany us?' Marcus said.

They were at the rear of the little column. Falx walked his donkeys in front of the cart on which the two women rode. The father and his teenage son took it in turn to lead the pair of mules.

'Anyone can go down a public road.'

'Cato the Elder was talking about visiting a brothel,' Marcus said.

Ballista grinned.

'I read it in Plutarch.' Marcus knew his face was colouring.

'All of these troubles can be blamed on Cato.'

Marcus was lost.

'You forget that I was also educated on the Palatine. When I married your mother, and first came to her estate in Sicily, I tried to read Cato *On Agriculture*. He was a hard old man, and a cruel master. Cast out your slaves when they are too old or ill to work. Even if few still read him, his authority set the attitudes of Romans to their slaves.'

'And things are better with *your* people?' Marcus did not try to hide his scorn.

'Actually, yes. We have fewer slaves, and we treat them as a part of the family – in practice, not just in words. Most are given a plot of land to work. And, like it or not, the Angles are *your* people, too.'

Marcus changed the subject. 'With all those notices at the temple, why is Falx leaving Enna?'

'It could be that he just wants to return home, like us?'

To Marcus, his father sounded unconvinced by his own words. He looked at Falx out in front. The fugitive-hunter's head continuously turned from side to side, scanning the surroundings like a great lizard searching for prey, or others of its own kind. Sometimes Falx glanced back at the family. It seemed to Marcus that his gaze lingered with an inappropriate focus on the two females on the cart.

'What happened to the last eunuch?' Marcus said.

'I think he got away.'

'And the priests' slave?'

'Not so sure.'

'He could have been an accomplice of Falx's. It could have been him who started the rock fall.'

'The avalanche was natural,' Ballista said. 'Although certainly a life of brigandage might have appealed to the slave. The Galli treated him badly, used him as a beast of burden, and in ways more demeaning to a man.'

'He could have led them to Falx, just as Falx is now leading us to him.'

'I do not think so. It could be Falx paid him off, and let him run.'

'But why has the fugitive-hunter attached himself to this family?'

'Maybe they are just heading in the right direction. If he fell into the hands of rebellious slaves, imagine what they would do to a man of his calling.'

The family kept at a short distance behind Falx. His was not a respectable profession, or one that encouraged intimacy in others. After a time, the father dropped back to Ballista and

Marcus. Again, he respectfully asked permission to speak to a man of equestrian status. When it was given, he proved voluble, volunteering information. Aulus liked to talk. His father had been a freedman. When manumitted, he had bought a smallholding, Aulus himself had added a pottery. The family grew flowers for the tables of the wealthy, and made earthenware for the less endowed.

'Why did you travel to Enna?' Ballista asked.

Aulus beamed, delighted to hold forth on the subject. Marcus had the impression that there was nothing the loquacious potter and market gardener would like to discuss more.

'My daughter was born blind. Two years ago an old crone came begging at our door. My wife is pious, and led her into the kitchen, had the servants prepare her a meal. There was something odd about the old woman. She did not have the stench of a vagrant. Instead there was a scent like cinnamon or frankincense. When I came into the kitchen, I noticed at once that she never blinked. We had a bed made up for her in the stables. In the morning she was gone. The porter swore that the gate was locked all night. When my daughter woke, her sight was restored.'

'Not to everyone do the gods appear,' Ballista said, without irony.

'The gods are hard to cope with when manifest. My wife knew that it was the Lady Demeter. Every year on the anniversary we make a pilgrimage to the temple at Enna.'

'Even in times such as these,' Ballista said.

'The goddess will hold us safe in her hands.'

Marcus envied his simple faith.

'It is not far.' Aulus became businesslike. 'Soon we will reach an inn. We will be safe for the night there. Tomorrow we will reach Centuripae. It would be an honour to have you as our guests. Your company would be a pleasure, and the gods reward hospitality to strangers.'

It all went as Aulus had predicted. The inn was clean – not one of those where the guests should make a will before staying. There was no suggestion that they might be fed anything repugnant, let alone the cooked flesh of previous unfortunate wayfarers. That sort of thing was only said to happen in the more barbarous provinces. The next day's journey was entirely without incident, until they reached Centuripae.

A man was masturbating in the marketplace. He was emaciated and filthy, with long matted hair and beard, barefoot and clad in just a cloak. His staff and wallet were on the steps of the town hall. He stood at the top, where all could see him.

Aulus' wife closed her eyes, then opened them, as if hoping the offensive sight might have vanished.

'Eat a raw devilfish or squid and die!' a voice in the crowd shouted.

The man took no notice. His hand moved faster, then he jerked his hips and ejaculated.

'Get out with you!' The crowd jeered.

'See how the tyranny of lust is overthrown!' the man shouted. 'I am a liberator of men, a physician to their ills. If only I could conquer hunger as easily by rubbing my belly.'

Aulus hurried his family away.

'Something should be done about those indecent Cynics. They are everywhere. A man cannot take his family to the agora without being outraged. They are not philosophers – nothing but impudent and disgusting thieves and beggars.'

'Not long ago, the emperor had one burnt alive in Rome,' Ballista said.

'Best thing for them,' Aulus said. 'Let us get home.'

The house was not ostentatious, but comfortable and spacious enough. Ballista and Marcus were given a room on the first floor overlooking the courtyard. The fugitive-hunter bedded down in the stables. Aulus accompanied his guests to a bathhouse a few paces from the house, then went off to attend to their needs.

Marcus lay in the warm water next to his father. Falx made no attempt at conversation, but his baleful presence was unrestful. Marcus was relieved when Aulus bustled back into the room.

'Good news and bad,' Aulus announced. 'I have secured three mounts at a reasonable price from a friend of mine, and I can promise a good dinner.'

'And the bad news?' Ballista said.

'Is very troubling. The road to Catana is closed. The slaves have risen at Hybla. The bridge over the Symaethus is in their hands. The pass there is narrow. There is no way round.'

CHAPTER THIRTEEN

'THERE IS ALWAYS A WAY ROUND,' BALLISTA SAID.

The five horsemen were riding north-east up through the foothills towards Etna. They had left Centuripae at dawn. In November there were only nine and a half hours of daylight. It was necessary to cover as much ground as possible before evening.

The land here was close-set with vines. In small clearings were beehives, their occupants cloistered for the winter. Here and there were strips of clover and saffron and various herbs. The volcanic soil was fertile, and it was a well cultivated landscape. Yet the riders seldom saw its workers. Instead, plumes of smoke, dotted across the valleys, indicated the bonfires where they were burning the season's vine trimmings. The handful of people they sighted watched them pass without comment. The labourers were all alike, clad in rough hooded work cloaks, and with clogs on their feet. All were silent and equally watchful. Men on horses often spelled trouble. The appearance of the rustics gave no indication of their status. Some would be peasants, proprietors of a few *iugera*, others tenants or sharecroppers of big estates, and the rest would be slaves. All except the latter would have the three names of a citizen of Rome. They might be poor, but they possessed all the rights and pride that citizenship entailed. The slaves, on the other hand, had nothing. To many of their owners they were little more than beasts of burden, *animals with voices*. Ballista wondered how many of these *animals* might aspire to regain their humanity, might answer the siren call of Soter the Syrian wonder-worker, and the messianic promises he held out to the rebels.

The horsemen forded an upland stream. Its green waters were fast and shallow and foamed white over the rocks. Coming out of its declivity, they saw Etna ahead. The day was overcast and cold. It was still in the foothills, but above a north wind pulled away the isolated column of smoke from the ever-active volcano.

In the milder months, the inhabitants of Centuripae made money guiding sightseers to Etna. Many visitors liked to watch the sunrise from the summit. Through the smoke, its rays shone many-hued, like a rainbow. The guides told them the story of Empedocles. So that he might be thought a god, the philosopher wished the manner of his death to be unknown. Empedocles threw himself into the fires of the crater. But his plan was undone when the volcano spewed out one of his sandals. Likewise, they enacted solemn rituals for them. If the mountain accepted their offerings the omens were good, but if it rejected them, cast them out like Empedocles' sandal, the portent could not be more dire. Unsurprisingly, Ballista had never heard of the omens being bad.

Aulus had instructed one of his men to show them the path to the upper slopes. His son had wanted to come, too. They would take the horses back down the mountain when the going got too tough. Of course, Ballista had not wanted Falx to travel with them, but the fugitive-hunter had said that in times like these a man should be at home to protect his dependants. There was no answer to that.

They had packs loaded with provisions for three days. Falx had left his donkeys with Aulus. He would collect them when the crisis was past. Some of his belongings, however, the fugitive-hunter had wrapped and sealed and entrusted to the safekeeping of the priests of the temple of Demeter. Despite the sacrilege to another goddess, Ballista thought it was probable that the golden chalice taken from the eunuchs had been left in the sanctuary.

As they got higher, the air smelt of sulphur. In places, mounds of old lava thrust up like anthills through the undergrowth. Now that they were at the edge of the cultivated land, the peak of Etna was in clear view. Its bare slopes were black under the dark clouds, except where snow lay in the depressions. The snow gleamed, and seemed to hang in swags, as if sculpted.

'Last month there was a big eruption,' Aulus' son said. 'In his forge under the mountain, the god Hephaestus was making weapons. No one heeded the warning of the uprising.'

'There is a natural explanation,' Ballista said. 'Sicily is hollow, honeycombed with underground tunnels. It is just the wind forcing fires to burst out from those subterranean caverns.'

'On the mountain, it is unwise to doubt the gods,' Aulus' son said.

'No, Ballista is right,' Falx said. Surprised, everyone looked at the fugitive-hunter. Falx seldom spoke, and hardly ever ventured any opinion unprompted. 'In primitive times, rulers invented the gods to maintain their power, to keep their subjects oppressed by supernatural terrors. But there is a terrible truth in the story of Typhon, the giant who tried to overthrow the gods, and was imprisoned beneath Etna. The fires are his never-ending death agony. Typhon was condemned to eternal suffering for trying to free mankind from the tyranny of superstition.'

The fugitive-hunter stopped talking and rode ahead, resuming his ceaseless scanning of the terrain. Aulus' son covertly made a sign to avert ill-omened words. Ballista watched Falx, surprised by such unexpected compassion.

They made camp that evening in the lee of an outcrop of lava. Long ago the molten rock had thrust its way down the mountain, burning the vegetation, incinerating everything it touched. Now it lay, black and cold and forbidding, across their path.

Their horses rubbed down, fed and watered, and tethered for the night, the travellers ate their own meal. Beyond the campfire the darkness was absolute. Owls called to one another across the slopes of the mountain. They were always active at the onset of winter, but both Aulus' son and his servant appeared uneasy. To the pious, the hoot of an owl was a bad omen. After the abduction of Persephone to the underworld, her release was ordered, provided she had not tasted the food of the dead. Ascalaphus, a servant of Hades, revealed that she had eaten a few pomegranate seeds. Then it was ordained that she must return to the darkness for three months of each year. In revenge, her mother Demeter had turned Ascalaphus into a long-eared owl.

They fell asleep to the sounds of owls mourning their lost humanity.

In the grey light of pre-dawn they broke camp. The land ahead was too broken for the horses. Aulus' son and his servant said farewell, and led the animals back the way they had come. Marcus watched them go. For a moment he wished that he were returning to Centuripae with them. Then he shouldered his pack, and set off after his father and Falx. The remote heights of Etna were notorious as a refuge for outlaws, and a third armed man might bring a measure of greater safety. Yet the brooding presence of the fugitive-hunter still made him uncomfortable.

They journeyed through the trackless scrub between the cultivated valleys below and the bare ash of the slopes above. The land here was fractured, cut by ravines. Not long after they had scrambled up out of one, they had to negotiate another. Where the ground was flat it was choked with stunted pines, junipers and brambles. The soil was friable. Every step raised a fine dark dust. It clung to their boots, worked its way into their clothes, clogged their nostrils and irritated their eyes.

Today the mountain grumbled and groaned. Tendrils of smoke coiled up across the sides of the cone, seeping out of hidden vents in the rocks. Sometimes it seemed to tremble, even slightly shift beneath their feet. The agony of Typhon was increased, or the labours of Hephaestus redoubled. Unlike the fugitive-hunter, perhaps unlike his father, Marcus had a healthy respect for the traditional gods.

The plan was to skirt around the upper slopes of the west of Etna. It was a harder route, but more direct than sticking to the foothills. There was a risk of broken men, fugitives from the law, but there was nothing up here to attract gangs of rebellious slaves. When they reached the northern side, they would find mining camps. There was a flourishing trade in black basalt to make corn mills. Ballista knew that region. He had hunted those slopes. From there, they would follow a miners' trail down to the coast and Tauromenium. At Tauromenium Falx would leave them, and take the coast road down to Catana.

After midday, a towering cliff, the relic of some huge eruption, forced them to detour downslope away from the peak. Sliding on the seat of his trousers down into yet another declivity, Marcus indulged in the fantasy of metamorphosis. It could be no more than twenty miles – at most twenty-five – in a direct line over the mountain to Tauromenium. If a god changed him into a bird, he could be there in an hour or two. In a few myths the gods gave back a man's original form.

Struggling up the other side, they saw a stag lying in a clearing. It was injured, but still breathing. From above came the baying of hounds. In its flight the stag must have toppled over the cliff. There were terrible stories of packs of wild dogs in the lonely places of the mountains. Huge and savage and cunning, they stalked travellers. Silently they padded up behind a man, pounced before he knew they were upon him. Once he was down, sharp fangs tore him to pieces.

Two dogs appeared at the top of the cliff. Then there was a shout, and the hounds fell silent. The figure of a man was outlined against the sky. There was a spear in his hand, a bow slung across his back. This was worse than any feral dogs. Only one type of man haunted this wilderness.

Marcus saw his father drawing his own bow, reaching for an arrow. Falx had taken cover behind a boulder. Marcus rushed to join the fugitive-hunter. Falx was looking at the treeline below. So far there was no sign of anyone else. But obviously

Falx was apprehensive that they had walked into a trap and were surrounded.

'Have no fear!' the man called down. 'I am a herdsman, not a brigand!'

'No great difference,' Falx muttered.

'Are you alone?' Ballista shouted.

'Wait there, I will come down!'

The dogs following, the man climbed down, nimble and goat-footed.

Feeling foolish cowering behind the boulder, Marcus got up. Then he saw that his father still had a notched arrow, and Falx had not ceased peering down the slope.

The man was heavily bearded with long hair. Over his shoulders he wore a wolf skin. He drew a long curved blade.

'There is nothing to fear,' the man said. 'All the brigands have gone down from the mountain to join the slaves at the bridge by Hybla.' He went to the stag, and deftly cut its throat. 'If one of you might help me?'

Ballista put down his bow. Together they skinned and butchered the carcass.

'If you will accept my hospitality, my home is not far.'

'Do you live alone up here?' Ballista asked.

'No, my family and I live with another. There are seven of us.'

'We are in a hurry.'

'Where are you going?'

'Tauromenium.'

'Then my home is on your way.'

They divided the joints of meat. Marcus slung a haunch of venison across his shoulders.

The going was easier following the hunter. Evidently he knew every deer trail on the mountain.

'Can we trust him?' Marcus whispered to his father.

'Let us find out.' Ballista increased his pace to walk close behind the strange guide. 'How do you come to live in this remote place?'

'My neighbour and I have always lived here. Our fathers were herdsmen. The wealthy man who owned the estate was executed. The stock was driven off. Our fathers were hired hands. They were free men, so were not sold with the slaves. Most of the land was poor grazing. No one came to claim it. Our fathers took it over. At first they lived by hunting. Then they caught and bred wild goats. It was a hard life, but they survived until old age. My mother is still alive. I married my neighbour's sister, and he married mine. Of the four children, two of the girls are married. One lives in the village at the foot of the slope. The other has a husband in Centuripae. My youngest daughter and my neighbour's son remain with us.'

Like many who live in some solitude, the hunter enjoyed the chance to talk.

'We sell the furs we catch in the village. We have bought a milch-cow, fenced a meadow, and dug a garden for vegetables, a few vines and a little grain. We will never be rich. There was no dowry for our daughters. Yet they found husbands all the same. The girls are frugal and hard-working, modest and blessed with good looks.'

Marcus noticed an unfathomable emotion swim below the surface of Falx's normally blank eyes. It was the same look he had given the women on the cart as they left Enna.

'No, we will never be rich, but we have everything we need – eight she-goats, the cow has a pretty calf. We have four sickles, four hoes, three spears, a bow, and each of us has a good hunting knife.'

Ballista raised his eyes, and grinned at Marcus. Like a dam that had broken, there was no stopping the flow of words.

'There are sides of bacon and venison, three bushels of wheat, six of barley, and the same amount of millet, but only four quarts of beans, since there were none this year.'

The rest of the journey passed in an endless recital of the rustics' meagre possessions and the rounds of their occupation.

The settlement was exactly as the huntsman had described. Two thatched huts with drystone walls covered in daub, and a small barn of the same construction, stood by a stream in a sheltered vale. There was a vegetable garden and a field, and the cow and her calf and the goats grazed in the meadow. Some chickens scratched around the yard, and further up the hillside were some vines, and half a dozen pigs rootling about under the trees. Marcus must have missed the last items in the rustic's lengthy monologue.

The other herdsman was as taciturn as the first was talkative. In the presence of strangers, the four females maintained a proper and demure silence of old-fashioned manners. A fire was already burning, and cauldrons of water were placed to heat.

The herdsmen insisted that their guests strip to bathe. The three travellers were black with grime from head to foot. As there was no oil, the younger women rubbed them down with tallow. The wives massaged Ballista and Marcus, and the daughter Falx. The hunter had not exaggerated the prettiness of his daughter. She had long black tresses, skin the colour of pale honey, and an innocent face. Her homespun tunic did not disguise the shape of her body. She was just of marriageable age, probably not long turned fourteen. Marcus tried not to be caught staring. As she worked on his back and shoulders, Falx had his eyes shut. If anything, her ministrations seemed to do nothing but increase the ever-present tension of the fugitive-hunter. After the aches had been kneaded out of their muscles, the warm water sluiced off the tallow.

Dried, they put on the clean tunics from their packs. As the son turned the spit of the roasting venison, the women spread boughs as couches. The men reclined and ate parched chickpeas, and drank wine.

'You said all the outlaws had gone down to the bridge by Hybla,' Ballista said. 'Do you know if there have been any other slave risings in the east of the island?'

'Seldom we get any news up here,' the herdsman said. 'None since the outcasts left. Only hear things when we go down to the village. Not been there for a while.'

'Nothing about Tauromenium?' Ballista persevered.

'Nothing. We get few visitors. Although you are not the first to come this way.' It was natural as host that the loquacious hunter should take the conversation where he wished. 'Only last year we found a philosopher.'

Both of the herdsmen smiled at the recollection.

'He had gone up to think profound thoughts while gazing on the fires – the fleeting nature of life, the immortality of the soul, things like that. He had become disorientated. The fumes sometimes do that. On the way down, he had got lost, and taken a fall. The poor old man was in a terrible state, limbs all grazed and cut, and his tunic ripped to shreds. Half-dead, he was. We cleaned him up and fed him. Had nothing with him but a staff and a wallet. Nothing decent left to wear. Could not let him go on his way like that, not a venerable old man like him, so I told my daughter to give him her tunic. She had a scrap of cloth to cover herself. Praised us to the skies, the philosopher did. Said he had never been treated better in the palaces of governors or kings, called it *true* philosophy, a philosophy of actions, not words.'

I bet the old lecher did, Marcus thought, imagining the girl taking off her tunic.

The venison came on wooden platters with wheaten bread and cabbage and bacon. The son joined the men. The girl sliced the bread with a little knife. When she had served the food, she retired to join the older women eating at a distance. Quite frequently one of the herdsmen held up his cup, and the girl would refill everyone's cup. The women themselves drank water. Each time Marcus watched her discreetly, not letting his eyes linger too long.

'How do you protect yourselves from the brigands?' Ballista asked.

'My dear sir, there is little need. Poverty is the surest guard.' Behind his beard and fringe, the hunter's eyes were full of mirth. 'And the dogs and our spears take care of the rest.'

He gestured for more wine. Quite a lot had been drunk. This time one of the wives brought the pitcher. Marcus had noticed the girl slip into the woods, perhaps to round up the pigs. He had very much wanted to follow.

'They are not all bad men.' The huntsman suddenly grew earnest in his cups. 'Often they have been forced to flee the towns. Crooked judges have confiscated their possessions, or corrupt tax gatherers have taken all they own. They are left with nothing. The old philosopher said it was hard for a poor man to live a virtuous life in a town.'

Falx got up from his couch, excusing himself for a call of nature. Marcus watched him walk into the treeline where the girl had gone. No one else seemed at all concerned. Marcus looked over at his father. Listening to his host expounding the vices of urban life, Ballista did not notice. It might be nothing. But Marcus had to be sure.

Muttering some pleasantry, Marcus also got up. He tried to walk casually up the hill. A mixture of wine and apprehension made that difficult.

Inside the trees it was already near dark. Marcus stopped and listened. Nothing but the last few songbirds and the low grumbling of the mountain. The sounds of the feast were almost inaudible. His eyes grew accustomed to the gloom. He went deeper into the timber. Again he stopped and listened. If Falx was merely relieving himself, there was no need to have gone so far. Marcus was about to move on when he half-heard something. A voice, low and urgent, off to his right.

Marcus set off in that direction. Ducking under branches, placing his feet quietly, he tried to move without noise. If there was an innocent explanation, he would look a fool. For once, that did not matter.

Another voice – higher pitched and frightened, cut off suddenly.

Marcus started to run, sweeping aside the foliage, bursting through the undergrowth.

The girl was on the ground. Her tunic was pulled up around her armpits. Falx stood over her. With one hand he was unbuckling his belt, in the other was a sword.

The fugitive-hunter heard Marcus coming. He turned his head, but kept the tip of his blade at the girl's neck.

'Best walk away, boy.'

The fugitive-hunter's eyes, usually so flat and devoid of emotion, shone in the half-light.

'Leave her alone.'

'Walk away, keep quiet, and no one gets hurt.'

'No one gets hurt!'

'This little pig won't say anything. Be grateful she has been broken in ready for her marriage bed.'

'What?'

'A Roman takes what he wants. Romulus and the Sabine women. It is in our nature.'

Falx attacked with no warning. Two steps and a thrust. Marcus leapt backwards. A rock caught his heel. He went sprawling, rolled away, and scrambled to his feet, dragging his sword free. Falx thrust again. Somehow Marcus got his weapon in the way. The force of the blow almost tore it from his grip.

'Run!' Marcus shouted. He had no idea if the girl was still there.

Falx closed with neat, balanced steps, like a dancer. He feinted at Marcus' face, altered his angle and aimed for the torso. At the last moment, Marcus recognised the trick, sidestepped, and ducked round the trunk of a tree.

Relentlessly, with an awful calm, Falx followed. Marcus gave ground. He realised that the fugitive-hunter had turned him, like a greyhound would a hare. Now he was retreating uphill, away from the settlement.

The girl was still there, huddled on the ground, clutching herself.

Marcus had no breath or attention to shout again. His whole being was focused on his assailant. He blocked another blow, the impact jarring up his arm. The fugitive-hunter was much stronger than him. Sooner or later Falx would wear him down. You did not win a fight just parrying. Marcus tried to remember everything the sword-masters on the Palatine had tried to teach him: *keep your feet moving, watch the blade, wait for your opportunity.*

Far off, one of the pigs or some other large animal was crashing through the wood.

Marcus had been wrong. His father had been wrong. They had misjudged Falx. The fugitive-hunter was not beyond human passions. Here in the gloom, there was a light in the fugitive-hunter's eyes. This was his pleasure: raping and killing, acting out his power over others, witnessing their fear and pain. Blind to the consequences, Falx was intent on killing Marcus. Nothing else mattered. Nothing was going to stop him.

A pale shape moved in the darkness.

Falx stopped, swivelled his body, and unleashed a backhand blow behind himself. The girl was there, just out of reach. Falx looked at her, then at the small dagger protruding from the back of his right thigh. He plucked the dagger out, tossed it away. The pain made him stumble, trying to regain his balance. He looked back at Marcus. But it was too late. Marcus had taken his opportunity. A wild slashing blow cut into the fugitive-hunter's other leg. Falx doubled up, his free hand instinctively clutching at the new wound. The other still held the sword. Marcus brought the edge of his blade down on the back of his skull. Now Falx dropped the sword. Two, three more times, Marcus struck, all his strength behind the blows. Hot blood splashed up into his face. The hideous intimacy of killing. Falx was down on his hands and knees. Marcus raised his arms, steadying himself to strike again. The fugitive-hunter collapsed. Marcus was never going to stop. Strong arms seized him, pinioned them together. Marcus yelled, incoherent in his fury and terror.

'Enough,' Ballista said. 'That is enough. He is dead.'

CHAPTER FOURTEEN

THE NEXT DAY THE MOUNTAIN ERUPTED in earnest. A great cloud of ash, in the shape of a pine tree, thrust high into the sky. The wind was still from the north, so the ash was not a danger. But lower down, lava was spewing out. Thick gobbets of molten rock could be seen bursting from the cone. In recent times, the lava had ploughed down the eastern slopes towards the sea. Usually it went slowly. Yet neither its course nor its speed were ever certain.

The herdsman was leading them round the shoulder of the mountain to the north. They had been walking for hours. Marcus was tired, but was not going to be the one to call for a halt.

Once, long ago, when Etna had revealed its true fury, great rivers of fire had flowed down through the territory of Catana. They had moved at a terrible pace. Two young men had to abandon their country house and flee to the city. Their aged mother and father were too infirm to keep up. The young men, not giving the slightest thought to gold or silver or any of their possessions, and not considering their own safety, took their parents up on their shoulders. They were progressing with difficulty when the flames raced ahead, and cut them off. Even so, they would not abandon their parents. When all seemed hopeless, the gods heeded this example of filial duty, and parted the flood of molten lava.

As a child, Marcus had attended the festival where the people of Catana celebrated the piety of their forebears. There was drinking and feasting, a procession and sacrifices. At the Palatine school, Marcus had read several versions of the story. Oddly, the names of the young men were given differently. For Strabo the geographer, they were Amphinomus and Anapias, while Aelian the Sophist called them Philonomus and Callias. Perhaps two or more separate incidents had become conflated. It was the sort of detail that interested Marcus. Often on the Palatine, he had found a refuge in reading. Especially when the other pupils had taunted him as a *mixo-barbarus*, a half-caste barbarian.

Losing himself thinking about books might have freed him from the teasing of children, but it would not work today. Not after the things of last night. They had not been the things of children. Falx had been left where he had fallen. At first light they had returned. Others had been at the corpse. Birds already had pecked out the eyes. Nocturnal animals had nibbled away the tips of some of the fingers and other choice morsels. The herdsmen and Ballista had fashioned a sledge out of two branches, and lashed the carcass aboard. Marcus had helped drag it away from the settlement. It was hard work, but they had gone a considerable distance. It was important to avoid polluting the stream. Eventually, they reached a crevice. Marcus had been surprised that Ballista placed a copper coin between the teeth of the dead man before they tipped him over the edge. Again, before they buried the fugitive-hunter under rocks, Ballista gathered a handful of dust, and sprinkled it over the head of the corpse.

'He is not worth such respect,' Marcus had said.

'All the dead deserve respect.' Ballista scooped up a second handful. 'Otherwise their spirits find no rest.'

'It was self-defence. His ghost will not pursue me.'

'No, probably not.' Ballista had shrugged as if trying to cast off a burden or dismiss a memory. 'It is terrible for a man to be haunted by a *daemon*. The worse the man, the more malignant the *daemon*.'

After disposing of the corpse, the men had washed downstream from the settlement. There was neither the time nor paraphernalia for any elaborate rituals of purification after touching the dead. Among the possessions of the fugitive-hunter, sure enough, they had found the golden chalice. Despite its value, when its provenance was explained, the herdsmen would not accept it. Ballista suggested they rededicate it to whatever deity they thought best. After that, they had left. The farewell from the women had been brief and formal. The girl had looked drawn and close to tears.

The herdsman, so loquacious the previous day, now guided them in an inhibited silence. Yesterday he had thanked Marcus for saving his daughter. But his thanks had seemed constrained. No doubt he blamed Marcus and his father for bringing the fugitive-hunter to his home. Marcus very much hoped that the rustic idyll had not been permanently tainted. Such an assault could leave scars that would not heal.

At dusk, the three weary walkers came to the mining camp. The mine was opencast. Its workings had gouged great troughs out of the mountain. The sheds and the barracks were dark and silent.

They approached cautiously, crept soft-footed through the camp like thieves.

The place had been abandoned in a hurry. Shovels and panniers lay where they had been dropped in the diggings. There was a half-prepared meal in the kitchen. Evidence of violence could be seen. The wood around the lock on the door of the barracks was splintered. The chains which had confined the miners inside at night had been severed. There were no bodies, but the quarters of the guards were ransacked and stinking. The possessions had been picked through. The valueless items that remained – clay lamps and cups, broken buckles and letters – were strewn around the floor. Everything that could be smashed had been ground underfoot. In each bunk, someone had defecated. Not a single pick or axe remained in the tool shed, or knife in the kitchen.

Marcus thought his father looked aghast, as if confronted by some personal tragedy. But Ballista said nothing.

Everyone was long gone. The ashes in the fire were stone-cold. There was no reason to think anyone would return. Whatever had happened, it should be safe enough to spend the night in the camp.

They raked out the grate, lit a new fire, and ate a subdued meal. The night was cold. No one suggested mucking out the guards' room, and the associations of the barracks were unappealing. They laid out their bedrolls by the fire in the kitchen. Before turning in, they stood in the chill wind and watched the eruption. Tongues of fire flickered from the summit. Above, the clouds were tinged blood-red.

The three silent figures were dwarfed by the mountain, like survivors of some primordial apocalypse.

Ballista thanked the herdsman. He found it hard to find the right words. It was impossible to say *we are sorry your daughter was assaulted, and it was our fault*. He thought about offering the man some money, but, even if it did not offend his pride, it looked too much like paying blood-guilt.

As he watched the herdsman depart, Ballista wondered how the next lost wayfarer, philosopher or not, would be welcomed. Trying to put that – and far more pressing worries – out of his mind, he told his son that they should get moving.

They crested a ridge, and saw the sea. It was slate-grey under a lowering sky. In the distance – seven or eight miles off – was the Hill of the Bull, its quarters and shoulders and head sloping down towards the coast. Even from so far away, he could make out a thin grey line against the dark green of the hillside. The buildings were invisible, but there was Tauromenium. After last night, he dreaded more than ever what he would find when he reached his home.

At least it was not far. He knew the way from here: down into the valley of the Asinius, follow the river to the sea, cross the bridge, and pick up the Via Pompeia north. A walk of just a few hours.

'Will it be all right?' Isangrim asked.

'How in Hades should I know?' Ballista snapped. Then he regretted his flash of temper. 'I am sorry. I hope so. Yes, I think it will be all right.'

Never in his life had he hoped for something so much.

Allfather, let it not be a tragic homecoming.

Once they had descended to the bank of the river, the Hill of the Bull was lost to sight. It did not reappear for hours – not until they rounded the flank of an outcrop on the coast road. At last, they were no more than a couple of miles from the town. A steep climb and they would be there.

They entered the town through the Catana Gate. But Ballista had known everything was wrong for some time. The Via Pompeia had been deserted. Rubbish was scattered along its length: smashed amphorae, discarded flasks and scraps of food, broken straps and bits of leather – all the detritus left by a mob or an army.

Tauromenium was empty. They walked up the main street, the acropolis high above to their left, glimpses of ravines and the sea between the buildings to their right. They saw no one. There was a stillness to any town that had been sacked. Yet usually there were furtive movements or noises. Sometimes you heard women weeping. Here, there was nothing. If anyone remained, they were hiding.

Ballista unslung his bow and notched an arrow. Isangrim drew his sword.

They reached the forum. The doors of the temples and the public buildings gaped open. Abandoned loot was strewn across the square. There were tapestries and rugs, statuettes and a painting – acquisitively grabbed, then tossed aside as not worth the trouble.

Not far now. Ballista felt his heart thumping. There were no corpses. Not one. That was something.

They turned into the street running to the theatre, then halfway along into the alley backing onto the house. Oddly, the garden gate was shut. The hinges had been oiled not long ago. They did not squeal when Ballista pushed it open. The gatekeeper's lodge was empty, but the garden was unchanged.

Ballista stood still, afraid to go further. He shut his eyes, listened to the birds in the shrubs and flowerbeds. Like a child, he wanted everything to be different when he opened them.

This was no example to set Isangrim. No matter what they found, he had to show courage for the sake of the boy.

Ballista opened his eyes. Isangrim was regarding him. Ballista could not tell what the boy was thinking. He slung the bow over his shoulder, and drew his sword.

'Ready?'

Isangrim nodded.

They walked through the garden to the house.

Again, the door was closed. It was locked. They looked at each other. Neither dared to hope. From the pouch containing his coins, Ballista produced the key. Under the circumstances, there was something ridiculous about the homely gesture.

As soon as they opened the door they knew the house had been plundered. The Corinthian bronze was not on its plinth. The antique weapons no longer hung on their pegs. Yet the tapestries were still on the walls – too bulky to be worth stealing. They shut the door behind them.

Their footfalls echoed as they walked down the long corridor. It was dark. The shutters were drawn. The painted vases were missing from their niches. But there was nothing broken. The corridor smelled of cedar wood and polish. It looked as if it had recently been swept.

In the atrium, the small gold and silver statues were gone from the shrine of the household gods. Otherwise everything looked normal.

In the corridor they had left, a tapestry shifted in the wind. Isangrim went to go deeper into the house. Ballista stopped him with a gesture. The door was shut. There was no breeze.

Not trying to disguise his approach, Ballista walked back into the corridor. Isangrim followed. The tapestry trembled ever so slightly. Isangrim brought up his blade, ready to thrust. Catching his eye, Ballista silently mouthed *no*.

'Come out,' Ballista said.

He thought he heard a muffled sob.

'Come out now.'

A head popped from behind the tapestry. An old man, terrified out of his wits. Vaguely familiar, but Ballista did not recognise him.

'Is that you, Hilarus?' Isangrim said.

The old slave peered out myopically. In his fear, he could not look beyond the drawn swords.

'Hilarus, it is me,' Isangrim said, 'with my father.'

Recognition dawned on the wizened face. And Ballista knew him, too.

'Master.'

Julia's chamberlain got down and embraced Ballista's knees. He might have kissed his boots, if Ballista had not raised him to his feet.

'They did not touch your books, but all the mistress's treasures . . . they took them all. I could not stop them.' The old slave looked ashamed, and started to cry. 'I was too frightened to try and stop them. At first I hid in the attic. When they found me, I did nothing, just watched.'

'The mistress?' Ballista said, his voice tight. 'My other boy?'

'The mistress?' Hilarus repeated as if his reason had deserted him.

Ballista had to stop himself shaking the old man.

'Where is she? Where is Dernhelm?'

'Gone.'

'Gone where?'

'Everyone left before the rebels arrived.'

Ballista felt his heart leap. He had to keep calm. Too soon to be sure.

'Where?'

'They took a boat.'

'To where?'

'Syracuse.'

Ballista exhaled. His legs were unsteady.

'The mistress wanted me to go, too. But I said I would stay. Someone had to remain at the house. When the rebels came, I was so afraid, I hid.'

They were alive. Julia and Dernhelm were alive. Ballista was weak with relief. But why Syracuse? *Allfather, why not Italy?* They would have been completely beyond harm there.

'But I have tidied up the things they damaged. They took the precious things, but not that many things were broken.'

'You have done well.' Ballista patted Hilarus as he would a horse. 'Very well.'

They were alive, and in Syracuse. They would be safe there for the moment, safe enough provided Ballista could reach them before the slave army.

The ruins of Naxos were a couple of miles south of Tauromenium. They stood on a promontory jutting out into the

Ausonian Sea. It was a safer place to spend the night. The main body of the slaves was gone, but there was the danger of stragglers or isolated bands, perhaps like the miners from the camp. Unlike Tauromenium, there was nothing in the ancient and broken walls of Naxos to plunder.

The slaves had left two days previously, Julia and Dernhelm two days before that. Ballista had missed his family by just four days. From where Ballista stood, he could see both Tauromenium and the mountains of Calabria across the sea. Lit by the evening sun, the mountains looked so very close. Hilarus said that Julia had waited until the last moment, then she had hired a fishing boat. But she had not gone to Italy – she had gone to Syracuse. Exasperation competed with relief in Ballista's thoughts. Maximus or one of the *familia* should have made her see sense. Although, the gods knew, it would not have been easy once Julia had made up her mind.

At least, thanks to Hilarus, he knew where they had gone. Nothing could have been worse than if they had vanished. If you never discovered what had happened to your loved ones, you would spend the rest of your days in torment. You would never even have the threadbare comfort of mourning.

Ballista and Isangrim had gone down to the docks. On the way they had seen a few people – looters or householders emerging from hiding or returning to the city. At the waterside there had been no boats, nothing seaworthy, not even a leaky skiff. Likewise, although they searched, there was not a horse or mule left in Tauromenium, not a riding animal of any sort.

They would have to walk. By now the rebel force would be approaching Catana. Ballista and Isangrim would have to follow. Etna meant there was no way round, no short cut. Somehow they would have to skirt the slaves' camp, or even slip through their ranks. Whatever the risk, they had to reach Syracuse before the rebels.

Ballista looked at his son. Isangrim was building a fire for the night. Of course, there was another choice. Ballista looked again at the sea and the mountains on the far shore. To the north, only two miles separated the island from the mainland. The straits of Messana were notoriously treacherous. For the ancients, it was the lair of Scylla and Charybdis. The currents were fast and powerful. The sea there smelt of the innumerable monsters in its depths. It drew sharks like nowhere else. But if they went north, surely they would find some sort of vessel in a remote fishing village or tucked away, overlooked, in a cove. Ballista had sailed all his life. He could get Isangrim safe to the mainland. But then it would be too late to return to Syracuse.

It was a terrible choice. To convey his eldest son to safety meant abandoning the rest of his family. To go to their aid was to place Isangrim in mortal danger. Ballista felt crushed by the weight of that choice.

Isangrim placed a skillet on the fire, and began to fry some meat. Old Hilarus had provided the steaks. The storerooms of the villa had not been stripped completely bare. Hilarus had shown extraordinary courage. Staying on when the *familia* left, he had gambled that, as a slave, he would not be harmed. The old man had wagered his life, and he had won. This afternoon, again he had remained in the house. Ballista hoped he would be all right. The danger was less than before. Before leaving, Ballista had granted him his freedom.

Hilarus had said that after the villa had been plundered, he had gone out into the town. In the forum, he had mingled with the slaves. Although many of the rebels were barbarian Alamanni, no one had challenged him. He had listened to their leader address them from the steps of the town hall. Soter, the self-styled *Saviour*, had spoken of a return to the age of Saturn, a golden age before slavery. They would take the whole of Sicily, and they would found a City of the Sun, where no man would bear the shackles of servitude, where every man would be equal, and every man would be free.

The reported speech fascinated Ballista. No rebellious slaves had ever succeeded. They had never left any record of their hopes. Their story was always written later, by their conquerors. They were always condemned by history as ferocious and irrational savages bent on revenge. Beyond a bloody vengeance, all they wanted was to turn everything upside down, to remake the world with themselves as the masters, and their former owners, those they had not massacred, reduced to serving as their slaves.

Here was proof that history books did not tell the whole story. Many slaves, like Soter, were educated. They could draw on philosophy, on ideals of equality, of the brotherhood of man. They could change them to suit their purposes, bring them out of the darkness of inner morality, and make them a rallying cry to create a better world. Even the illiterate knew of a time when mankind lived according to nature, a time before slavery was invented. Even the meanest intelligence could hear the siren call of freedom, and not just for themselves.

To break the train of his thoughts, Ballista shook himself, like a dog emerging from a stream. No matter how noble the motives of the uprising, he remembered what had happened at the villa of Caecilius, remembered being hunted across the hills outside Enna. He would kill every one of the rebels, wade ankle-deep through their blood, before he let them harm his family.

'You are quiet,' Isangrim said.

'It's nothing.'

'The food is ready.'

They sat and ate with their backs resting against the wall of what had long ago been a house. The masonry was rough, huge and irregular cyclopean stones. The fire made their shadows flicker, deformed over its surface. Naxos was very old. The first settlement of the Greeks on the island. A thousand years since the first men sat and ate here. All those generations now dead. Some men found comfort in the immensity of time. What were their troubles measured against that? No more than a heartbeat, or the blink of an eye in eternity. Ballista found it no comfort at all.

'How many men have you killed?' Isangrim asked out of nowhere.

'I cannot remember.'

Isangrim said nothing.

'Are you all right?'

'Don't worry.' Isangrim smiled. 'I have not become a Christian, or anything like that.'

'Killing is not something to be taken lightly. Never take pleasure in the act.'

Again Isangrim was silent.

'You did well, Isangrim. Did what was necessary.'

'Marcus – I prefer to be called Marcus.'

Now, taken aback, Ballista did not speak.

His son looked embarrassed.

Ballista broke the silence. 'When you were young, I started to teach you the language of Germania. Do you know why?'

'Pride in your ancestors.'

'Only in part. They were not all good men.' Ballista laughed, changed tack. 'You know the story of the Parthian prince Meherdates in Tacitus?'

The boy furrowed his brows in thought, then remembered and beamed.

'A hostage, educated in Rome. When the emperor sent him back to take the throne, the Parthians killed him because he was a stranger to their customs. No, that is wrong. They would not accept him as one of them, and they cut off his ears.'

Ballista watched as his son spoke, and saw the realisation dawn.

'But the emperor would send you, not me.'

'I am getting old.'

Isangrim looked appalled.

'It may never happen . . .' Ballista caught himself. 'Marcus.'

CHAPTER FIFTEEN

A T FIRST, THEY WALKED IN SUNSHINE. The road ran close to the shore. Waves crashed on the pale grey sands. Gulls shrieked in the bright air. Scattered across the beach were groups of stones. They were large and dark grey and rounded. Their smooth surfaces glistened like the coats of seals.

The mountain was quieter than yesterday. The pious would think that Hephaestus rested in his forge, or that Typhon had a respite from his torment. A rationalist would argue that the subterranean winds must have dropped.

As the morning wore on, a cold breeze got up at their backs, and storm clouds were gathering in the north. By midday the sun had gone, and the first rain had started to fall. Big fat drops dimpled the dust of the road. They ate some salt pork and biscuit sheltering under the boughs of an ancient olive tree.

Ballista looked at his son. The boy was licking the grease from his fingers.

Marcus, I must remember to call him Marcus.

And he was not a boy anymore, but a young man. It was not the killing of the fugitive-hunter. Given the right circumstances, anyone can kill. A lucky blow, or a tile dropped from a roof; anyone can kill – even a child or an old woman. It was the conversation they had had last night. Ballista had set out the choice they faced. Go north, find a boat, cross the straits to safety, trust that Syracuse would not fall, or that Julia and the others would also manage to take passage to Italy. Or go south, somehow skirt round or pass through the rebel forces, get to Syracuse before it was besieged. If they chose the latter, there was always the chance that the family would have left Syracuse – that the two of them would run the risk for nothing. Marcus had not hesitated. They would go south.

In the afternoon the rain got heavier, turned to sleet, then snow. The initial flurries were succeeded by a steady enveloping blanket. It was too damp down by the sea for the snow to settle. But if it continued to fall, soon it would lie in sweeping folds and drifts across the higher slopes of the mountain. They trudged on, cold and wet, enshrouded by the storm.

The road curved away from the sea, and they went through sodden olive groves and fields of vines. They saw no one. It was a long day's walk from Naxos to Catana – twenty-five miles or so. There was one settlement, not far from Catana. They would take to the fields to avoid the hamlet. It would be dusk, if not full dark, when they reached the city. Ballista had not decided, but thought it might be best to slip through the rebel lines under cover of darkness. It would be good if the storm had not abated. Even the disciplined sentries of a Roman legion were less alert in a foul night. With luck the slaves might have abandoned their outposts, and sought the warmth of their campfires and whatever cover they could find. The gods willing, the two of them might pass through unchallenged.

You could not see far through the snow, and it deadened all sound. They were lucky. In a brief lull, they heard the jingle of harness and the thud of hooves. There was just time to throw themselves flat in the slush of a ditch.

Ballista let them pass before he peered over the edge. The dozen horsemen were already disappearing north into the driving snow. They wore bulky cloaks. Most were hooded, but a couple wore broad-brimmed hats over long, braided hair. They rode at a trot, in a column of twos, looking all around. In no time they were out of sight and hearing, vanished into the storm.

As soon as they were gone, Ballista and Marcus climbed out of the ditch, brushed off as much of the clinging mud as they could, and pressed on down the road. There was no point in discussing what they had seen.

Despite the delays, both hiding from the patrol and then cutting through the fields to circumnavigate the small village, they reached Catana at twilight. The storm had blown away to the south. The fading sky was a clear and washed-out blue, the sea luminescent. They left the road, and ascended a low hill not far from the city.

From their vantage point they could take in the whole city: the curve of the walls; the imposing gates; the citadel crowned with temples and the amphitheatre carved into its northern flank; the half-moon of the harbour. Catana had not fallen. The rebel camp lay all around the perimeter, and stretched inland to the far side of a small lake. There was a large pavilion by the lake, with some smaller tents and horse lines set out neatly close by. Otherwise there was little indication of order. The rebellious slaves had pitched their shelters wherever seemed best to them. Smoke from cooking fires drifted across the encampment. Yet there was no sign of any women or children.

'How many of them are there?' Marcus asked.

'A lot.'

'You can't tell?'

'No. In a regular army there are eight to ten men in a tent. You estimate the number of tents, multiply it by ten, then, depending how long they have been in the field, deduct a percentage for casualties, stragglers and deserters. But this is not a regular army.'

'But they are all fighting men.'

'Yes, they must have left their families somewhere on the north coast. It does show a certain control. And you see the horse lines by the big tent? Whoever Soter really is, he is building something out of nothing. There are pickets set, and the mounted patrol also indicates a measure of discipline.'

'How many of them would you guess?'

'Too many for comfort. Several thousand, maybe as many as ten thousand.'

'What are we going to do?'

Ballista gazed inland, beyond the lake. 'We could work our way around across country, then get back to the road. But it would take a long time. We do not know how long Catana will hold out. Our other option is to brazen it out, and walk straight through the camp.'

Marcus squared his shoulders. 'Then that is what we should do.'

'You are not too tired? It has been a long day.'

'Fear will keep me going.'

Ballista grinned. 'Just for tonight, you had better revert to Isangrim. If we are challenged, we are two German tribesmen. Call me Dernhelm. Do you remember any of the language?'

'A little,' Marcus said.

His attempt at the tongue of northern *barbaricum* was heavily accented. It would not convince anyone who spoke the language.

'Better let me do the talking.'

The two muddied and bedraggled figures walked straight down the road to the outpost.

'*Libertas!*'

The challenge was in Latin. There were ten guards, half of them lounging by the fire, the others standing in the road.

'I do not know the password,' Ballista replied in the same language, but let his pronunciation betray his northern origins. 'Soter sent us on a scouting mission up onto Etna after we all left Tauromenium.'

'What are your names?' A big German asked the question in his native language. His face was hidden by the brim of his hat. He gave the impression of being in charge.

'Dernhelm of the Angles, and this is my son Isangrim.'

The warrior did not answer at once. Studying them closely, he pushed his hat to the back of his head. He was bearded, and his hair hung in braids to his shoulders. The letter *F* was branded on his forehead.

'We have met before.'

Ballista's heart sank. Of all the chance encounters in the world.

'At the beach beyond Panormus.'

'I remember.'

'When I said we would meet again, I had no idea who you were.'

'But now you do.'

'Yes, now I do.' All the warrior's followers were on their feet. They were all northern tribesmen. They had ringed Ballista and his son. Every one had drawn his sword. 'Disarm them.'

Marcus' hand went to his hilt. Ballista shook his head. The odds were impossible. The warriors took the weapons from their belts.

'There is no blood feud between our peoples,' Ballista said.

'You Angles are allies of Rome. We Alamanni fight the empire.'

'That is how it is now,' Ballista said. 'But it has not always been. A warrior does not choose who he fights. You and me, we are the same, like snow blowing from one tree to another.'

The warrior smiled. 'Except you are my prisoner.'

'What will you do?'

'Let Soter decide. You might be killed, or you might be useful.'

They were marched to the lake.

'*Libertas.*' The guards at the pavilion made the challenge.

'*Virtus,*' the Alamann answered.

One word, Marcus thought. *If we had known that one word, we would have walked clean through the camp. Even now we would be on our way.*

There were a dozen more Alamanni guarding the entrance to the big pavilion, although none patrolling around its perimeter. They waited by the entrance. Marcus was puzzled. He had no doubt that the guards would cut them down if they resisted or tried to escape. Yet the leader of the outpost treated his father almost with deference. They were talking in their own language. From his distant lessons, Marcus could understand some of the words. They were talking about the rebel leader, Soter. His name was coupled to that of the goddess Aphrodite. The warrior used the Greek word *Epaphroditus* – beloved of Aphrodite. Yet he and Ballista seemed more interested in some physical deformity. If Marcus understood correctly, Soter had only one eye.

A chamberlain came and summoned the leader of the picket into the tent. Marcus and his father were left waiting outside with the other guards.

After a time, the chamberlain returned and ushered them through the entrance of the pavilion. There was an antechamber with passages running off around inside the walls of the tent. The chamberlain pulled back the inner hangings, and they entered the main room. The air was fragrant with incense. Soft lamplight shone on rich tapestries and antique statues. At the far end was a dais raised some feet off the ground. In the centre of the dais was the curule throne of a senior magistrate. On the throne sat a man robed in a purple toga, and wearing a golden crown. The crown was radiate like the sun. Its wearer had long white hair and a deep white beard. One of his eyes was covered with a patch.

'*Proskynesis*,' the chamberlain whispered.

Marcus looked at his father, then followed his lead. They bowed, then raised their fingertips to their lips, and blew the figure on the throne a kiss.

Soter might have modelled his audience on that of a monarch, Marcus thought, but at least the leader of the rebellious slaves had not insisted on full adoration, had not made them grovel on their bellies like the subjects of an oriental potentate.

The slave-king regarded them with his one eye.

In front of the dais a fire was burning on a low altar. It was flanked by a dozen men holding axes bound up in a bundle of rods. Off to one side, several secretaries waited with their writing materials. Up on the dais, behind Soter, were ranged seven councillors. Six of them were Alamanni, one the warrior who had captured them. The final councillor wore a toga with a broad purple stripe, the mark of a Roman senator. The lictors; the radiate crown; the advisors: the whole was a barbaric simulacrum of the council of a Roman emperor.

Marcus looked around, as if some divinity might reveal some way to escape. There were three other openings: two at the sides, which must open onto the passageways running around the outer walls, and one to the rear, which must give onto smaller, private chambers. Somehow Marcus knew there were guards on the other side of the hangings of each.

'You are Marcus Clodius Ballista.' The slave-king spoke well-educated Attic Greek. 'The one known to the Germans as Dernhelm. And you are here as a spy.'

'No,' Ballista replied in the same dialect. 'We are travellers on our way to Syracuse.'

'To organise the defence of the city.'

'To be with our loved ones. The boy's mother, his brother and the rest of our *familia* are there.'

A movement caught Marcus' attention. A tame raven perched on the arm of the throne shifted to groom its wings. As if sensing his gaze, the bird stopped and fixed him with a glittering eye.

'You own slaves.' It was impossible to tell if it was a question or a statement.

'I have freed all my slaves,' Ballista said.

'And your wife and her family?'

'All those blessed with wealth own slaves. It is natural.'

'There are others who hold that controlling another human being is contrary to nature.'

Ballista said nothing.

'It is only by convention that one man can be a slave and another free. There is no natural difference, and therefore it cannot be just, as it is based on the use of force.'

Marcus wondered if his father had recognised the quotation was from Aristotle.

'I am no philosopher,' Ballista said.

'It is the same in Roman law. Slavery is an institution by which a person is put into the ownership of someone else contrary to the natural order.'

'I am not a lawyer.'

'For nine days and nights I hung on the cross. Unlike the false god of the Christians, I did not die. From that tree of life, I learnt wisdom. When I was cut down, I let myself be enslaved to learn evil. The man who thought he was my master made me his secretary. Now I have revealed myself to make men free.'

'No slave revolt has succeeded.'

Marcus thought his father's words ill-considered. Soter might be educated, but he was obviously insane.

Soter appeared not to take offence.

'This is not a slave revolt. This is my kingdom. There will be no slaves in the Island of the Sun.'

'It is just a dream of philosophers.'

'The other Island of the Sun lies in the Ocean, four months' sail south of Arabia. Like its righteous rulers, I make no claim on other territories.'

'The emperor will send an army to retake Sicily.'

Soter smiled. 'That is no certainty. You were a friend of Gallienus. You know the emperor is beset with troubles – Postumus in the West, Odenaethus in the East. Can he spare troops for an expedition to the South? And what about the North? For now, the Alamanni are quiet. But only five years ago they reached the gates of Rome. My councillors, the warriors in this pavilion, reached the gates of Rome.'

'Odenaethus rules the East in the name of Gallienus,' Ballista said.

'And I am prepared to do the same in Sicily. The Island of the Sun is rich. I will send grain and wine to Rome, once Gallienus has recognised my right to Sicily.'

Marcus thought Soter might be deluded, but he was no fool.

'My friend here' – Soter pointed to the only councillor in a toga – 'the Quaestor Caius Maesius Modius, was going to travel to Gallienus. But how much better if the embassy is headed by a friend of the emperor?'

Marcus looked at his father. Ballista stood very still, his face a mask.

'Of course, that will wait until we have taken Syracuse and secured the whole island.'

Ballista nodded gravely, then spoke dispassionately, as if discussing some theoretical proposition.

'The walls of Syracuse are strong, too strong to take by storm. Its granaries will be well stocked. Your army will starve before its citizens.'

The slave-king clapped his hands with pleasure.

'And that is why fate has sent me a general experienced in siege warfare. *You* will take Syracuse for me.'

Ballista did not reply at once.

The only sound was the fire hissing on the altar.

'If my family are spared,' Ballista said, 'I will give you Syracuse.'

Marcus stared at his father in horror.

The slave-king beamed at Ballista. 'We are close, you and me, close kinsmen. As they say in the North, snow blowing from one tree to another.'

CHAPTER SIXTEEN

'HOW COULD YOU?'

Ballista gestured for Marcus to be quiet.

'You took an oath!'

Ballista took his son by the shoulders. 'Lower your voice, and talk Greek.'

They had been given a tent near the pavilion. The two guards outside were Alamanni. Having been slaves, they would understand Latin, but perhaps not Greek.

'You swore an oath to serve the rebel,' Marcus hissed.

'An oath extracted under duress is not binding.'

'Soter made no threats.'

'The threat was implicit.'

Marcus was angry and appalled. 'You sound like a Sophist arguing black is white.'

Ballista looked away.

'You have done this before.'

Ballista nodded. 'More than once.'

'A man who goes back on his word has no honour.'

Ballista could feel his own anger rising. 'We are not the virtuous heroes of some Greek novel. I was trying to buy us time, keep us alive.'

'The gods are not to be mocked – their revenge is slow but certain.'

'You would be better off following the Epicureanism of your mother. If the gods exist, they are far away, and do not care.'

'But you do not believe that.'

'No, I don't think I do. If there is divine retribution, it should fall on my head.'

'Sometimes the gods are merciful.' Marcus' anger was waning. 'Anyway, the heroes of Greek novels are not always moral.'

'And those in Latin ones are all cheats and liars,' Ballista said.

They both smiled. The tension between them was gone.

'Now you have bought us some time, what are we going to do with it?'

Marcus reminded Ballista of Julia. It was the sort of practical thing she would say.

'I am going to become very ill. You are going to ask the guards to fetch me a doctor.'

'That old trick will never work. Anyway, there are two of them. They are both armed, and we are not.'

'I can't think of anything better. We will wait until after midnight, when the camp is sleeping.'

Ballista was lying under a blanket on one of the two pallets of straw. He had heated water on the small brazier, dabbed it on his forehead and neck to counterfeit sweat.

'Please, my father is ill. He needs a doctor.'

The flap of the tent was pulled back. The two Alamanni looked in.

'He is burning up.' Marcus sounded desperate. 'I think he has been poisoned.'

The guards looked at each other. They had been ordered to keep Ballista safe.

'Please, you have to help.'

The Alamanni were suspicious. One entered the tent. The other remained, watchful by the entrance.

'If he dies . . .'

The threat did not have to be completed. The anger of the slave-king would be terrible.

The one in the tent knelt and touched Ballista's face. Ballista flinched and groaned.

'He might have a fever.' The guard got up. 'Watch him, I will get the doctor.'

Ballista lay still for a short time, then started to moan and thrash about.

'He is having a fit.' Marcus flung himself on his father. 'For the gods' sake, help me hold him down.'

Still not totally convinced, the remaining Alamann came and peered down at the convulsing figure. Ballista lunged up, got him by the throat with both hands, dragged him down. The Alamann grunted with surprise. Ballista rolled his weight half on top of the man. The Alamann twisted. They rolled across the floor of the tent, grappling. A knee came up into Ballista's groin. The blow had little force, but Ballista felt a surge of nausea. They collided with the wall of the tent. Ballista was on top. Not releasing his grip on the man's throat, he jackknifed his body, got his knees up on his opponent's chest, pinning him down. With his right hand, the Alamann reached for the dagger on his belt. Ballista grabbed his forearm with his left hand, hung on to it like a dog with a rat. The Alamann opened his mouth, took a breath to shout. No sound emerged. Ballista's right hand was choking him. Nails raked Ballista's face, clawing for his eyes. Rearing back, Ballista used all his strength and weight to throttle the Alamann. The warrior's eyes were bulging, his face mottled. Unrelenting, Ballista crushed his windpipe – crushed the life out of him.

The limbs of the Alamann twitched; the heels of his boots drummed on the ground. Then he was still. Ballista got both hands around his throat, to make sure he was dead. His fingers were deep in the soft flesh.

'That is enough,' Marcus said.

Panting, Ballista collapsed onto the corpse. There was hot blood running down his cheeks. He was exhausted, his arms shaking. There was no time for weakness. Dragging air back into his lungs, he hauled himself to his feet.

'Watch outside.'

Like a warrior in a tawdry epic, Ballista stripped his fallen foe, took his sword and dagger, rolled his body over to free his cloak. The interior of the tent stank like a latrine. The Alamann must have voided his bladder and bowels. There was no dignity in death.

'They are coming!' Marcus ducked his head back into the tent. 'The doctor and the guard.'

Hades, why did they have to be so quick?

Ballista threw a blanket over the corpse, covering its head. He handed Marcus the dagger.

'You will have to deal with the doctor. Crouch over the body.'

Ballista put on the cloak, pulled up the hood, stood back to one side of the entrance.

'Help, I think he is dead.'

At Marcus' plea, the doctor bustled into the tent. The other guard crowded at his back. Ballista stepped forward, and hit the warrior with the pommel of the sword, full force to the temple. The Alamann went down like a toppled statue.

The doctor wheeled round, too surprised to yell.

'Don't make a sound.' Marcus had the dagger at the doctor's throat.

Ballista kicked the fallen man. The Alamann made no sound. Bending, Ballista touched his throat. A fluttering pulse. Unconscious, not dead. No threat for now – that was all that mattered. Ballista took his weapons, tossed them aside.

The doctor whimpered with fear.

'What is your name?'

'Evagoras. Please don't kill me!'

'Death is the last of your worries. Do as I say, and you will live.'

Ballista took the bag of medical instruments, searched his clothes methodically. The doctor had a knife, but nothing else.

'Give me your signet ring.'

The doctor handed over the ring.

'Please take me with you. I am a free man. I was forced to join them. Please don't leave me here.'

Ballista seized his face, forced his jaws open, felt his teeth, as if he were buying a mule.

'You are lying. You are a slave.'

'No, I am a free man.'

'Your teeth betray you. They are worn down from a lifetime of eating coarse slave bread.'

Ballista removed the doctor's cloak, used it to tie his hands behind his back, then forced him to his knees.

'You won't get away.' Now the doctor's eyes blazed defiance. 'Soter will kill you and your boy. Kill all your sort. He will torture your son to death while you watch. You two will die slowly, with refinement. You will both beg for the release of death.'

Ballista cuffed him round the ear. 'Don't try my patience, whipling. The quality of mercy is finite.'

Cutting a strip of cloth from the doctor's tunic, Ballista fashioned it into a gag. The doctor struggled, until pricked by the dagger Marcus still held. Ballista got the doctor on the ground, hogtied him with his own cloak.

'Take the other guard's weapons, get your pack, and put on a cloak.'

When they were both armed and cloaked, Ballista looked round the tent. He thought for some moments, then kicked the brazier over onto the unoccupied mattress of straw.

'We can't leave them to be burnt alive.' Marcus gazed at his father with horror.

'Probably someone will rescue them. We need a diversion.'

The encampment was quiet, slumbering in the depths of the night. No one challenged them until they arrived at the horse lines.

'*Libertas.*' The man in charge of the horse lines was a southerner, an ex-slave.

'*Virtus.*'

'Who are you?'

A lie might do more damage than the truth.

'Marcus Clodius Ballista.'

The stableman chuckled. 'It is all over the camp that you have joined us.'

'We need two horses. Soter has told us to go ahead to Syracuse.'

'I haven't received any orders.'

'*The Saviour* told his doctor Evagoras to give us his signet ring as a token.'

'I don't know . . .'

'We need two good stayers, comfortable saddles. Time is pressing.'

Ballista had spent a lifetime giving orders, the stable hand obeying them. Two grooms were told to fetch the tack.

'The mare and the gelding at the end are the best stayers in the string. Run all day, they can.'

As they waited for the grooms to bring the saddles and bridles, then tack up the horses, it was as if the gods had held back time. The head lad prattled away happily.

'The goddess Aphrodite favours Soter, talks through him, she does. The *Saviour* goes into a trance, breathes fire from his mouth, talks in strange tongues. Seen it myself, I have. It is wonderful to behold. Every prophecy he has made has come true.'

As he talked, Ballista thought about killing him and the two grooms. Nothing causes more chaos in a camp at night than if the horses get loose. But there were many shelters within earshot. It would be difficult to kill all three without making a sound.

At last the mounts were ready. The grooms gave Ballista and Marcus a leg-up.

'The gods hold their hands over you.'

'And you,' Ballista replied to the benediction.

As they rode away, Marcus grinned at his father.

Ballista smiled back. But it was too soon to rejoice. One obstacle remained.

The picket at the edge of the camp on the road south was once again manned by Alamanni.

'Halt! No one is to leave the camp.'

'I am Dernhelm, son of Isangrim the Himling, ruler of the Angles.'

'I heard Soter had confined you to your quarters.'

'He gave new orders. We are to prepare for our entry to Syracuse. This signet ring gives his authority.'

'No one leaves the camp unless Soter himself tells me. I will send a man to ask.'

Ballista caught his son's eye. There were ten Alamanni. The odds were bad, but the guards were on foot, five of them sprawling by the fire.

'What in Hell is that?'

One of those by the campfire jumped to his feet, and pointed back into the camp.

Down by the lake, men were shouting near the pavilion. Their black silhouettes flitted in front of a spreading blaze. Tongues of fire curled into the sky. Bright embers eddied in the updraught. Several tents were burning.

'Some stupid ex-slave must have kicked over a brazier.'

All the guards were gazing at the disturbance.

'Fucking southerners.'

Ballista nodded to Marcus. As one they booted their horses, flicked them on with the reins.

The warriors in the road stood their ground, then hurled themselves clear at the last moment.

The two horsemen thundered past, and were gone into the darkness.

CHAPTER SEVENTEEN

THEY RODE HARD INTO THE NIGHT, the hooves of their horses ringing like bells on the stones of the road. Away from the campfires, it was not that dark. The moon was waning, but the sky was cloudless. The road and the country were bathed in a cold, blue light. You could see a long way, but everything seemed flat and two-dimensional. Distances were hard to judge. Looking over his shoulder, Ballista saw the fire at the summit of Etna. It shone red and unblinking, as if it were the eye of some mythical being, or a huge beast of prey.

After half an hour, they reined in, dismounted, and stood listening. There were no sounds of pursuit yet. They checked their girths, made sure that the saddles had not slipped. Then they remounted and went on at a trot. Through the remaining hours of darkness they varied their pace, going from a trot to a canter, back to a trot, then getting down and leading the horses. It was slower, but they could not afford to exhaust the horses by galloping them into the ground. The spelling avoided the fatigue which would get into the muscles of the horses from the ceaseless repetition of one gait.

At first light they looked back. So far, the road was still empty. They moved into a canter. The countryside here was as flat and smooth as a marble table. Endless fields sown with wheat, and vines pruned for the winter. Living under the mountain was double-edged. Sooner or later Etna would rain destruction, but it created the most fertile soil. It was said that in the upper meadows of Catana, the sheep grew so fat that they had to have blood drawn from their ears every four or five days.

Ballista thought about the journey ahead. The plain of Catana was bisected by many rivers. They had already crossed the Symaethus in the night. The Terrias, Assia, Pantakyas, and other smaller and nameless streams remained. All were bridged. None posed any delay. They would pass to the west of Cape Tauros, and the abandoned town of Megara. They would go up into the hills, the Hyblaian Mountains looming to the right. And finally, a few miles past Point Thapsos, dead ahead would lie the Epipolae heights which guarded the approach to the city of Syracuse.

Pursuit was a certainty. Ballista had told the slave-king they were going to Syracuse. That had been a mistake. No point in crying over spilt wine. Hindsight was not a virtue. In any event, there was nowhere else they could go. They were bound to this road like Ixion to his wheel.

Soter had to send men to try to run them down. The authority of the *Saviour* rested on his charisma. His men followed and obeyed him because every prophecy he had made had come true. If the slave-king let himself be tricked, his prestige would suffer. If Ballista and Marcus escaped, Soter's tenuous hold over the thousands in his camp might begin to crumble.

Either they would reach the safety of the walls of Epipolae, or they would die. It was in the lap of the gods. Yet Ballista was not prepared to give way to blind fatalism. The gods, even the grim northern gods of his youth, favoured those who did not despair.

At mid-morning they halted at the river Terrias. They unsaddled the horses, rubbed down their backs, then led them down the bank to water. They did not let them drink too much, but tethered them away from the stream to crop the grass. The stable hand had been right. Both the gelding and the mare had stood up well to the rigours of the journey.

Ballista was not particularly hungry – they had been fed in the camp last night – but he chewed some air-dried beef. The Alamanni had taken their weapons, but left them their packs, and even their money and the other things on their belts.

'Do you think the Island of the Sun exists?' They had spoken little since their escape, but now Marcus wanted to talk. 'An island of freedom, where men are equal, and slavery does not exist?'

'It might, somewhere far away, but even there everyone is not equal. In the stories, the rulers have the power of life and death. They select their own successors. That is not freedom. It makes their subjects little better than slaves.'

'Then slavery is universal.'

'No, out on the Steppe the tribe of the Alans have no slaves. Men do not have to live the way they do.'

Ballista watched Marcus eat. Sometimes his son was old before his years.

'If Soter takes Syracuse and holds all Sicily, will the emperor negotiate with him, perhaps recognise his authority? Will he grant him some title, like he has Odenaethus in the East?'

'No, never.' Ballista was emphatic. 'Gallienus has to send an army. The cases are entirely different. Odenaethus rallied the men of his home town, Palmyra, and whatever Roman soldiers were left, to fight a Persian invasion. It was done in the name of the emperor. Now Odenaethus may act as an independent ruler in the eastern provinces, but he still pays lip service to the authority of Gallienus. Odenaethus was never a rebel like Soter.'

Ballista got up from where he was sitting, and lifted his saddle.

'Besides, Soter's Island of the Sun is not isolated in the middle of the southern Ocean. Sicily is in the heart of the Roman empire. The example of such a community without slavery could not but spread. It would draw runaways from all over the imperium, inspire revolts in other provinces. The emperor has to crush the revolt. If Gallienus were not in Milan, and if it were not the closed sailing season, the legions would be here already.'

They checked the horses' feet, smoothed the rugs on their backs, cinched tight the saddles, led them back up to the road.

Marcus was not yet done talking.

'Did the doctor burn to death?'

Ballista paused before answering. 'You have to remember that he would have killed us without hesitation. Sometimes it is hard to be as brutal as necessary.'

Marcus said no more, and they swung up into the saddle.

'Look!'

Ballista did not need to ask where. To the north, a tall column of dust on the Via Pompeia. Three, perhaps four miles off. Too far to see the posse.

They rode for the rest of the day. Every hour they halted, and looked back. They could see for miles over the plain. In the glare of the sunshine the long, straight road shimmered, as if it was burning. Once they thought the pursuit was over, but it was just a trick of the light. All too soon the hunters, black and malignant like insects, emerged out of the haze. They were closer now. Wearily, Ballista and Marcus rode on again.

From Catana to Syracuse by sea was some forty miles. It was further by road. A man on horseback could cover fifty miles in a day. Riders carrying imperial despatches routinely covered that distance. If it was urgent, the *cursus publicus* could convey the message much further, up to a hundred and fifty miles. Likewise, the tribal horsemen of the Steppe were capable of riding that far between dawn and sunset. But nomad warriors had strings of a dozen or more led horses, and the *cursus publicus* had remounts stationed every few miles. Ballista thought that once, in some emergency, Alexander the Great had force-marched his cavalry for forty miles several days running. Was it when he was chasing the defeated Persian king? The details eluded his memory. One thing was certain – their horses would have been good for nothing at the end.

In the evening they came into the hills. Before the light failed, they saw the posse was still there out on the plain. Ballista and Marcus plodded up under the trees. Their horses were sorely worn. As the shadows closed, Ballista racked his brains for a way to throw them off the scent. Turning a spare horse loose might create a false trail. If a lantern was tied to its saddle, it would draw attention. But he did not have a spare horse or a lantern. If he had a bow, or one or two more men, a sudden, brief ambush from the darkness would halt the pursuit in confusion. But the guards had taken his bow back at the encampment, and there were just the two of them. Another man called Alexander, a citizen of Emesa, had once been chased by soldiers somewhere in the East. He had faked a fall from his horse. His companion had built a pyre. The soldiers were convinced that he was dead, that they had seen him cremated. But the companion had burnt the carcass of a ram. Alexander escaped, and was never seen again.

Ballista knew his mind was wandering. He was bone-tired, but this was no good. To save them both – to save his son – he needed to think with clarity. In war, always consider the view from the other side of the hill. Long ago Flavius Vopiscus had drummed that into him. Put yourself in the boots of the enemy. What would you do in their position? Flavius Vopiscus had been a good commander.

The riders in the posse knew that Ballista and Marcus were armed. They knew they would not surrender, that they were desperate, and would not sell their lives without a fight. The pursuers had numbers, but they would be cautious. When they reached the wooded hillside, they would be apprehensive. None of them would know the terrain. The dark, closed slopes would be alien and menacing. What if their quarry turned on them, like a vicious beast at bay? Every bush, and every tree, might conceal an armed man. The sway of every branch in the breeze, the rustle of every nocturnal animal in the undergrowth, might be the furtive movement of an armed man run to ground and turning on his hunters.

Ballista reined in, and turned to his son.

'We need to build a fire.'

Marcus threw the last armful of fallen branches onto the fire. The wood was dry and rotten. It would not last long, but it flared and burnt brightly. Walking back to where his father held the horses, he gathered his reins and climbed into the saddle. They rode down through the timber. At the road, they again turned south, and moved off at a trot. The horses seemed a touch less exhausted, having had the weight off their backs for a spell. Marcus looked over his shoulder. Through the boughs of the trees, the fire shone like a yellow beacon.

It was a good idea of his father's. Their pursuers could not miss the blaze. They would not rush at it, like moths to a lamp. They would spread out, surround the site, edge in with utmost care. Perhaps they even had orders to take the pair alive. The slave-king might want to savour his revenge. Building the fire had taken time, but it should delay the men hunting them longer.

There was no doubting his father's resourcefulness or courage. Yet Marcus was troubled. His father had left the doctor to burn to death. Marcus had seen a man burnt alive before. It was a public spectacle in the theatre at Tauromenium. The man was a brigand, and, of course, he deserved to die. Someone had told Marcus beforehand that the smoke usually suffocated the condemned before the flames reached them. That had not been the case in Tauromenium. The man had been alive when the fire turned the skin of his legs black and crisp. He had screamed as his flesh burst apart. Through the air, among the audience seated on the elegant marble benches, had wafted a terrible sweet smell, horribly like roasting pork. For months after, the reek had been in Marcus' nostrils as he woke, soaked in sweat, from yet another nightmare.

No Roman man could be squeamish about killing. Taking life was in their blood. Romulus had been suckled by a she-wolf. The founder had killed his own brother. Their Trojan ancestors had cut down myriads of warriors on the windswept plains of Ilion before the walls of the city. Aeneas had hacked and chopped his way through the inhabitants when he landed in Italy. On every triumphal arch and column, Roman soldiers piled up the corpses of slain barbarians. Gladiatorial combat was a moral lesson acted out in blood. If even slaves and criminals could show some fortitude close to the steel, how much more was expected of a free citizen?

Yet there was a world of difference between the honourable killing of a man in open battle, and the torture and execution of the defenceless. The former demanded manly courage, *virtus*, and that was the preserve of free citizens. The latter needed no more than expertise and inhuman cruelty. That was why their proponents were despised outsiders. Gladiators were locked in the cells of their barracks. The undertakers who carried out public executions and torture were consigned to live outside the walls. If these *libitinarii* should enter a town, it was the law that they wear distinctive colourful costumes, so that decent people could avoid them, and the pollution of their proximity.

Each act of brutality must leave a stain on the soul. They would fester and spread in the dark. If they were not cauterised, the soul itself must become putrid. It would be best, Marcus thought, if a man regulated his soul as if it were a city. Each act of unavoidable brutality needed to be confined, chained out of sight, or banished to the outer darkness.

Marcus glanced at his father. Behind the stubble of the last few days, Ballista's face was calm, almost serene in the moonlight.

Ballista turned, and smiled at his son. The smile was open, free of any guilt.

Despite everything he had done, his father was not haunted by *daemons*. Marcus Clodius Ballista was not a man who contended with himself or the world. When they reached the safety of Syracuse, Marcus would ask him how such equanimity was achieved.

If, of course, they did reach Syracuse.

CHAPTER EIGHTEEN

A MIST ROSE IN THE LAST HOURS of the night. It hung in swathes under the vines and the trees. They were close to Syracuse now, but the horses were nearly finished. Ballista and Marcus walked, leading them, saving them for one last effort.

Out of the moonlit fog loomed the statue of Callistratus the Athenian. After the defeat of the Athenian expedition, Callistratus had led his cavalrymen towards the safety of Catana. The Syracusans had overhauled them on this stretch of road. Ordering his men to ride on, Callistratus had turned to fight. His men had escaped; Callistratus had died. The clean lines of the sculpture – the jut of his horse's neck, the calm acceptance of fate on Callistratus' face – seemed to rebuke the anxiety of the filthy and exhausted creatures of flesh and blood trudging past.

The sky was getting lighter as they came out of the trees onto a broad field of saffron. Wearily they climbed into the saddle. Feeling the ache in his back and shoulders, the stiffness in his thighs, Ballista thought yet again that he was getting too old for the demands of life on campaign. At his age – forty-two winters behind him – he should greet the dawn in the comfort of his home, read a book in the quiet of early morning, then get shaved and dressed, eat a light breakfast, then perhaps walk in the gardens or stroll with friends down to the marketplace. A life of civilised leisure, the *otium* of a cultured member of the Roman elite, the alarms and dangers of public service left behind.

The mist shone translucent when the sun crossed the horizon. Then it retreated into the hollows, like a creature of the night retreating to the underworld. The few high clouds were marbled with purple and gold. There was an extraordinary clarity to the light. Every bead of dew on the grass was glistening and distinct. The air carried the sharp tang of the sea. It was going to be a fine autumn day.

They crested a rise, and there before them were the heights of Epipolae that guarded the approach to the city. Only a couple of miles. They were close enough for Ballista to make out the walls at the top of the slopes, and the towers by the Hexapylon Gate at the end of the Catana road.

A wild cry, like a hound baying catching sight of its prey. The slaves were coming out of the olive grove. No more than a couple of hundred paces behind. Dark, hunched figures urging their horses in pursuit. Ballista did not try to count them. A glance told him there were too many to fight.

Ballista saw the fear on his son's face as they booted their mounts.

'Just ride!' Ballista shouted. 'We are almost there!'

Ballista leant forward over the horse's mane, driving it onward with arms and thighs. Knee to knee, they raced down the road. Marcus was muttering. Perhaps encouraging his mount, or intoning a prayer. Ballista could not hear the words. The noise of their own passing drowned the sounds of pursuit. Almost halfway there.

Allfather, hold your hands over your descendants.

Marcus' mare pecked, stumbled slightly. Fear leapt in Ballista's chest, like a jagged shard. His son's mount recovered into her stride.

'Hold her up! Not far now!'

Ballista's words were snatched away by the thunder of hooves. It made no odds. They were pointless.

The road began to rise. Only another half a mile. Ballista could feel the energy draining out of his mount. But the gelding had a big heart. Despite having been hard used, it would run until it dropped. *Surely, by Hades, the horses of those chasing must be equally worn.* He glanced back. It was not as he hoped. The posse was gaining on them.

Marcus had fallen back half a length. Although carrying a lighter weight, the mare was failing. If Ballista reined in, held them back like Callistratus, his son might get clear. No, there were too many of the rebels. A handful might halt to cut him down. He would take one or two of them with him. The rest would ride round the melee, and continue the chase. His sacrifice would not let Marcus escape.

'Hold her up!' Ballista yelled at his son. 'She can get there!'

An arrow arced out from the walls. A ranging shot. It fell wide, but the distance was good. A ragged volley followed.

Hercules' hairy arse, they are not shooting at the slaves!

They were aiming for Ballista and Marcus. One arrow pinged off the road just ahead. The rest scattered harmlessly over the fields.

Thank the gods, they are poor shots.

Grabbing the corner of his cloak, Ballista waved it high above his head: the military signal for *enemy in sight*. The archers on the wall were not soldiers. It might mean nothing to them. They were drawing their bows again. A man wearing a scarlet-crested helmet was running along the parapet, gesticulating. Perhaps he was some retired veteran, and knew what he was doing. Another volley lifted from the battlements. The man must be a civilian after all. The irony – after all this way, surviving so many deadly threats – to be killed by the very people they were trying to reach. The flight of arrows sliced overhead.

Ballista looked over his shoulder. The shafts plummeted down around the rebels. The shooting was no better. None of the posse was hit. Yet one or two slackened their pace. Not enough were discouraged. At least a dozen were still riding hard, intent on slaughter.

'Open the postern gate!' Ballista was bellowing as loud as he could.

Arrows were flying thick and fast at the rebels, but both the huge main gate and the small postern remained closed.

'Open, for love of the gods!'

'Identify yourself.'

The officer with the scarlet-plumed helmet was peering down. There was something familiar about him.

'Ballista.'

The officer stared at him.

'Marcus Clodius Ballista! Now open the fucking gate!'

The officer disappeared from the parapet.

A javelin whistled past Ballista's shoulder. To hit an individual from a galloping horse would take the luckiest cast in the world. But if there were enough missiles . . .

Allfather, don't let them hit Marcus!

They were under the walls, in the shade of the flanking tower. Still all the gates were shut. More javelins whipped through the air.

'Dismount!' Ballista tried to sound calm as he yelled instructions. 'Use your mare as cover!'

Getting his left leg from the horns of the saddle, Ballista dismounted as he wheeled the gelding between himself and the rebels. The steel tip of a javelin thudded into the wooden boards of the postern gate. Crouched behind the shoulder of the gelding, Ballista drew his sword. Die blade in hand, and the shield-maidens would take him to the Hall of the Allfather. But would they take Marcus? He would trade Valhalla for the cold meadows of Hades, if he could remain with his son. The enemy were almost upon him. Time to die like a man.

'Come!'

Marcus was tugging at his arm. The postern was open a crack. Marcus darted through. Ballista followed. The little gate slammed shut behind them. The sounds of heavy bolts slamming home.

Ballista was standing under the arch of the gate.

'Are you all right?'

Marcus just nodded.

Suddenly Ballista was tired beyond belief. He sheathed his sword, and tottered to the wall. Leaning his back against the stonework, he slid down and sat with his head lolling between his knees. He shut his eyes.

A shadow blocked the sun.

Ballista opened his eyes, and squinted up at the elderly officer with the red crest.

'Flavius Vopiscus, it has been a long time.'

'Is it really you?' The old man put out a hand, and helped Ballista to his feet.

'Yes, it is me.'

Vopiscus folded him into an embrace. Like a child, Ballista fought back tears of relief. Marcus was safe! His son was safe!

'Gods, you stink.' Vopiscus held him at arm's length. 'You needed a bath, when I first met you at the siege of Aquileia.'

Ballista went to speak, but Vopiscus held up a hand to silence him.

'Your wife is here, and your other son. They are safe. All your *familia* are safe. They are staying in my house.'

Ballista took a deep breath, tried to control himself. But now he could not stop the tears. They ran hot down his cheeks.

'And a great nuisance your bodyguards are. They will keep seducing my serving girls. That Hibernian, Maximus, is incorrigible.'

Ballista was laughing through the tears.

Vopiscus squeezed his shoulders. 'Before you go to them, I need to know – where is the main force of the slaves?'

Ballista knuckled his eyes. 'The night before last they were camped before the walls of Catana.'

'And the city was holding out?'

'Yes.'

'Then at the worst we still have a few days. We will talk more tomorrow. Now one of the levy will take you to my house. I would take you myself, but you saw their shooting. They need all the training they can get.'

It was a long walk across the heights of Epipolae. Syracuse was said to be five cities in one. Although walled, the district of Epipolae was scarcely populated. Just a few rich Syracusans had built suburban villas up here to catch the breeze. At the highest point in the west was the fortress of Euryalus. It had been constructed by the tyrant Dionysius the Elder to block the only easy access to the plateau. It was through that pass, one night long before it was fortified, that the Athenian expedition had scaled Epipolae. Under the monumental walls of Euryalus was a maze of tunnels designed to let the defenders both move about unobserved and sally out without warning against any besiegers. Every time Marcus and his brother had played there, they had discovered new branches of the subterranean passages. It had driven their nurse to distraction as they had emerged in different places out of her sight.

They walked in silence to the cliffs, and took the steep path down. There were steps and a handrail. Unlike the fortress, Marcus knew these cliffs more from reading Thucydides than his own experience. After initial success, the Athenians on Epipolae had fallen into terrible confusion. In the darkness they had mistaken friends for enemies, and turned on each other, cutting down their kinsmen and fellow citizens. Panic had gripped them. They had taken to their heels, flinging away their arms, every man for himself. Many had toppled over the precipice to their deaths.

As they descended, Marcus saw the gloomy entrances to the quarries. Nowadays they were used as workshops by ropemakers. Their history was much darker. After the final defeat, seven thousand Athenian prisoners had been herded into the caverns. Exposed to the elements, each given just half a pint of water and a pint of corn a day, living with their own excrement and the corpses of those who died, few emerged alive after seventy days. Later the tyrants had continued to use the quarries as prisons for any they suspected of disloyalty. Whole families were confined for years on end. Children were born and lived and died there. They knew nothing else, no other life. It was said those few who were released had been scared by the sight of something as normal as a horse.

It had been strange seeing his father crying. Strange, but not earth-shattering. In every account that Marcus had read, Alexander the Great was prone to tears. Strong emotions brought tears to the eyes of strong men. It was no cause for embarrassment or shame. Yet somehow it seemed against the natural order. A father should comfort his sobbing child, not the other way round. And Marcus had not moved to comfort his father. Perhaps, he thought, in the future he would regret that failure of compassion.

At the foot of the steps was the district of Tyche. The streets here were crowded and noisy. Schoolteachers held lessons, and barbers trimmed their clients in the open air out on the pavements. Hawkers threaded through the crowds, calling their wares. A juggler performed on a street corner. Carts rumbled over the flagstones, and a peasant drove a herd of goats to market. All the activities of a peaceful and prosperous city continued, as if there was not an army of rebellious slaves just up the coast. After the last days, it all had an air of unreality for Marcus.

They turned left before they reached the district of Neapolis, and the great public monuments. Instead they passed through the gate of Achradina. The walls of this district were picturesque, festooned with ivy, and ramshackle with houses and outbuildings built up against their face. After Epipolae, they were the second line of the defences of Syracuse. A couple of the civic Watch lounged in the gateway. They did not bother to question anyone entering. Marcus looked at the crowds. There were men of all sorts – countrymen and city dwellers, rich and poor. Of the latter, it was impossible to be sure who was free, and who a slave. Anyone of the throng might be a runaway sent ahead by Soter. Anyone of them might be there to spy out the weak places of the city, to incite insurrection among the unfree of Syracuse, or, when the rebel forces arrived, to slyly open a gate.

After crossing the agora, they came to the causeway that linked the island of Ortygia to the mainland areas of the city. Off to the right, the sheltered waters of the Great Harbour sparkled in the sun. Along its quays were moored many large ships, laid up for the winter. These were bulky merchantmen with tall masts and wide beams. In the summer months they plied their trade across the whole of the Middle Sea. To the left was the half-moon of the Lesser Harbour. The vessels there were the small undecked skiffs and smacks of local fishermen. Most of these were drawn up out of the water, waiting to go out that night with the offshore breeze.

Ballista had stopped, and was gazing at the harbours. Marcus and the guide waited. After a time Ballista nodded, and they moved on. Marcus saw that some thought was troubling his father.

The causeway was closed off by a tall stone wall, the final line of the defences of Syracuse. Unlike that at Achradina, its masonry was clean and uncluttered. In the gateway there were more of the Watch. This time an officer was present, and he asked them to identify themselves and state their business, before waving them through. The check could not have been more perfunctory. They had been neither closely questioned or searched. The heights of Epipolae were a natural strongpoint, and as a capable commander Vopiscus was trying to instil discipline into their defenders. But here in the city the Syracusans appeared to be merely going through the motions, as if they had not accepted the reality of their position. It struck Marcus that the city was no more impregnable than an egg: a tough outer shell, but if that was pierced the centre was soft. For the first time, he thought that they might not be safe in Syracuse.

The first building on Ortygia was the Temple of Apollo. It was squat and dark and very ancient, the original shrine erected by the colonists when they landed on the island. It smelt of dried blood and the smoke of centuries of sacrifice. This did not evoke sanctity in Marcus' mind, but something more ominous. A deity who inhabited such a place would be primitive and vengeful.

The streets of Ortygia were broad and well laid out, the houses spacious. After the city had spread out onto the mainland, the island had been turned into a stronghold. With the coming of Rome, and the imposition of peace, the affluent had taken over Ortygia. The Roman governor had his palace here. Overlooking the sea at the end of the promontory, the residence of the senator Flavius Vopiscus rivalled it in opulence.

They walked along by the Great Harbour. Marcus found something soothing about being down by the water. Evidently it was not having the same effect on his father. Ballista's lips were compressed into a thin line, and his every movement expressed barely suppressed tension.

They passed the Temple of Athena. Tall and airy, topped by the gilded statue that acted as a beacon to mariners, Marcus thought that was how a holy place should look. It was easy to imagine that the grey-eyed goddess would hold her hands over the people that showed her such honour.

Just before the house of Vopiscus, set in a tree-shaded park, was the sacred spring of Arethusa. It bubbled up sweet and clear into an ornamental pool. In Arcadia, when the world was young, and gods walked openly among mankind, a huntsman called Alpheus had fallen in love with the nymph Arethusa. Not wanting to marry, she had fled across the sea to Ortygia, where she had been transformed into this freshwater spring. A deity had changed Alpheus into the river that ran through Olympia. His love undiminished, Alpheus crossed under the waves of the ocean, so that his waters would mingle with those of Arethusa. The credulous believed that an object thrown into the river in Greece would re-emerge in the pool on Ortygia. Whatever its truth, Marcus thought the story propitious to the occasion of his father's return to his mother.

At the house they thanked the guide, and he departed.

A liveried doorman barred their way with all the hauteur of the servant of a great man. Doubtless their travel-stained attire did not help.

'I am Marcus Clodius Ballista, and this is my son Marcus. I believe my wife and *familia* are guests of Flavius Vopiscus.'

An unctuous civility instantly replaced the disdain. The doorman ceremoniously ushered them along panelled corridors and across open spaces where fountains splashed. Part of the time he actually walked backwards, as if leaving the presence of royalty.

Marcus' mother was reading in the sunshine on a balcony overlooking the sea. His brother was playing on the floor. She looked up, peering from the brightness into the shade of the room.

They walked out into the light. Julia gasped and leapt to her feet. Then she stopped. Very carefully she put down the papyrus roll, marking her place. With the self-control of a Roman matron, she went to her husband, and took his hands in hers. Raising herself on tiptoes, she kissed him briefly on the lips, a mere peck.

'You are here,' she said.

'And so are you,' Ballista said.

'And so is our son.'

Letting go of her husband's hands, she enfolded Marcus in an embrace. He was half a hand taller than her now. Her face was on his shoulder.

Ballista held out his arms to his younger son. The boy did not move.

'Lucius, go to your father,' his mother said.

'In the *Iliad*, Hector's son burst into tears at the sight of him,' Ballista said.

'Lucius,' Julia said.

Somewhat reluctantly, the boy got up and went to his father. Ballista took him under the armpits, and lifted him off his feet. He kissed the boy on the top of his head, then set him down again.

'You smell strange,' Lucius said.

'Your brother and I have been on the road some time.'

'You have just missed his seventh birthday,' Julia said.

Marcus felt a terrible pity for his father. He had imagined their homecoming would be less constrained.

Julia released her eldest son. 'Lucius is right. You both need a bath.'

Marcus sensed people in the room behind him. Julia glanced past him, then looked back at her husband.

'Will you want food before bathing?'

'That would be good.'

'I will see to it. Boys, come with me.'

'Let Marcus stay,' Ballista said.

'As you wish.'

'It is time he took the toga of manhood.'

'He is not yet of age.'

'He is ready. We will hold the ceremony tomorrow.'

There was a look of deep sadness on Julia's face, but she said no more. She took Lucius' hand, and they left.

As soon as they were gone, his father's bodyguards crowded forward. The four barbarians were a strikingly ugly crew. Maximus the Hibernian had the end of his nose missing. The two from the northern tribes, Rikiar the Vandal and Grim the Heathobard, were both lame from old wounds to their left legs. As Maximus often said, you could not make a whole man out of both of them. By comparison, Tarchon, the foul-mouthed one from the Caucasus mountains, was almost handsome.

Marcus watched as, without any formality or respect, they hugged his father, slapped him on the back, sometimes even cuffed him round the ear. With the lack of restraint of barbarians, they all seemed to be weeping. *You old bugger*, they kept saying, in tones of the deepest affection.

'And you brought your puppy, too,' Maximus said.

Ballista gestured Marcus over, took him by the scruff of his neck, dragged him into the huddle.

'It was as much he brought me,' Ballista said. 'And he is not a boy anymore.'

They all knew what his father meant. In their world it was a violent rite of passage.

'Young to be killing,' Tarchon said. 'Very promising. Fucker probably very bad man, much needed killing.'

'Very bad man,' Ballista agreed.

'Like your first girl, you never forget the first time.' Maximus looked at Marcus with an unexpected tenderness. 'A lot less pleasurable to remember. Best not dwell on it.'

Marcus doubted the fugitive-hunter would ever cease to haunt his dreams.

'Unless, of course,' Maximus continued, 'you are a demented savage from the Caucasus, like Tarchon here. In which case, you never stop boasting about how . . .'

Maximus stopped in mid-sentence. They all fell quiet.

Julia had returned. Looking at them, her expression was unreadable.

'The food is ready,' she said.

CHAPTER NINETEEN

'YOU WERE QUITE TOUGH ON THE BOY,' Ballista said.

They were in bed. The lamp was lit. They had made love.

Julia raised herself on an elbow. She was naked, and Ballista admired the smooth sheen of her skin, and the sway of her breasts.

'Children are like clay,' she said. 'They need to be moulded. It does them no good to see weakness in their parents.'

Ballista looked at the ceiling. *Return with your shield, or on it.* The Romans had taken as their own the ancient injunction of Spartan women. The past was full of moral examples of stern Roman matrons. Cornelia had sent her children, her *jewels*, to die for philosophical principles. Lucretia had committed suicide, even though both her husband and father had pleaded with her to live; the rape had not been her fault. When her husband had been reluctant, Arria had opened her own veins: *See, it does not hurt.*

All the exempla had been written by men. But women read or heard the stories. They lived their lives in the shadow of such an unforgiving morality. It was how things had always been. Few would not judge themselves against such exacting standards.

Julia traced the line of his jaw with her fingertips, turned his face to hers. She smiled into his eyes.

'This time I thought I had lost you, the boy as well.'

Ballista smiled back. 'And I thought I had lost you and Dernhelm.' He stopped himself saying more.

As often in their marriage, she seemed to know the words he had not spoken.

'Of course, when we heard of the approach of the slaves, I thought about taking him to safety in Italy. Your friend Maximus was insistent. But I knew you and Marcus would have already sailed for Sicily. The *Fortuna Redux* was overdue. I did not want you to find we had gone. I waited for you both in Tauromenium until the last moment. By then there were storms in the straits. It was safer to coast down to Syracuse.'

'And how are things here?'

She shrugged, and said something.

Ballista was distracted by the movement of her breasts. Men are simple creatures.

'What?'

She grinned, her eyes playful. 'Again? A man of your age?'

'It has been a long time.'

She reached down for him, but answered his question.

'Things here are not as good as I had expected. The governor has gone.'

'Gone?' Ballista was so surprised, he forgot what she was doing. 'Where?'

'Apparently, at the first news of the uprising in the West, he remembered some urgent task in Rome. He left on the only warship.'

'The emperor will kill him.'

'Perhaps not – his family are influential. But then we heard that the quaestor had been captured by the slaves.'

'And to save his skin, he has turned traitor.'

Now Julia was so startled her hand stopped what it had been doing.

'The coward! How could he join a mob of rebellious slaves? It will not save him long. Gallienus will nail him to a cross.'

'No wonder Gallienus mistrusts all senators,' Ballista said.

'We are not all like that. Our friend Vopiscus knows his duty.'

'So Vopiscus has taken charge of the defence of Syracuse?'

'Not alone, unfortunately. The city council has saddled him with the other chief magistrate, a man called Lucullus, another Roman senator with a home here. Gallienus would be right to doubt him. Lucullus is vain, indolent and stupid. His only talent is for squandering money on his fish ponds and racehorses. That is why Vopiscus wants you to tour the walls with him tomorrow, the first hour of the day.'

Ballista sighed. After all he and Marcus had endured, he had so hoped they might be left in peace. Let someone else deal with the insurrection. Now, already he felt the weight of responsibility being thrust onto his shoulders.

She kissed him. 'Are you sure Marcus is ready to take the toga of manhood?'

'Certain.'

She looked sad. 'I do not want to lose my child.'

'You will not lose him. Like a caged bird, you have to let them free, and hope they will return.'

'And nothing I can do can change your mind?'

Ballista grinned. 'Nothing.'

She grinned back. 'Then I had better do my duties as your wife anyway.' Her head dipped down to where her hand had been.

'No matter how dutiful, I am not sure a modest Roman wife would do that. Certainly not with the lamp lit.'

She looked back up at him. 'I could stop, if you want. But how dull would that be?'

Ballista was alone with Vopiscus on the battlements of the tower of Galeagra on the north-eastern extremity of the heights. It was the last site on their tour of the defences. As Syracuse was immense, even mounted, it had taken hours.

The view was spectacular. To the west was the road from Catana leading down to the Hexapylon Gate. To the south-west were the great walls of the fortress of Euryalus. Turning south exposed the whole plateau of Epipolae. It was filled with squads of the levy being drilled. Beyond the heights, parts of the mainland districts of the city were hidden by the lie of the land. But the island of Ortygia was in clear sight, thrusting out into the water towards the opposite promontory of Plemmyrium, narrowing the entrance to the Great Harbour. There was a haze on the sea to the east. Not a ship was to be seen, although Ballista estimated that visibility was no more than a couple of miles. Finally, to the north, the small cove of Trogilus lay at the foot of the tower.

It was here that the Romans had first stormed Syracuse. At a parley, a sharp-witted officer had counted the regular block-work, and realised that the walls at this point were lower than around the rest of the heights. Even so, it had taken treachery. The first attempt, where traitors were smuggled out of the city hidden under the nets of fishing boats, had failed. The second had succeeded. An informer had revealed that lavish amounts of wine had been issued to the half-starved defenders for the festival of Artemis. In the dead of night, a storming party had placed their ladders and climbed to the battlements. They had made their way along the parapet, silently despatching the sleeping guards. At the Hexapylon Gate they had descended, and opened the postern through which Ballista and Marcus had entered yesterday. Ballista did not believe, unlike some, that history repeated itself. But there were lessons to be learnt.

A trumpet down on the plateau broke the reverie. A group of about a hundred conscripted citizens were hacking at wooden posts set in the ground. A well-dressed – indeed, elegant – young man was putting them through their paces. They went at it with more enthusiasm than skill. But sometimes in the tumult of combat, that was enough. They were being watched by Vopiscus' staff, who were holding the horses. Maximus and Tarchon were among them, doubtless full of wry contempt for the efforts of the civilians. This morning, without any instructions, the bodyguard had divided. Maximus and Tarchon had announced that from now they would accompany Ballista, while Rikiar and Grim would remain with Julia. It made sense. Due to their old injuries, the two northerners were far from mobile, only hobbling about, and under the circumstances Julia would not be straying any great distance from the house.

It was not just their widespread geographic origins that made the bodyguards such a disparate group. Their characters were very different: Maximus, with his endless jokes and amiable lechery; Rikiar, serious and reciting poetry; Tarchon, an enthusiastic killer of men, who mangled several languages into a foul-mouthed patois all his own; and old Grim the Heathobard, who hardly ever spoke. Yet they had one thing in common. They had all sworn the sword-oath to Ballista. It extended to his family. Not one of them would face the shame of living, if they failed to protect their lord or his wife or children.

'It is getting late,' Vopiscus said. 'We need to get back for your son's coming of age ceremony.'

But he did not move. Ballista knew they must talk, one officer to another.

'How many of the five thousand in the levy have military experience?' Ballista said.

'Just a handful of veterans who have happened to settle here. A dozen, no more. Sicilians do not serve in the army.'

It was as Ballista had feared.

'There is an imperial procurator called Ollius, who was running an estate of the emperor's down near Agrigentum. He was a centurion, promoted to the equestrian order. He commanded an infantry cohort, a wing of cavalry, and was an officer in the Third Legion Gallica.'

'But apart from him and you and a dozen veterans, no one has any military experience?' Ballista felt it needed making clear.

'The case is not hopeless,' Vopiscus said. 'We took care to conscript about a thousand Syracusans who are or had been *ephebes*. We have distributed them throughout the ranks.'

Ballista looked dubious.

'It is not exactly like the real army,' Vopiscus admitted, 'but *ephebes* should be trained in archery, throwing javelins and stones, and fighting with shields.'

'They are clubs for rich youths,' Ballista said. 'In the shade of the palaestra they wrestle and oil each other. It is nothing but posing and pederasty.'

'We have to work with the tools available.'

'What about weapons?'

'All hunting weapons and private collections of antiques have been requisitioned. The blacksmiths and bow-makers and fletchers are working through the night. Carpenters are fashioning wicker shields on wooden frames. And we have confiscated everything from the amphitheatre. There is one troop of fifty gladiators owned by Lucullus. They are disarmed, and locked in their barracks, guarded by the Watch.'

'Siege engines?'

Vopiscus shook his head. 'Even if we got engineers to build them, there is no time to train their crews. But the slaves will not have them either.'

'We cannot be sure,' Ballista said. 'Some of the Alamanni might have served in the Roman army.'

'It makes no difference,' Vopiscus said. 'The slopes of Epipolae are too steep to deploy them.'

'Supplies?'

'Water will never be a problem. Arethusa is only one of many potable springs in the city.'

'Food?'

'Xenophon, the aedile who oversees the markets, has secured the civic granaries, and has bought up the grain in the private warehouses. All ships that have docked have been impounded, and any foodstuffs in their cargoes seized. None are allowed to leave. The fishing fleet is still operating. Both harbours are patrolled by men of the Watch. Norbanus, the leader of the Watch, is reliable, even if his men can be negligent.'

Ballista leant on the crenellations. The stone was warm under his hands. The conversation could not be left there. He had a bad feeling.

'And you share command with Lucullus, the other chief magistrate.'

'I hold the outer walls of Epipolae, and Lucullus the inner at Achradina.'

'From what I have seen yesterday and today,' Ballista said, 'he is taking his duties lightly.'

'Lucullus is a rich and influential man, but lethargic, very much devoted to pederasty.'

Ballista did not smile at the joke.

'A divided command is never good,' Vopiscus said.

Ballista was quite sure where this was heading. The prospect was not pleasing.

'And that is why tomorrow morning in the council, I will propose that you, Marcus Clodius Ballista, be appointed in sole command of the defence of Syracuse.'

Ballista gazed down at the distant harbours. 'I would rather take my family and sail away.'

'By my order, no vessels are leaving.'

Vopiscus' smile transformed his face. Only then did Ballista realise how tired and careworn his old commander had been looking.

'You are the senior man,' Ballista said.

'No, I am the *older* man. You rose to higher command than me. Defended cities, fought battles, held the fate of emperors in your hands, even assumed the purple.'

Although they were quite alone, both men instinctively glanced round the tower, as if some informer might be lurking.

'This is not my fight,' Ballista said.

'You always were reluctant to put yourself forward, always questioned your own abilities, even when we first met at Aquileia. It is one of your finest qualities.'

Ballista said nothing.

'This is your fight, my old friend. None of us can leave – not me, not you or your family. If any of us tried, it would start a panic. Would you rather have the fate of those you love in someone else's hands?'

Ballista shook his head, although he knew Vopiscus was right. Still, he made one last effort.

'I am an equestrian, and a stranger. You are both senators, and this is your home.'

'All the more reason for your appointment. You are above petty local interests and squabbles.'

'Would the council accept your proposal?'

'Of course Lucullus will oppose it. His *dignitas*, or vanity, will be cut to the quick. Yet I am not without influence. Once they have met you, Xenophon and Norbanus will support your command. Which is why I have taken the liberty of inviting them to attend your son's taking the *toga virilis*. Now that is settled, we should get moving.'

'I was not aware that I had agreed,' Ballista said.

Vopiscus laughed. 'You agreed as soon as you arrived. A man cannot fight his destiny.'

A boy's coming of age granted a freedom as keenly anticipated as the manumission of a slave. It was a happy day, marked by prescribed rituals, and surrounded by family and friends. Ballista had not returned when the barber arrived to give Marcus his first shave. Marcus did not mind. He was entering into manhood, and his father was performing the duties of a man. There was something Marcus had to say to him, and discretion was necessary. But it could wait until the dinner this evening. It would be childish to be resentful, or to make a fuss about Ballista's late arrival. By her frigid demeanour, it appeared that his mother was altogether less forgiving about the absence.

The barber put towels around his neck, bathed his face with warm water. As he tipped his head back, and the razor scraped across his exposed throat, Marcus understood why some tyrant of old had only let himself be shaved by his daughters. He could not remember which tyrant – perhaps one who ruled Syracuse. There was something else. After his daughters had married, the anxious tyrant, instead of shaving, had his beard singed.

As the barber addressed the delicate task of removing the hair from his upper lip, Marcus was glad it was happening in the privacy of Vopiscus' house. Those who were shaved at the street barber shops were at greater risk. Gangs of urchins liked to throw stones to try to jog the barber's hand. Marcus himself had done it in Rome. Now it seemed a less harmless prank.

The barber was skilled. There were only a couple of nicks that he had to staunch with cobwebs. When he had finished, he carefully gathered the trimmings and gave them to Marcus' mother, who placed them in a small gilded box.

Next, Marcus should have formally put off the striped toga of a child. It had been left behind in the villa at Tauromenium, so two domestic servants began to engulf him in the pure white *toga praetexta* of an adult. They were busy with the elaborate swags and folds when his father arrived. Ballista bounced into the room with the Hibernian, Maximus. Both were beaming with such good cheer, it seemed almost forced.

'I knew you would be detained.' Julia looked far from pleased. 'I said the ceremony should wait until next March. The festival of Liber is the traditional date, and Marcus would have been fourteen.'

'Needs must,' Ballista said, and called for his toga and that of Maximus.

Julia left the room as both men stripped. Marcus thought it odd that after today he should never see his father naked, never go to the baths with him. The Romans were not prudish, like eastern barbarians. They exercised naked. Statues of the emperors often depicted them like gods without clothes. Perhaps it was all the alluring flesh on display at the baths. No man wants to see his father's erection.

When all three were encumbered by the dignified drapes of their togas, they walked out into the atrium. Vopiscus was waiting with Julia and a crowd largely unknown to Marcus. Although a follower of Epicurus, when they left Tauromenium, Julia had made sure that the *lares*, the gods of the household, had been packed. His mother might not believe in the gods, but she was tolerant of the faith of others. Besides, Marcus knew, she was hidebound by senatorial tradition. The statuettes had been placed in a makeshift *lararium*. Julia handed Marcus the golden charm that he had worn around his neck as a child. Feeling self-conscious with everyone's eyes on him, he placed it on the altar. As all the onlookers, even his mother, placed their right hands flat on their chests in reverence, he dedicated the bulla to the gods with a pinch of incense and a libation of wine.

The sun was getting low when the procession left the house, and made the short walk to the temple of Athena. Here, Julia gave Marcus the golden box containing the shavings of his first beard. These, like the bulla, he offered to the gods. Duties to the gods satisfied, it was the turn of mankind. In front of witnesses, Marcus Clodius Isangrim – his third name uncouth on the tongue – was enrolled as a citizen of Rome.

Marcus walked back in the twilight, past the spring of Arethusa, as a man. If they had been in Rome, the ceremony would have taken place on the Capitol. But Syracuse was an ancient Roman colony. There was no doubting the legality of his new status. He was a man, and now must take responsibility as such among other men. He would say what he had to say to his father over dinner.

The meal was sumptuous. Course after course, the wines excellent and plentiful. The centrepiece was an entire swordfish, freshly caught in the early hours of that morning. Marcus was glad the fishing boats were allowed out. He had been given the place of honour on the top couch. It would be many years before he reclined in that position again – not until he had done deeds that deserved the honour. And that was what he needed to discuss with his father. Yet much to Marcus' irritation, Ballista was on a different couch, deep in quiet conversation with Vopiscus and two lesser magistrates of the city. Both had been introduced to Marcus when they arrived. One was Xenophon, the aedile in charge of the markets, the other Norbanus, the chief of the Watch.

Patience was a virtue, Marcus counselled himself. Now he was a man, he would not blurt things out like a child. He took a sip of wine. Later that night, when the guests had departed, he would speak to his father man to man. He caught the eye of his mother. What he had to say would not be said in her hearing.

CHAPTER TWENTY

THE COUNCIL HOUSE WAS AN OPULENT BUILDING on the agora in the Achradina district. The doors were open so spectators could listen to the debate. Ballista saw Maximus and Tarchon were with his eldest son among the throng in the doorway. They were standing by a man in a flashy embroidered cloak. With his oiled ringlets and hooked nose, he looked like a caricature of a Phoenician merchant.

In the chamber, motes of dust moved in the band of sunshine. There was space for perhaps two hundred on the benches. Ballista counted about sixty councillors. Evidently many must have fled Syracuse before all vessels were confined to port, although others might be cowering in their homes. Lucullus had the floor.

'We have heard the proposal to appoint Marcus Clodius Ballista to sole command of the defence of our city – an extraordinary proposal to grant him plenipotentiary power for the duration of the coming siege. Yet what is most extraordinary are the many things left unsaid in the proposal of Flavius Vopiscus.'

Lucullus was a heavyset man in his sixties. His face wore an expression of supreme confidence in his own opinions. This was not a man to be troubled by doubts, or swayed by contrary arguments, no matter how cogent. His toga was so bleached it almost hurt to look at him as he paced in the sunshine.

'Every man of culture knows what is expected in a speech of commendation. Every councillor here has spoken recommending candidates as magistrates of the city, or as new members of this august body. Many have had the honour of welcoming governors to the province, or undertaken embassies and addressed the emperor himself. You all know that the first topic in the eulogy of any man is to praise the city of his birth – its antiquity, its monuments, its exploits in war, its famous sons. Vopiscus made no mention of such origins. Why? Because this man Ballista was born in a mud hut somewhere beyond the Rhine. The second item in a panegyric addresses the subject's glorious ancestors. Again, Vopiscus was silent. How could he speak about fur-clad and savage barbarians?'

Lucullus made a grand gesture of contempt straight from the schools of rhetoric.

'Third, an orator enumerates the virtues of his subject. Here Vopiscus talked at great length of the integrity and courage and intelligence of his protégé. But these are mere words. Vopiscus would have us take them on trust, because this Ballista is an outsider of whom we have no personal knowledge. Vopiscus would have you entrust your safety, the safety of your families, not to one of your own, but to a complete stranger.'

Ballista noted a few heads nodding, not just the coterie around where Lucullus had been sitting.

'Finally, Vopiscus has made much of the military record of Ballista – how he defeated the Persians at some remote place or other in Cilicia, how he saved Miletus and Didyma from the Goths. We will pass over the truth of these skirmishes. We were not there, and nor was Vopiscus. Let us instead bring out into the light the other side of the coin, the battles where this Ballista has led Roman forces to crushing disaster. Wisely, Vopiscus chose not to mention the battle beyond Edessa, where our emperor's father Valerian, misled by bad, if not treacherous, advice, was captured by the Persians. And what now remains of the city of Arete in Syria defended by Ballista? Nothing but ruined temples and empty houses where jackals roam, and wolves make their lair.'

As the selective and biased account of his service continued, Ballista's attention wandered. If these men were fools enough to believe this pompous windbag, let it be on their own heads. Ballista would find a way out of the city for his *familia*. Vopiscus had a skiff moored at his villa. To Hades with them all.

Ballista glanced over at Marcus. The insults about his father's barbarian origins would have stung the boy. No, not a boy, not since yesterday. After the dinner, Marcus had asked to talk to him in private. Ballista should have seen it coming. Julia would be livid when she found out what her son intended. She would demand that Ballista put a stop to such dangerous wilfulness. She would insist that a father could still control an adult son by *patria potestas*. In point of law, she was right. But it would be hard to deter Marcus.

'Before you vote on this unprecedented and unconstitutional proposal, consider its consequences.'

Ballista started listening again. Lucullus was working up to his conclusion.

'If, as I suspect, Ballista is the tool of another, you must ask yourselves who gains? The answer is none other than Flavius

Vopiscus! With your vote, he gains control of our city. At a stroke he can dispense with all forms of law, and rule through his barbarian creature. This proposal is a covert attack on me, the colleague whose equal powers stand in the way of his ambition, the lawfully elected colleague whose restraint he can no longer endure. An attack on me is an attack on the freedom of all of you!'

Those councillors well-disposed to Vopiscus cried out shame.

'If, however, Vopiscus has misjudged Ballista, and the barbarian turns out to be his own man – and there are things in the past best left unsaid about his vaunting ambition – you are handing over yourselves and those you love to an alien tyrant. You might as well open the gates and offer the city to the mercy of Soter and his rebellious slaves!'

In the ensuing hubbub, before Lucullus had reached his seat, Vopiscus was back on the floor.

'Lucullus says that I ask you to take my words on trust, and, for once – perhaps only once – in that long speech, he was telling the truth.'

Vopiscus paused for the audience to settle. When he continued, his words were so quiet they had to lean forward to catch them.

'No, I was not at Arete, but I was on the council of the emperors that sent Ballista to that city. His orders were to delay the army of the Persian King, and that is what Ballista did, and by so doing saved the eastern provinces of the empire. I ask you to take my words on trust, because I know the truth of the things I say, and because you know me. I was born and bred in this city, and have lived here since my retirement from imperial service. Lucullus speaks of strangers. How long is it since he himself bought a house in our city, for no better reason than the climate and seafood here is better in winter than in his usual domicile on the Bay of Naples? Is it five years or six? Did he retire here full of honours from a life of public duty? No, he arrived worn out from gluttony and wasting his patrimony tending his ornamental fish ponds. How his cowardly soul must wish that this storm had broken when he was safe back in his other home.'

Vopiscus took a deep breath, then spoke at full volume.

'The vote is straightforward. Would you rather the defence of Syracuse was in the hands of Ballista, an officer who has shed his blood for years in the service of Rome, or Lucullus, a man notorious for breeding exceptional lampreys?'

With such a demolition of Lucullus, the outcome was no longer in doubt. After the vote had gone against him, Lucullus stormed out. The man with the hooked nose in the loud cloak trailed after the outraged councillor.

'Politics never makes a man friends.'

They were sitting in the empty theatre in the Neapolis district. Ballista was looking out at the Great Harbour, and did not answer.

'Admittedly, it is my fault that Lucullus is your enemy,' Vopiscus continued, 'but now the majority of the councillors will have turned against you. Many of them will be thinking that there was some truth in Lucullus' speech.'

Ballista looked at his old friend. 'How long are the walls of Epipolae?'

'The complete circuit must be fifteen miles, perhaps more.'

'Even if all five thousand of the levy were trained soldiers, they could not defend that distance. The next wall at Achradina is much shorter. Neapolis and Tyche are indefensible. They have to be evacuated. The householders have time to remove their most precious possessions.'

Vopiscus gestured at the theatre, the great altar and the palaestra.

'But to abandon all this to the slaves?'

'A temporary necessity. Men will be sitting in this theatre in two thousand years' time.'

'But will they be watching Aeschylus or Euripides?'

'Perhaps they will be listening to Thucydides? "My work is not a piece of writing designed to meet the taste of an immediate public, but was done to last for ever."'

The first thing Ballista had done once appointed *strategos* – the Greek word was thought safer than any Latin term for general that might presume upon imperial titles – was to dismiss Lucullus from command. Defence of the inner wall of Ortygia now was entrusted to Vopiscus, and that of Achradina, where the rebels must be held, to the imperial procurator Ollius, as he was just as experienced a military officer, and somewhat younger. As had been agreed at the dinner before the council meeting, Xenophon the aedile remained in charge of supplies. Likewise Norbanus, the leader of the Watch, continued to oversee security, above all of the harbours.

For the moment Ballista had left a skeleton guard of a thousand men on Epipolae. The other four thousand conscripts and volunteers were labouring on the Achradina wall. Ollius had divided them into gangs of two hundred, and assigned each a section of the defences, under the instruction of a master stonemason. They were tearing down the buildings that had grown up against the sides of the wall, and repairing the areas where the structure was decayed. Ollius had offered prizes for those gangs that completed their work with the greatest skill and speed. Ballista had ordered that, when the task was finished, the rubble, along with the cranes that had lifted it, were to remain close behind the wall.

There should be enough time to complete the work. Vopiscus had mounted scouts watching the rebels. Catana had fallen two days before. A traitor had opened a postern gate. The slaves had settled down to an orgy of rape and plunder. Another three days would be the very soonest that they could arrive at Syracuse.

'How many horses are there in the city up to the weight of an armed man?'

Vopiscus thought before he answered. 'Not many – perhaps sixty. When we heard the slaves were advancing on both the coast roads, we sent most of those pastured out on the plain up into the interior. Don't worry, your own string should be safe. The lads sent with them are reliable, all free men.'

'I was thinking we would need them when we break the siege.'

'If we break the siege,' Vopiscus said.

'*Let me at least not die without a struggle, inglorious, but do some great thing first, that men to come shall know of it.*' Ballista looked solemn. 'It will be unpleasant, but if we do not hunt them down, those that escape will take to the hills. The embers must be stamped out with exemplary cruelty.'

'Here they come,' Vopiscus said.

A file of some four dozen men, chained hand and foot, were shuffling past the Great Altar towards the amphitheatre. They were guarded by about half their number of the Watch.

'Lucullus will take this as a personal affront,' Vopiscus said.

'He sees everything as an insult to his *dignitas*.'

'This might push him over the edge to madness.'

Ballista grinned as he got to his feet. 'That is a problem for his doctor, not me.'

The gladiators were lined up on the sands of the arena. The majority of them were big, heavy men. There was a belief that layers of fat shielded the vital organs. They looked both mutinous and apprehensive. As he prepared to address them from the place of the official presiding over the games, Ballista scowled like a fierce and merciless barbarian.

'*Burnt with fire, shackled with chains, whipped with rods, and killed with steel.* One or two of you may not have been criminals or slaves condemned to the arena, may once have been free men, but you have all sworn that terrible oath. Doubtless every one of you dreams of winning the *rudis*, the wooden sword of freedom. In your hearts you know that it will remain just a dream. You are destined to die on the sands for the pleasure of the crowd.'

Ballista paused, as if contemplating ordering their execution.

'Today you are owned by Lucullus. But that can change. I offer you a choice. Those of you who wish can return to the barracks, return to the fire and chains and whips. There, as the property of Lucullus, you can wait for the day when you are dragged out through the gate of death.'

Again, Ballista stopped talking. The breeze raised little eddies of sand down on the floor of the amphitheatre.

'Or you can turn your skill in arms from the entertainment of others, and the aggrandisement of one man, to a noble cause. If you take an oath to defend Syracuse, you will be compulsorily purchased by this city. If you obey orders, and fight with courage, when the coming siege is lifted, you will be granted not just your freedom, but a sum of money to set you up for the rest of your life. You will live out your days, not as despised outcasts, but as freemen, respected by all.'

A gladiator, slighter than most, shuffled a pace forward. Probably he was a *retiarius*; an unarmoured fighter with trident and net needed to be nimble.

'How can we know that it will be as you say?'

'As you will take an oath to me, I will take one to you.'

The other gladiators looked at the *retiarius*. In every barracks, just as in every army tent, a natural leader emerges.

'I, Ganymede the *retiarius*, will take your oath.'

One by one the others stepped forward.

Idem in me, they said: *the same for me*.

'You are a fool!'

They were on the same balcony where Ballista had first seen Julia reading. Now she was standing, and rigid with fury.

'An absolute fool!'

Ballista looked away at the skiff moored below the balcony.

'You cannot let him volunteer.'

'Marcus has taken the *toga virilis*.'

'No one under sixteen can join the army.'

'The militia is not the army. There are *ephebes* little older than him already serving.'

Julia angrily snatched up a jug and poured a drink. Some of the wine splashed on the table.

'As his father, you can forbid him.'

'I am not sure that would be the best thing to do.'

'This is Rome, not your barbarian backwoods. In the name of the gods, he is still a child.'

Ballista turned and looked at his wife. 'He has already killed a man.'

Now Julia looked away. 'Exactly – he has already been in enough danger.'

'Maximus and Tarchon will keep him safe.'

Julia sighed. 'And then who will watch over you?'

Ballista moved towards her. She looked up into his eyes as he put his hands on her shoulders.

'Marcus will be safe,' he said.

She did not remove his hands, but ignored the reassurance they were meant to offer.

'And there is something else,' she said.

Ballista said nothing, hoping her anger would soon blow over.

'You do not see how your friend Flavius Vopiscus has outmanoeuvred you.'

Ballista waited for her to explain.

'If you save the city, you will be a hero for a fleeting moment – until you leave. When you are gone, everyone will praise the wisdom of Vopiscus in choosing you. Yet when they remember what they have suffered – their wrecked houses and stolen goods, their fear and the weakness it exposed – they will look back, and they will blame you. All the odium will fall on you, the *barbarian* general, and Vopiscus' hands will be clean.'

'What else would you have me do?'

Julia turned away in irritation. 'Just keep our son safe, or, I swear, you will have the same homecoming as Agamemnon.'

CHAPTER TWENTY-ONE

'THEY ARE HERE!'

Marcus was with Ballista in the council house in Achradina. It had been requisitioned as Ballista's headquarters. His new guard of gladiators were quartered here. Why he trusted them, the gods only knew. Sometimes, Marcus thought, his father was going out of his way to alienate the councillors of Syracuse.

'There are thousands of them!' The messenger was shifting from foot to foot in agitation.

'Thank you,' Ballista said. 'Return to the wall, and tell Ollius to have the men stand to arms. We will join him presently.'

The messenger left, looking as if he had expected a more dramatic response.

Ballista turned to the leader of the gladiators. 'Ganymede, send one of your men to Flavius Vopiscus and another to Norbanus. Tell them that I would be grateful if they would double the watch on Ortygia and the harbours respectively. If the slaves have acquired any boats, the forces at the wall may be intended as a distraction.'

The *retiarius* saluted, and gave the orders. 'You want the rest of us to come with you?'

'No. I will summon you if they look like assaulting the wall. I suspect this is just a probe to gather information about our defences. Let them think they face just a bunch of civilians. No need for them to know that we have your squad of trained combatants.'

Ballista settled his helmet on his head.

'Maximus and Tarchon with me. You too,' he said to his son.

Marcus grabbed his own helmet. It was new, and felt unnatural. His fingers fumbled as he tried to tie the laces under his chin. Gods below, he had never felt so nervous.

It was a short walk to the wall. Once they left the agora, the streets were deserted. Both Achradina and Ortygia were overflowing with those displaced from the abandoned districts of Tyche and Neapolis. Those who could were staying in the houses of relatives or friends. The rest were camped wherever there was space, in temples and porticos, and empty warehouses down by the docks. Thousands of refugees, but none were to be seen. The houses lining the street, like those of any city in the empire, presented a blank face to the world. No windows looked outwards. The only openings in the blank walls were doors, which were shut and barred. The effect was oppressive, even claustrophobic, like being in a maze.

Near the wall, a haze of fine, gritty stone dust still hung in the air. The last of the new masonry had been embedded just three days earlier. It was December, seven days before the Ides. The slaves' plundering of Catana had given time to finish the repairs to the defences.

Inside the main gate stood two cranes, next to a heap of broken beams and jagged stones from the demolished buildings. They went up the steps to the wall walk. Ollius was waiting for them.

'All in order?' Ballista asked.

'We will do what is ordered, and at every command we will be ready.'

Despite years of peaceful employment running an imperial farm, the procurator slipped naturally back into the language of the army.

Ballista walked to the parapet with Ollius. Marcus went to join them. Maximus caught his arm.

'Our place is behind the main men,' the Hibernian said.

Marcus peered out round his father's shoulder.

The view was a wasteland. All the buildings for almost a hundred paces had been flattened to their foundations. The ground was scarred and jagged, like a desert of rocks. Marcus knew that its surface was treacherous, concealed carefully disguised traps.

On the far side were the rebels. There were hundreds, perhaps thousands, closely packed together, grouped under various standards. The flags over the Alamanni bore strange representations of animals: wolves and bears and fierce, nightmarish beasts from the northern forests. Imitations of Roman military standards fluttered above the other rebellious slaves. The latter might hate Rome, but it was the only thing they had in common. All the insurgents were armed with spear and shield. Many carried swords, but few had helmets or armour. Their improvised equipment mirrored that of the defenders. Jumbled together, they would be hard to differentiate.

The rebels stood waiting. A quiet but incessant murmur came from their ranks. They were well within bowshot. Marcus wondered why his father did not order the archers to shoot. Of the four thousand militia assigned to the wall, a quarter had bows, some had slingshots. Then he noticed that many of the slaves also had bows. He forced himself not to flinch behind Ballista or Ollius.

Everyone was waiting for something. Perhaps for the other side to make the first move, perhaps for something Marcus did not know. It was like being in a theatre before the play started. Marcus found he was biting his lip.

A deep *hooming* sound drifted across the wasteland. It was men cheering. The throng parted. A man came into view, riding a pale grey horse, and followed by a dozen mounted men. The man was dressed in a purple robe, and his beard and hair were long and white. Even at that distance, Marcus could see he had an eyepatch. Soter, the *Saviour*, the slave-king who would be emperor, had come to Syracuse.

'Sure, it looks like your horse,' Maximus said to Ballista.

'Pale Horse is safe,' Ballista said. 'Vopiscus sent him into the interior with the others.'

Marcus had forgotten his father's favourite old gelding.

'What is the half-blind old fuck thinking he is about?' Tarchon said. 'If killing him too easy, it will not be a thing of most exquisite pleasure.'

Ballista and Maximus laughed. Marcus was not sure why. Tarchon clearly was not joking. And how could the three of them be so calm, as if chatting in a bar?

'Marcus Clodius Ballista.' Soter's voice carried well. 'It is time you fulfilled your oath, and delivered to me the city of Syracuse.'

All along the parapet the men of the militia turned to each other, asked questions.

'Silence in the ranks!' Ollius roared. The order was not entirely successful.

'Nothing to say?' Soter called. 'No matter – there are those in Syracuse happy to talk. They have pointed their fingers at the weak places in your defences, named your unguarded hours. When I give the word, they will open the gates.'

Ballista spoke quietly to Ollius. 'Have the word passed down the line from man to man. No trumpets or orders. On my command, and not before, one volley from the archers, all aiming at the man on the grey horse.'

'This is a new dawn, a new age,' Soter continued. 'We are the masters of the Island of the Sun. We decide what man does what labour, who lives and who dies.'

Marcus sensed rather than heard his father's order ripple along the battlement.

Across the wasteland the slave-king made a gesture, and two naked men were pushed forward from the crowd. One was thin and lithe, the other overweight and out of condition. The ankles of both were shackled.

'Tell Vopiscus on Ortygia that one of his scouts has returned.'

That would be the slightly built man. *How in Hades*, Marcus thought, *did the rebels know the arrangements of the defence?* It gave a horrible credence to the presence of traitors within the walls.

'You set a bad example with your treachery, Ballista. Although he, too, had sworn an oath to me, the Quaestor Caius Maesius Modius was inspired to desert. As you can see, his flight was less successful than yours.'

Two swords were thrown out by the feet of the prisoners.

'If the winner fights well, I will grant him his life.'

Both men reluctantly picked up the weapons.

The combat, Marcus thought, *could only end one way*. This was indeed the world turned upside down. A quaestor forced to fight as a gladiator, humiliated before the mob, his life at the whim of a slave. A senator, a magistrate of Rome, no matter what his crime, no matter how heinous his treason, was entitled to dignity in death. Even the worst tyrannical emperors respected that privacy, and allowed the condemned man to open his veins in his own house.

An Alamann stepped forward and lashed a whip across the quaestor's back. The naked man stumbled. The slaves jeered.

'Hades! What fool . . .?'

A single arrow arced out from the walls. The aim was poor. It fell nowhere near the rebel leader. But more followed. Not a co-ordinated volley. The shafts flew wildly. Marcus heard Soter shout a command. As one, the insurgent bowmen loosed. And then Marcus was shoved down to the wall walk. Tarchon was crouched over him, covering him with his shield. Ballista and Maximus were still standing, but they had their shields up. Marcus saw an arrow glance off his father's shield. Then he felt one thump into the wooden boards over his head. The impact jarred down through Tarchon. Marcus noticed that Tarchon had some fingers missing from his right hand, which held the shield.

Like a summer storm, the rain of arrows suddenly ceased. Marcus peered over the crenellations. Behind a screen of archers, the rebels were withdrawing. Under the slave-king's eye they went unit by unit in reasonable order.

'A dangerous man, that Soter,' Ollius said. 'Hard to control that mob. Without him they would be nothing.'

Ballista had a faraway look in his eyes. 'Without him they would be nothing,' he repeated.

Out in the wasteland lay the corpses of two naked men. They were riddled with arrows. The unknown hero and the coward together in death.

'Why try to storm the walls?'

Ballista did not answer the Hibernian's question straight away.

'They will die in droves. Even if they succeed, the casualties will be enormous.'

Ballista stopped studying the enemy ranks drawn up on the other side of the wasteland, and turned to his friend.

'If they know Vopiscus commands Ortygia, they will have been told the city has good supplies. And we can get more. If prices are high enough, merchant ships will risk winter storms. The rebels have no boats. They cannot blockade the harbours. Maybe Soter thinks his men will starve before us.'

'Who is telling them?' Maximus asked.

'Many slaves in town, many resentments,' Tarchon said. 'Or maybe one of the council thinks to save own skin. Weak men devoted to selves, much given to hating.'

Ballista ignored their speculation. 'It could be Soter has little choice. We saw the other slave force come in from the southern coast road yesterday. Some of the mounted rode on up to the Euryalus fort, where Soter has pitched his pavilion. There may be rival leaders among the insurgents.'

Ollius joined the discussion. 'As I said before, they are nothing without him.'

'Not all of them might recognise that,' Ballista said, 'especially the newcomers who have been campaigning without him in the South. For all his magic tricks, Soter has to deliver success after success to maintain his position. Any delay in taking the city might undermine his authority. Anyway, he did not strike me as a leader who would be too troubled by the deaths of other men.'

Like a large animal waking from slumber, the rebel host stirred. A dozen or so stepped out of the throng. They were tall men with long fair hair. After pausing, hands held to the heavens, they took up their weapons, and began to dance.

'What in Hades are they doing?' Ollius asked.

The dancers were lunging and leaping, twisting in the air, thrusting at imaginary foes.

'It is the custom of the North,' Ballista said.

'All my postings were in Africa and the East,' Ollius said.

'Those Alamanni are dedicating themselves to the gods. Dancing themselves into a frenzy, they draw into themselves the ferocity of wild beasts – wolves or bears. It encourages the others. My father was a beast-warrior.'

Perhaps he had said too much. Ballista caught his son looking at him, as if for a horrible moment Marcus did not know him at all, maybe half-expected him to start howling at the sky.

'The gods have never possessed me.'

The presence of his son unsettled him. Marcus was well armoured: helmet, mail-coat and shield. Maximus and Tarchon would protect him. But if anything happened to him . . . At the thought, Ballista felt fear almost physically overwhelm him.

The homecoming of Agamemnon. It was not every day that your wife threatened to kill you. But Julia was right. He should never have let Marcus take the *toga virilis*, never have let him enlist as a combatant. Still, all he could do now was try to keep the boy safe, stand between him and the enemy. Julia would have no need to play Clytemnestra. Ballista would die before he let harm come to their child.

With wild gyrations, the dance of the Alamanni was moving to its climax. Not long now. Without conscious thought, Ballista went through his own silent pre-battle ritual: his right hand went to the dagger on his right hip, pulled it an inch or so out of its sheath, then snapped it back; his left hand on the scabbard of his sword, his right hand pulled the blade a couple of inches free, then pushed it back; finally, his right hand touched the healing-stone tied to the scabbard.

It was good to have his own sword again. Battle-Sun had been forged in the North before the mists of time. It had been passed down from one warrior to another. If its owner fought with courage, Battle-Sun would never let him down. Ballista would not let down the men who had carried the blade. Sometimes, as he gazed on the colours in the steel, or felt the hilt in the palm of his hand, he thought those long-dead heroes communed with him.

This was no time to dwell on the past. Ballista looked along the battlements. Ollius' men were in place. Four thousand of them, a quarter archers, perhaps two hundred with slings. Enough to put a lot of missiles in the air. Ganymede and the fifty gladiators were below, in the lee of the wall, as a mobile reserve. Fires were lit along the wall walk, at intervals of about fifty paces. Bronze cauldrons, suspended by chains from metal tripods, hung over the flames. The fires had been lit at the first news that the slaves were forming up for an assault. The contents of each cauldron would already be scalding hot. Two sets of long iron tongs were ready by each fire. Pitchforks were leaned against the crenellations every twenty paces. There were two other gates besides the main one where Ballista was stationed. Behind each were two cranes. Each was overseen by an engineer, and crewed with experienced builders.

Satisfied the defences were ready, Ballista gave his attention to the enemy. They were formed up in a solid block, many ranks deep. The standards marked their divisions. Yet the units abutted each other, left no room for manoeuvre. The only tactic would be one massed advance. Their numbers were uncertain. Ballista estimated that if there had been about ten thousand with Soter, perhaps another five thousand had joined them from the south. Odds of somewhat more than three to one. Usually enough to take a defended position. But any certainty was impossible. Neither side were soldiers. The morale of both defenders and attackers would be fragile. If the slaves established themselves on the wall, the militia would break and run. Yet, on the other hand, would the insurgents have the fortitude to endure the carnage necessary to reach and get onto the battlements?

It was the Alamanni that worried Ballista. They might have been defeated and captured by Gallienus at Milan, but previously they had reached the outskirts of the city of Rome itself. They were trained warriors, not unaccustomed to the fury and horrors of battle. Much depended on their numbers. There were several Germanic flags among the insurgent standards. At Catana the Alamanni had been prominent in the besieging army, at guard posts and on patrol, and as officers and councillors. Ballista hoped that it signified no more than Soter had recognised that they were his only reliable combatants. With luck, only a thin crust of Alamanni, backed by a mass of slaves, stood under the northern standards.

The rebels had been busy. Large wooden mantelets screened their front ranks. Each of the big shields would have to be carried by several men. Even so, they would be heavy and difficult to manage. They would slow the advance down, keep the attackers in the killing zone for longer. Yet they looked robust enough to stop most arrows and sling stones. *If only*, Ballista thought, *Syracuse possessed just one piece of stone-throwing torsion artillery*. It would soon have reduced the mantelets to firewood. Battering rams stood opposite each gate. The frames from which they hung were covered by wheeled penthouses. Raw and dampened ox-hides were stretched over the boards of the mobile sheds to protect them from fire. It was a sensible precaution. Looking at the metal beaks of the rams jutting out from under the penthouses, Ballista doubted it would be enough. It was the many siege ladders, lying on the ground in front of the besiegers, waiting to be lugged forward, that most worried Ballista.

A gust of wind from the sea snapped the standard flying above the gatehouse. Ballista looked up at the White Horse of Hedinsey, the symbol of his family in the North. Julia and her maids had embroidered the flag. Whatever her feelings about his barbarian origins, she understood something of what it meant to her husband. No Woden-born man of his dynasty fled the field while that standard still flew. Ballista grinned. What Julia could not know was the effect it might have on the Alamanni. They could have no doubt who they fought. There was no warrior from Germania who did not recognise that white horse on a green field. For many generations, the Himlings of Hedinsey had inspired fear on the battlefield.

A trumpet rang out. And there in clear view, mounted on his grey, overtopping his men, was Soter. Either he genuinely believed he was touched by the divine, or he had a reckless courage. The slave-king gestured, called out to his army. The wind did not let his words carry to the defenders.

'Pass the order,' Ballista said. 'Prepare to loose.'

Ballista had walked his lines earlier. Every few paces he had stopped, and spoken words of encouragement to his makeshift troops.

You are fighting for your homes, the temples of your gods, your families. You are free men, they are nothing but slaves. You are protected by battlements, they are exposed to every missile. Everything is in your favour. Do not let them gain the wall. Do your duty, and you will win.

Now he saw no reason to let his opponent make any such speech.

'Loose!'

The sound of hundreds of thrumming bowstrings, of whirling slings. Like vicious insects, the missiles hissed across the desolate expanse, the arrows thin black lines, the stones from the slings almost too fast to see.

The slave-king's guard had closed their shields around him. Almost all the projectiles thumped harmlessly into the big mantelets.

'High trajectory!' Ollius was shouting. 'Aim high, drop the arrows on their heads! Slingers, wait for gaps to appear in the line of shields.'

Another volley. More ragged, but at a better angle. Now Ballista saw a tremor run through the enemy, like a breeze shifting through a field of barley. Behind those big shields men would be falling.

It was enough. Without orders, blocks of the enemy were stung into movement. Better attack than stand impotent to be shot down. They came forward with no cohesion. At once the line was broken. The penthouses cradling the rams weighed a ton. Already they were lagging a little behind.

As the slaves advanced, their bowmen started to shoot back. Ballista raised his shield, peered around its rim.

'Slingers, aim for their unshielded sides!' Ollius was roaring. 'Their unshielded sides!'

Now Ballista could see men struck down. They crumpled, curling around the arrowheads embedded in their bodies, or crashed backwards, felled by unseen stones. They had eighty paces to cover before they came in range of javelins hurled from the wall. Some groups raced towards the town – anything to get through the torment – all order abandoned. Others edged forwards, huddled together behind the big shields.

Allfather, but there are an awful lot of them.

An arrow whipped by his face. It plucked a figure off the wall. In a moment of panic, Ballista swung round looking for his son. Marcus was there, warded by Tarchon's shield as well as his own. Ballista felt a lurch of fear at the two arrows embedded in the shield of his son.

Forcing himself to remain calm, Ballista turned his gaze out over the parapet at the rams. They had to approach down the three tracks leading to the gates. He was looking at the one heading towards the gate by the Little Harbour when he heard men cheering from the other end of the wall. The penthouse there was tipped at a crazy angle. Its front left wheel had sunk through the wickerwork covered in soil that concealed one of the pits that Ballista had had his men dig. The issue would be decided long before the unwieldy device could be freed. As Ballista looked back towards the Little Harbour, the penthouse there lurched to a stop as the ground gave way.

'Sure, that has taken care of two of the three,' Maximus said. 'Some people might be thinking you had done this sort of thing before.'

Ballista did not reply to the Hibernian.

The street to the main gate was paved. No hidden pits had been possible. That ram would have to be dealt with by another means in its turn.

A great roar, like a tidal wave breaking on a headland, rolled along the wall. Everywhere men were throwing javelins, rocks, anything that came to hand. Just a few moments, and the assault would have reached the foot of the wall. The crisis was at hand.

'Cauldrons!' Ballista shouted.

A trumpeter stationed on the gatehouse played the expected signal. It was relayed all along the line.

With the long iron tongs, hands wrapped in rags, men lifted the bulky and sizzling vessels. Gingerly they shuffled to the parapet, lifted the ungainly things high, then tipped. The sand, white-hot and smoking, poured down. From below came the sounds of men screaming in agony and terror. There had been no naphtha in the town, but sand was almost as effective. It sifted under armour, into clothes, stuck burning to the skin.

Not all the slaves had been stopped. Ballista saw ladders rearing up against the battlements, saw pitchforks trying to fend them off. There was no time to watch the results. The ram was almost at the main gate.

'First crane lift!' Ballista yelled down through the uproar.

A great tremor, like an earthquake, moved the flagstones under his feet. The immense impact of the ram striking seemed to have shaken the whole gatehouse. The boards of the gate were solid oak, bound with iron. Yet it would not withstand for long such force channelled through the steel tip of the ram.

As men worked the pulleys, the arm of the crane swung up and over the defenders and outwards. It bowed as it struggled with the load it carried.

Ballista peered out over the defences, then rushed back to gesture guidance to the engineer at the crane. Maximus flitted here and there – like some agitated *daemon* – trying to cover Ballista with his shield as his friend dashed back and forth.

'Left, left, a bit! Stop there! Now release!'

The enormous block of stone – once the lintel of a fine house – plummeted down.

From below came a satisfying noise of rending wood.

'Bugger!'

The stone had caved in the roof of the penthouse. Slaves could be seen crushed like beetles. But the structure of the frame remained intact.

'Second crane, lift!'

Its crew had been impatient. The arm was already overhead. *Take your time*, Ballista muttered to himself.

Heedless of the shafts slicing past, not noticing the ministrations of his friend, Ballista calmly issued instructions until he was convinced the crane was perfectly positioned.

'Release!'

This time the aim could not have been bettered. The second building block landed on the front apex of the frame of the penthouse. The edifice imploded in a cloud of dust. When the haze cleared, it was seen that the stone had neatly snapped off the metal point of the ram.

Now – once again fully aware of his surroundings – Ballista grabbed his son, and hunkered down behind the shelter of the crenellations. It was odd how the fear came after the danger.

'They are on the wall!'

Ballista prised himself off the floor. Two ladders, down by the gate to the Little Harbour. Alamanni climbing over the parapet. A confused scrum on the wall walk. The militia had not run yet. There might still be time.

'Ollius, take command.'

Ballista hurled himself down the steps. Ganymede was waiting at the bottom.

'Bring your men.'

Ballista had meant to leave his son with Ollius. Too late now.

It was only about a hundred paces to the little gate. They ran, their weapons and armour clattering. By the time they were there, the mail-coat was digging into Ballista's shoulders. Sweat was running down his face from under his helmet.

'Ganymede, get up there, and clear them off the wall.'

The gladiator did not move. Ballista saw the doubt in his eyes, and those of the men at his back. Somehow he knew they would follow, but not risk the ascent on their own.

'Follow me!'

The steps were wide enough for two men. Ballista went up with Maximus at his left shoulder, his son and Tarchon behind. There was no chance to check that the gladiators were following. Four Alamanni were coming down. If they opened the gate, it was all over.

The Alamann descending on Ballista brought his sword down in a huge overhand chop. Ballista staggered as he took the blow on the boss of his shield. Recovering his stance, he flicked the point of his sword out at the warrior's legs. The edge sliced open the left thigh. The Alamann crumpled, hands going to the wound. Ballista hurdled two steps clean over him. Someone else would finish the injured man.

Now Ballista was adjacent to the one fighting Maximus. Tucking his shoulder into his shield, he threw his weight sideways. The Alamann grunted with surprise, then yelled as he was driven off the side of the steps. He fell, arms clawing for some non-existent purchase.

The manoeuvre had left Ballista off balance and exposed. The remaining pair both lunged at once. In their haste, they impeded each other. Twisting, Ballista blocked one thrust with his sword. The other missed his face by a hand's breadth.

Now Maximus leapt forward. In a fight the Hibernian's movements were smooth and instinctive, like those of a big cat, or some other rapacious animal. A couple of deft stabs, and both Alamanni were down, choking out their life breath.

'Come on!'

A quick look back. The gladiators were pounding up the steps.

There was a lull in the fighting at the top of the steps. The militia were in a huddle a few paces to the left, the Alamanni to the right. A red standard showing a golden wolf showed above the tribesmen. The wall walk was broad enough for four men abreast. Ballista realised that his son was on his left shoulder; beyond Marcus was Tarchon, then Maximus by the outer parapet. Before he could order Marcus to the rear, the Alamanni were on them.

Watch the steel.

Ballista had to force himself not even to glance at his son. The warrior facing Ballista was cautious, jabbing and probing for a weakness. The noises of steel on steel, of steel on wood, to his left were torture to Ballista. He needed to finish this fast. A strong warrior would soon beat down the defence of a thirteen-year-old boy.

Deliberately Ballista stumbled a pace backwards, as if something had turned under his boot. His guard dropped a fraction. It was enough to draw his opponent in. As the Alamann thrust at his torso, Ballista pirouetted, and smashed the pommel of Battle-Sun into the bridge of his nose. There was a horrible sound of delicate bones breaking, like the body of a small bird. As the warrior reared back, Ballista killed him with a thrust to the throat.

Knuckling the stinging blood out of his eyes, Ballista turned to rescue his son. It was too late. Tarchon was standing over Marcus' assailant. Since he had lost those fingers on his right hand, Tarchon had trained himself to become a fine left-handed swordsman.

There was a moment of peace. The Alamanni had given ground.

Where is Maximus? Ballista gazed round frantically. *There he is!*

The Hibernian was in the midst of the enemy. Like some sprightly ghost avid for blood, one of those that in its hatred of the living tears them limb from limb, Maximus hacked his way to the wolf standard. A sweep of his sword cleaved the standard-bearer's shoulder. For a grotesque moment, the fingers of the severed arm still clutched the shaft of the flag. Then Maximus grabbed it, and hurled it to the ground.

And that was the end. Their proud symbol reduced to a rag, the Alamanni turned in flight. As they fought one another to reach the ladders, Ganymede and the gladiators launched themselves at their defenceless backs.

A wave of cheering rolled along the battlements. The militia, almost insane with relief, hugged each other, screamed abuse down at the insurgents fleeing back across the wasteland.

Ballista found Marcus. 'You all right?'

His son's face was white, his eyes wide with the enormity of survival. Unable to speak, Marcus nodded.

'Good.' Ballista turned away. 'Tarchon, go and tell Ollius to organise two parties to get pitch and torches, anything inflammable, and go out and burn the rams and penthouses while the slaves are still in disarray. We have weathered the first storm, but the siege is not over.'

CHAPTER TWENTY-TWO

THREE HOURS TO MIDNIGHT. It was very dark. Great banks of black clouds scudded across the few stars and the thin crescent of the new moon. A storm was coming from the north, but for now there was no breeze down in the Great Harbour. Its waters were as still and glassy as a millpond. The oars of the small boat were muffled, but their splash and creak seemed so loud they must carry back to the city or out to the shore.

Lights were burning up on the heights of Epipolae. The marsh ahead was indistinct in the gloom. It was Lysimeleia, where the doomed Athenian expedition had made its camp. Its pestilential vapours had brought disease. In its fetid mud the Athenians had abandoned their dead and wounded. A bad portent. Was their clandestine mission tonight fated to meet with similar disaster?

The marsh was close now. No sign of life. Would the men be waiting? Without the horses they could not reach Euryalus, and the camp of Soter, before dawn. And that would be far too late.

The boat nosed into a tiny creek. Reeds and stunted trees lined the banks. The air was thick with the smell of stagnant water and rotting vegetation and mud. Something plopped into the water in their wake. The boatman turned into an even narrower inlet. Here willows overhung the stream. Those not rowing brushed them aside with their arms.

After a time, the boat was run ashore on a shelf of firm ground. Marcus got out with the others. His father thanked the crew. They had been promised a large reward. They would only collect the money if they waited through the night, and delivered their passengers safely back to the wharfs of Syracuse in the morning.

The guide led them off through the marsh. They followed in single file: Ballista, Marcus, and Tarchon, with Maximus bringing up the rear. Their course was circuitous. Often they detoured around slimy pools, doubled back on themselves. Although the guide gave every impression of knowing exactly where he was, now and then Ballista stopped, and looked back the way they had come.

Eventually they came to a stand of alders at the edge of the marsh. The guide gave a low whistle. It was answered from within the trees. The horses were hobbled, contentedly cropping the grass. Their handlers were tense.

'We will see you at first light,' Ballista said. 'No point in letting the rebels take our mounts.'

They murmured agreement. Marcus wondered if they would remain all night. Flavius Vopiscus had sent a message into the interior for them to bring the horses. He said they were reliable men. But waiting through the long hours of darkness, so close to the camp of the insurgents, would fray anyone's courage. Apart from losing the horseflesh, it did not matter. As long as the guide did not lose his nerve. Without him, surely it would be impossible to find their path back through the marsh to where the boat was hidden. That was, if the boat was still there tomorrow.

They mounted and set off. It was a good six miles to the Euryalus fortress at the western end of Epipolae. They went across country. The ground was flat. Most of the time they could keep to a canter. They did not speak. Just the drumming of hooves marked their passing across the darkling plain.

Marcus felt his spirits lift – an animal surge of well-being. This was much better than sitting helpless in the boat, or creeping through that stinking marsh. His father had not wanted to bring him. Marcus had argued that Ballista had no knowledge of the tunnels under Euryalus, whereas he knew them intimately from childhood, every twist and turning, every dead end, every entrance and exit. His father had said there must be others in the town familiar with the subterranean passages, preferably grown men. But could they be trusted, Marcus had countered – could they be trusted like a son?

They had told next to no one that they were going. Among the officers, just Vopiscus and Ollius, and only Grim and Rikiar in the *familia*. But, of course, Julia had found out. His mother had been white-lipped with anger. Marcus was sorry that he was causing her such anxiety. But he was not a child anymore. Although, if he did not make it back, it might be best if his father also failed to return.

It was five days since they had driven the rebels from the walls. Many among the garrison had been sure that the defeat would cause the insurgents to disperse. Such confidence had been misplaced. Marcus had known they had nowhere to go. If they failed to take Syracuse, their only future was to be hunted down. Some might hide in the mountains for a time, maybe for months, but their end would be inevitable. His father had divulged the hope that the reverse might so tarnish the image of

Soter that he would be overthrown by his own men. That had been answered on the second morning. Daylight had revealed six crucified men facing the walls. At least four of the men nailed to the crosses appeared to be Alamanni. Presumably that was the slave-king taking his revenge on those of his officers who had dared to question his authority.

Without him they would be nothing, Ollius had said. The veteran procurator was right. Only the charisma of Soter held the rebellious slaves together. Without their *Saviour* they would not be any form of army, but a disparate and uncontrollable mob. *Cut the head off the snake*, Maximus had said. Marcus thought that, for once, the Hibernian was right.

The dark cliffs of Epipolae loomed ahead. There was a grove sacred to Hercules. Tarchon would wait there with the horses. Marcus knew he should be afraid – very afraid. This was a desperate venture. If they were captured alive, their deaths would be slow and agonising. Yet that had an air of unreality. His father and Maximus were great warriors. With them it was impossible to imagine failure, let alone coming to any harm.

They reached the grove of Hercules without encountering anyone. Ballista had not expected any patrols would be out at night on the plain. The rebels had nothing to fear from inland. All their precautions would be directed against a sally from the walls of Syracuse. If the little craft had been spotted crossing the Great Harbour, it would not have been seen as posing any threat. Most likely a rebel sentry would have dismissed it as a fishing boat, or, as it carried no lights, as some faint-hearted inhabitant who had bribed a boatman to let him furtively flee the siege for the imagined safety of the interior.

The great oaks of the sacred place were bare of leaves. Yet they were ancient – perhaps they had been saplings when the Athenians invested the city – and in the darkness their thick trunks provided good cover. The nocturnal travellers tethered the horses by the altar in the centre. Tarchon was left in charge.

Marcus led Ballista and Maximus towards the ditches of the fortress. One or two torches burnt high up on the walls, where sentries paced their rounds. The flaring torches would make the darkness more profound beyond the small circle of their light. There was little danger of the guards seeing the three figures, faces and hands blackened with burnt cork, and clad in black hooded cloaks, who were stealing through the night.

Down in the ditch, Marcus went slowly, working along one bank, hunting the concealed entrance to the tunnels. Part of Ballista hoped that his son failed to find the opening. It was not unlikely. Things always looked different in the dark, and it was years since Marcus had explored the passageways. If they turned about now, they could be back in Syracuse within the hour. There would be no shame in such a retreat. Anyway, it was iniquitous to place on a youth the heavy responsibility of guiding them into the fortress. And what sort of father would put his son in such danger?

Ballista had another reason for wanting the opening to remain elusive. Since childhood, he had hated confined spaces. There was something terrifying about being hemmed in, unable to move freely. Underground chambers were the worst of all, with the thought of the immense weight of earth and rock pressing all around, straining to crush the life out of you.

They made no sound as they crept along the ditch. All three wore soft leather-soled riding boots. Their mail-coats had been oiled, and all ornaments stripped from their sword-belts and the cases of the short composite bows that they wore on their right hips.

'*Eleutheria!*' The sentry, previously unseen, above them on the wall, called the challenge.

They froze, pressing themselves into the shadows at the bottom of the ditch. Not far to the grove. Still time to run.

'*Parrhesia!*' The answer, somewhat fainter, also came from somewhere on the battlements.

Ballista could see the white of Maximus' teeth, as the Hibernian grinned with relief. *Freedom* and *Free Speech*, suitable watchwords for the revolt – things unknown to the slaves under the previous order, even if the Greek might mean little to the Alamanni.

They waited for some time before moving on again. For the first few steps they expected an outcry. None came. The stillness of the night remained undisturbed.

'Here!' Marcus hissed.

Hades, Ballista thought.

Behind a bramble was a small, black opening in the side of the ditch. Ballista eyed it with distaste. It was no bigger than a trapdoor into a loft. If it had once had a covering, it was long since removed or rotted away. The whole fortress had been derelict for centuries of Roman peace.

Marcus got down on all fours and wriggled into the entrance. Ballista let Maximus go next. They both had a slighter build than him. When the Hibernian's boots had disappeared, Ballista could find no reason for any further delay.

The opening was only just wider than Ballista's shoulders. Once his torso was inside, the light was blocked out. It was a cold December night, but he was sweating heavily. As he squirmed all the way in, his breath became fast and shallow, close to panic. Tons and tons of rock poised above his head. Nowhere to escape.

'Wait.' Marcus' quiet voice sounded strange, almost echoing.

Ballista's hands found the boots of Maximus. He lay in the inky blackness, striving to control his breathing, attempting to divert his mind from the surrounding rock. Think about anything, anything else.

A light flared briefly ahead, as Marcus used flint and steel. As soon as the wick of the storm-lantern caught, he narrowed the shutters to a chink.

They were in a tunnel of rough-cut stone, no more than two feet wide, and little higher. The sides were green and greasy. There was a reek of damp and rodents. The tunnel ran upwards at a steep angle. Some sort of drain. Beyond the others, Ballista could make out another blank hole, an entrance into another chamber.

It was hard and filthy work hauling himself up after the others. His hands and boots slipped; it was difficult to get any leverage. At last a hand reached down, and Maximus helped pull him up.

Ballista sat for a moment, getting his breath back. This was better. They had emerged into an underground passageway. Constructed of smooth, dressed blocks of stone, it was taller than a man, and almost wide enough for a small cart.

Marcus shone the lantern in both directions. The passage was utterly bare.

'They might not even know about the tunnels,' he said. 'Easy to get lost down here. It is a labyrinth.'

Ballista levered himself to his feet. He stank, and his cloak was thick with foul slime.

'Lead on,' he said.

As far as Ballista could tell, they were moving north. A couple of passages opened off to the right. His son ignored them. Then they came out into a chamber with half a dozen exits.

'There are connections all over the fortress and outside,' Marcus said. He thought for a moment, then entered one which also appeared to go north.

After a while the passage branched. Marcus took the right-hand turning. After that, Ballista lost all sense of distance and time. They just walked, seemingly without end, down one long subterranean path.

Eventually, Marcus stopped.

'Quiet now. The stairs are just ahead.'

The door, protected from the elements, still closed the passage. Thankfully, it was not locked, or bolted from the other side. When they pulled it open, however, its hinges gave an alarming squeal.

Once again they were very still, gazing up the steps, listening for an alarm, praying they did not see guards rushing down.

When the silence became too oppressive to bear, they started their ascent.

The staircase spiralled up inside the wall. At the top was another solid closed door. Ballista took the ring of the handle in his hands, and told Marcus to close the storm-lantern before he tried the door. Light suddenly spilling out might well give them away. Ballista waited in the pitch darkness. Satisfied that his night vision would have returned, he turned the iron ring. The bar lifted with a clunk. He opened the door a crack – the gods were with them, this door was not locked either – and peered through. Dark shapes moving near the wall, too bulky to be men. As his sight adjusted, he saw they were nothing more menacing than cattle. But no men nearby, no immediate threat. He quietly shut the door again.

Ballista thought about the lantern. They should have brought two. Easy to be prescient after the event. If they left it shuttered, it should have enough oil to burn for another hour. But, if they were delayed, Ballista could not face descending into the total darkness.

'Marcus, put out the lantern,' he said. 'We will leave it here.'

Light flooded the chamber, splashed their shadows across the walls, before Marcus snuffed out the wick, and they were back in utter blackness.

Again they waited, so they would not be night-blind outside. Ballista recited the Greek alphabet twice, then he opened the door.

After the tunnel, the ambient light seemed as bright as day. Marcus had brought them out where he had predicted. Off to the left was the old main gate of the fortress. Ahead, Ballista could see the ridge of the big pavilion. A couple of hundred paces, no more. It stood above the cluster of smaller tents, silhouetted against the sky. The herd of cows had been penned against the interior of the wall. By the gate, rank after rank of wagons were drawn up. They were laden with sacks of grain, and barrels and amphorae of wine and oil. The slaves had gathered together all the produce plundered from the fertile island through which they had passed. It was never easy to stop the individual looting and the general wanton destruction of an army on the march. Ballista admitted a grudging admiration for Soter.

Pinpricks of light up on the wall showed where the scattered sentries paced through their tedious watch. There were a few more among the wagons, just one on the far side of the animals.

'Let's go.'

They walked slowly. Unalarmed, the cattle regarded them with mild, docile curiosity. Their warm, sweet breath hung on the air. That and the scent of hay. Halfway through the herd, while the doorway was still in sight, Ballista stopped and looked back. He noted its position relative to a notch in the battlements, where the crenellations had fallen. The other two waited as he took his bearings, then they all went on.

The pair of herdsmen with the torch were some way off when they ducked through the fence. No one else appeared to challenge them. The smaller tents were in darkness. No one was stirring at this hour. They did not skulk, but walked openly down the lines, as if merely out for some innocent late night stroll.

They halted in the deep shadow of the last tent. The pavilion was about thirty paces away. They were looking at its side. The big tent was exactly as it had been outside Catana. A dozen guards off to the right, partly hidden by the corner, outside the only entrance. Like before, no doubt there would be more armed men inside, but there were none walking around the outside. Grown accustomed to having the initiative, always being the aggressor, the insurgents' security was slack. On the other hand, muted voices and light came from the interior. Soter was awake, and had company. That could not be helped.

'Cover me,' Ballista said.

Maximus and his son drew their bows, and fitted arrows to the strings.

Trying to walk normally, as if he had every right in the world to be there, Ballista went to the rear of the pavilion. While he was still in sight of the others, he looked all round, then dropped to his knees. Beyond the wall of the tent should be the passageway that ran around the structure. He listened intently, but could hear nothing except the muffled voices from deep in the interior. No shadows moved against the wall. He pulled the dagger from its sheath. This was the crux. If anyone was in the passage, they would shout, and he would just run. In the darkness, it was quite likely they would be able to get back to the tunnel and escape. Ballista smothered the cowardly thought.

The canvas was taut. Ballista punched the razor-sharp point of the dagger through it, a couple of feet from the ground. No immediate outcry. A tearing sound as he dragged the edge of the blade to the bottom. Then, holding the material tight, he sawed another couple of feet along the floor. Yanking back the flap, he stuck his head through. The passageway was lit by lamps. They revealed an empty walkway.

Ballista crawled through. The bow case on his hip got caught. He was stuck. Tugging at the canvas, he freed himself, and got to his feet.

A man walked round the corner of the passage. He was carrying an unopened wine flask and unarmed, some sort of domestic servant.

'*Eleutheria!*' Ballista said with all the authority he could raise.

'*Parrhesia!*' the man replied.

As Ballista strode past him, he saw the man wrinkle his nose. Of course, the cloak stank of the drains.

Ballista turned into where the passage ran along the side. As he had suspected, a guard was stationed outside the hangings of the opening into the main chamber, halfway along. It was an Alamann.

Allfather, be praised, just the one.

'*Eloo . . . ther . . . ia.*' Ballista pronounced the word in a thick German accent.

The guard smiled. 'Ridiculous language. *Parrhesia.*'

'What is he doing?' Ballista pointed over the man's shoulder.

The guard turned. The Alamanni were not renowned for their quick intelligence. Ballista got his left hand over the warrior's mouth, and cut his throat with the dagger in his right.

He held the man against him as his body convulsed, then lowered him gently to the floor.

Ballista wiped the blood from his hands, got his bow from its case, selected an arrow, and notched it. With the hand holding the bow, he pushed the hanging back just far enough for him to see into the main room. There was Soter at the high table. The slave-king was feasting. Seated by him was a man with a hooked nose, clad in a vulgar tunic. The other diners close to Soter were all Alamanni. One with an *F* branded on his forehead was looking with disfavour at the man with the distinctive nose.

'Hey, you!'

Perhaps it had been the foul reek of his cloak that had aroused the suspicions of the servant, had persuaded him to retrace his steps and follow. No one would ever know. Ballista turned and shot him through the chest. The aim was good.

Yet, as the man crashed backwards, he collided with the wall of the inner chamber, and managed one last inarticulate yell.

Ballista plucked another arrow, and peered again through the hangings. The oily haired man with the extraordinary nose was gazing about in confusion. Soter, however, was invisible behind a wall of bodies of the Alamanni, who had all leapt to their feet.

Ballista heard the alarm being shouted as he started to run.

Jumping the corpse of the servant, as he reached the turning he heard men tumbling out in pursuit. He turned and shot. The Alamanni dived to the ground. Ballista raced round the corner.

Skidding to his knees by the torn canvas, he dropped the bow, and hurled himself through. Heavy boots were pounding after him. The fucking bow case snagged again. Ballista frantically ripped it free and, swearing repetitively, hauled himself clear.

In the torchlight, the guards from the entrance were coming round the corner. The two arrows that whistled out of the darkness at them both missed. But the unexpected attack gave the guards pause for thought. They stopped, ducked behind their shields, scanning for the unseen threat.

'Over here!'

Ballista heard Maximus. Coming out of the lit passage, he had been heading off at the wrong angle.

'There!' The guards had seen him.

Another brace of arrows made them again duck behind the boards of their shields.

Ballista reached the others. As one, they fled between the lines of the lesser tents. Here and there, behind their walls, men were stirring, calling out to their neighbours, asking what was happening.

They threw themselves over the cattle pen. The urgency of their flight communicated itself to the animals. Lowing and bellowing, they parted before these intruders, then began to stampede in all directions. Ballista looked up. Flames streamed back as sentries up on the wall walk converged. There was the notch in the battlements. No sentries there yet. Behind, men were roaring at the thundering beasts impeding their chase.

They bundled themselves through the door. Maximus went to slam it shut. Ballista grabbed his arm.

'Marcus, light the lantern.'

'No time,' Maximus panted.

'Light it!'

As his son fumbled with the flint, Ballista looked back at the torches bobbing and weaving through the maddened beasts.

The lantern flared. The pursuers gave a shout. Maximus slammed the door. A quick glance revealed no bolt.

'Run!' Ballista said.

They tumbled down the staircase – Marcus leading, then Ballista, Maximus at the rear. They raced down the long curving passage, the shadows of their flying cloaks like huge bats on the walls. How much further? It seemed never-ending.

When they reached the fork, Marcus unhesitatingly took the left-hand branch. Now, even above their own cacophony, the sounds of their hunters echoed down the tunnel.

They burst into the broad chamber. Marcus pulled up, uncertain. Which of the half-dozen passages?

'This one,' Maximus said.

'No.' Marcus sounded unsure. 'I think this.'

'Are you certain?' the Hibernian said.

Marcus did not answer, but set off. Ballista and Maximus followed.

Dear gods, let the boy be right.

If not, Ballista thought, they could run in circles down here, like dormice in a jar. No way out. Run until they were found and butchered.

An opening to the left. Then another. Surely this was the right way?

'Here!' Marcus shone the beam down onto the drain.

'You first.' Ballista took the lantern as his son slid into the hole.

'Now you.' Maximus got his boots over the edge.

Best let them go first. Ballista was afraid his wider frame might get stuck. At least let his son and friend get away. He opened the lantern, pinched out the flame, and was plunged into absolute blackness. *Where in Hades is the drain?* He got on all fours, feeling with his fingers, panic surging in his mind. Now he realised it was not totally dark. Torchlight was approaching. They were almost on him.

There was the awful narrow gap. Feet first, he went to get in, then remembered the bow case. There was no time to untie its thongs. Muttering meaningless curses, he squashed himself down into the drain.

Sure enough, the bow case wedged itself between a jagged chunk of rock and his side. Whimpering with fear, he wrenched out his dagger, slashed at the bindings. Above, there was light in the passageway. It rang with booted, running feet. The leather gave, and Ballista slithered to the bottom. Strong hands grabbed his legs, dragged him out.

It started to rain as they ran along the ditch. Not far now to the grove. Not far to Tarchon waiting with the horses. The chasers would not catch them.

They had failed, but they were alive. They were going to get away. His son would be safe.

But the slave-king was still alive. They had failed. And what Ballista had seen told him something very desperate would be necessary to save the city of Syracuse.

The moon was still small, just a few days old. Inside the Little Harbour the waters had been calm, but once they rounded the breakwater, it was choppier. Spray came inboard. Some of it reached the man lying on the deck hidden under the fishing nets.

Gods below, it stank down here in the bilges. It would take days to get rid of the smell of fish guts. It might never come out of his clothes. Ganymede debated the wisdom of what he was doing. It was fraught with danger, and it was not his decision. He could have refused. After all, he could have stayed and defended the city and earned the freedom he had been promised. But he had been born into slavery. A lifetime of doing what he was told had left its mark. A lifetime of obeying orders or suffering the bite of the whip. Half a lifetime of obeying the orders of Lucullus. In most ways, he had not been a bad master. Ganymede had already been condemned to the arena before Lucullus purchased him. He could not blame Lucullus for that. And Lucullus had treated his gladiators well – made sure they were well fed and clothed, had the best doctors dress their wounds, had sent women to their cells. They had been cheap, thin whores, accustomed to brutality, but Ganymede had enjoyed them. Of course, such kindness of Lucullus had had nothing to do with philanthropy. The behaviour had been untouched by humanity or fellow feeling. It flattered the vanity of the senator to own a troop of well-turned-out gladiators in peak condition. They had fought and bled and died so that the mob would chant Lucullus' name, praise his generosity, and give him their votes. While all the time Lucullus' wealthy rivals in Syracuse would be consumed with impotent envy. *Hubris* was the pride that took pleasure in humbling others. Despite such insight, Ganymede accepted that he was conditioned to obey orders. *Burnt with fire, shackled with chains, whipped with rods, and killed with steel.* This was no worse. When this new order had been given, Ganymede had just dumbly nodded his head.

'You can come out now.'

One of the fishermen pulled the nets off, and gave him a hand up. Unused to boats, Ganymede shuffled uneasily to the back. The thing rocked horribly with his movements, seemed likely at any moment to tip over and throw him into the sea. It was easy to imagine the water closing over his head, what little light there was vanishing, as he sank into the depths. He sat down near the helmsman. Keeping a good grip on the side, he looked back across the black water to the lights of Syracuse. It had not been hard to arrange. A few coins to the skipper of this boat, rather more to a junior officer of the Watch to look the other way and conduct an inadequate search. He was not the first, and he would not be the last to slip out of the besieged city.

The fishermen lit the lantern on its pole. They cast the nets to catch the fish drawn to the light. They were fishing well away from the rest of the fleet. They would drift further off. After an hour or so, as arranged, they would douse the lantern and, in the dark of the night, run to shore.

The most dangerous moment would be back ashore, when he first encountered the rebels, stumbled across some patrol or picket. They might just kill him out of hand. But hopefully they would accept him for what he was – a slave running to join them.

It was nothing to do with freedom, or loyalty, or any such insubstantial concept. Ganymede was doing this for money. Of course, back in the amphitheatre, that great, hulking semi-barbarian Ballista had promised him money, along with his freedom, if he fought courageously on the battlements. But not enough – not a quarter as much as he had now been offered to desert to the rebels, and betray the city.

CHAPTER TWENTY-THREE

CROCUS THE ALAMANN WAS AFRAID. It was like a deep fever in his bones.

The moon was waxing, almost half-full. The night was far too bright. Not a cloud in the sky. Outside the house, the wasteland before the walls of Syracuse was bathed in bone-white light. It picked out every broken brick, every piece of the foundations of the levelled buildings. A killing ground which offered no cover.

In the gloom of the gutted house, the other Alamanni warriors were very quiet. Crocus sensed they shared his fear. They would lead the way. Very few men ever came back from a storming party.

Crocus did not trust the deserters. He had not trusted the Phoenician with the too colourful clothes, the too ingratiating manner and the hooked nose. And he certainly did not trust Ganymede the gladiator. Neither were men of honour. They were *nithing*. Yet Soter had accepted them at face value, welcomed them to his councils as slaves keen, for different motives, to betray the city. Nothing had come of the confident words of the Phoenician. The messages on scraps of papyrus tied to arrows shot out from the defences had produced nothing but delays and excuses: the guard on the gate had changed; his master was closely watched; wait until the festival of Larentalia at the end of the month; just have patience. It had encouraged Soter to grasp at the offer of Ganymede, like a drowning man clutching for a sliver of driftwood.

There could not be a worse time to venture blindly into the city. The defenders were active. They must have increased their guards. Recently not a single message or deserter had come out. For the past few nights – since the night that Ganymede had appeared – sounds had drifted across the wasteland: the sounds of people and carts moving about, and the hammering of construction work. On a night darker than this, Crocus had crept close to the walls and listened. He had reported to Soter, but the slave-king had dismissed his concerns, and continued to put his faith in the plan of the gladiator. Now Ganymede remained safe in the camp at Euryalus, as better men ran all the risks.

From the rear raised voices, arguing in Greek, disturbed the silence. Crocus sent one of the Alamanni to quieten them. The slaves were fools, *nithing*. They had no discipline. They were cowards who would run at the first sign of danger. If they thought of anything beyond the satisfaction of their brutish desires – rape, plunder, the infliction of mindless cruelty – it was an ill-defined re-creation of the world before the revolt. The only difference would see them as the masters, and their former owners reduced to painful servitude. All Soter's talk of an Island of the Sun, where all were free, and all were equal, was incomprehensible to them.

Roman slavery corrupted everyone, masters and slaves alike. It was different in Germania. Of course there were slaves. Yet they were not treated like beasts, robbed of all humanity. The young masters and slaves lived together among the same flocks and on the same earthen floors. When maturity set them apart, each thrall was given a holding and a home of their own. A stated quantity of grain, livestock or cloth was demanded of them, and he lived with his own family, as if he were a tenant. Even in the halls of the greatest chiefs there were few domestic servants. To flog a slave, or punish him with imprisonment or hard labour, was rare. If one was killed in a fit of rage, a blood-price had to be paid.

Usually Crocus tried not to think about home. He had a wife and children, two sons and a daughter. He would never see them again. There had been talk among the Alamanni freed from servitude of seizing some ships. It had been just talk. Even if they had been Franks or Angles, seafaring people who lived on the coast, the task would have been near impossible. But the Alamanni were not seamen. They lived in the Ten Cantons between the headwaters of the Rhine and Danube, separated from the Ocean by hundreds of miles and hostile tribes. None of them would again walk in the wooded hills and valleys of the Agri Decumates. Sooner or later they would all die on this island, unless they were coward enough to let themselves be captured alive. Then they might die in the arena at Rome.

Crocus knew his fate was bound to that of the so-called *Saviour*. It was not a good thing. Someone had told him how the trick of breathing fire was performed with naphtha and a hollow walnut shell. Any cheap magician in the marketplace had the sleight of hand to cast off chains. Now Crocus wondered how he had ever mistaken the Syrian wonder-worker for the Allfather. Perhaps the hard months in the mill had robbed him of his wits; perhaps the gods had blinded him. Crocus had heard enough to realise that Soter was no *Saviour*.

The ambitions of the Syrian were personal. He had shown that when he had crucified those men who had come in from the southern road, and questioned his leadership. Four of the executed had been Alamanni. The intention of Soter was to make himself a warlord. No shame in that, but a leader must be honest with his followers. If he became ruler of Sicily, Soter hoped he could negotiate his own survival with Gallienus, the hard-pressed emperor.

The hope was delusory. After the devastation of the island, Gallienus could not negotiate. The emperor had to take vengeance. Crocus had known that back in Catana, as the slave-king had outlined his scheme to Ballista. From the look on his face, the Angle had known it, too. Now Ballista was a leader you could follow. A man of courage, a man of his word, yet cunning enough to deceive his enemies. If the Fates had spun the threads of his life differently, Crocus would have been proud to stand beside Dernhelm the Himling, the son of Isangrim, the one the Romans called Ballista.

But the Fates had woven his life another way. Crocus was bound to Soter. That the Syrian was unworthy made no difference. Crocus had freely sworn an oath. There had been no compulsion. It was a matter of honour. In the Ten Cantons, a man might stake his freedom on the throw of a dice. If he lost, he allowed himself to be bound and sold.

'There!'

On the dark wall of the city a light showed – once, twice, three times.

'Pass the word.'

Crocus hefted his shield, and walked out into the moonlight towards the gate that guarded the Little Harbour. The

Alamanni followed. There were still some three thousand of them, grouped in war bands of a thousand. They would lead the way. The slaves would bring up the rear. Their numbers had dwindled since the repulse from the walls. Bands of them had drifted to Etna and into the other mountains to become brigands; individuals had sought safety in anonymous flight. It did not matter. They were *nithing*. If Ganymede had spoken the truth, the Alamanni would win Syracuse. If not, the revolt was over. It would be time to seek an honourable death.

The battlements of the long wall were dark. The sentries of the defenders never carried torches. Surely they could not fail to see the column of men crossing the exposed wasteland?

No trumpets rang out. There were no shouts of alarm.

The gate opened as Crocus approached. Under its arch was pitch-black. Gritting his teeth, Crocus went into the blackness.

He sensed, rather than saw, the shapes of men.

'What about the other guards?'

'They have been dealt with,' one of the gladiators replied.

There seemed to be only about half a dozen of them. He had expected more.

The first group of the Alamanni entered, treading softly, looking about.

Crocus ordered them to go right along the inside of the wall, and open the main gate. The other two thousand would go with him.

'Lead the way to the agora,' Crocus said.

'We have done our part,' a gladiator replied. 'We have earned our pay and freedom.'

There was no point in arguing. They had done all that Ganymede had promised.

'Down the road straight ahead, take the third street on the right. It will bring you to the agora.'

Crocus set off into the city. It was quiet, as quiet as that night in Eryx. The only noise was the tramp of Alamanni boots, and the subdued rattle of their weapons and shields. The sounds echoed back off the blank walls of the houses on either side of the road. It was as if all the townspeople were already dead, or had fled.

One street opening to the right, then another. Crocus counted them off on his fingers. It would be easy to get lost in the endless city. All the streets looked the same.

Noises now from behind. Doors being kicked in. Men shouting. Things being smashed. The slaves were in the city. True to their nature, they had abandoned their duty, and turned to looting. The uproar would wake the dead, warn the defenders.

Crocus moved to a jog. The Alamanni pounded after him. Something was missing. The slaves were sacking the populous district of Achradina, but he could hear no women screaming.

Preoccupied, Crocus almost missed the turning. He swerved into the street. Ahead, hemmed in by a hundred paces of blank walls, he could see out into the open space of the agora. Still no resistance. He started to run.

Half the market place was in deep shadow, the other half bright. It was surrounded by tall civic buildings. There was no one in sight. The second war band would seize the buildings. Their broad stone walls would make strongpoints. Crocus led his men diagonally across the agora to take the street that led to Ortygia.

The houses here were tall. They threw black shade across the street.

Crocus stopped running, slowed to a walk. The Alamanni behind him barged into one another. It was a dead end. A barricade blocked the street. There were men behind the barricade. Crocus looked up. There were men on the roofs of the houses.

And then he realised the depth of the betrayal.

'Loose!'

The thirty archers behind the barricade released as one.

Trumpets relayed the command through the city.

The street was dark, the bowmen nervous. At a warning shout, the Alamanni had hunkered down behind their shields. Not many were hit.

The real damage came a few heartbeats later, from above. Innumerable bricks, stones, chunks of masonry plummeted down, clattered off shields, thumped into bodies, cracked into skulls. Those that missed shattered on the paving stones, sent razor-sharp fragments slicing across the road. Men reeled as if at some insane midnight revel. Pain and shock rendered them oblivious to their danger – until, struck by other projectiles, they sank to their knees, or crashed straight down, measuring their full length on the ground.

If it was hard for a man to guard against the wicked barbed steel flying at his chest, and at the same time the jagged weights that sought to crush his skull like an eggshell or mangle his shoulders, it was impossible to see the shards hissing thigh-high to tear open flesh and muscle or punch deep into groin or buttocks. The Alamanni were warriors, not soldiers.

Desperately they sought to shield themselves and their close companions, acting in small groups, not as a whole unit. They bunched up, left gaps, offered ever more targets.

The clamour lifted to the heavens. Even in the gloom, the rivulets and spreading pools of blood seemed to shine.

'Amazing,' Maximus said. 'A stratagem of yours that actually worked.'

'Not yet,' Ballista replied. 'Not until the Alamanni break.'

As a good Roman general should, Ballista had stationed his command group to the rear of the fighting line. Backing the archers at the barricade were two lines of spearmen; backing them, four of swordsmen. For sure, they were only militia, but it was a strong position which screened the place from where Ballista watched with the others: his son and Tarchon, Maximus and Grim the Heathobard – now raising the White Horse standard – and a couple of trumpeters, the latter now all but redundant in the tumult. Their mounts were further back, held by the other selected fifty horsemen. If the night went well, they would play their allotted part later. If not, they would lead the rout back to Ortygia.

'Sure, it was mainly my idea anyway,' Maximus said.

'Utter bollocks,' Tarchon said, adding thoughtfully, 'you vainglorious Hibernian gobshite.'

'As if you could find your arse with both hands,' Maximus replied without animosity.

'Will the two of you shut the fuck up,' Ballista said.

Whoever led the Alamanni had good sense. Ballista heard him yell to his men to get into cover in the houses. The warriors scuttled, bending like men caught in heavy rain, to the various doors. While some held shields over their heads, others tried to break open the doors with their shoulders, their boots, the pommels of their swords.

Ballista looked at the roof above the nearest doorway. Two men were straining to lift a large building block over the parapet. He watched as, with an awful inevitability, they pushed it clear. The massive weight dropped into the abyss. It shattered the flimsy roof of shields, and dashed two warriors to the ground. Ballista thought he heard their bones snap above the general cacophony. Their companions stepped over them, and resumed their assault on the stubborn wooden boards. They could batter away until the end of time. The Alamanni were not to know that behind the woodwork, the doorways had been bricked up.

It was the same almost all the way back to the Little Harbour Gate. The trap had been carefully laid in the last few nights. Just two roads had been left open – the one here, to the agora, and one halfway to the main gate. The side streets had been barricaded. All the inhabitants along both routes had been evacuated to Ortygia. The first few houses inside the city had been left empty, to entice looters, and not to arouse suspicion. The ground floor openings of the others were sealed. Their roofs were crammed with defenders, not just the militia, but thousands of volunteers – old and young, men, women, even children. A brick dropped by a child can kill as effectively as one dropped by a trained soldier.

The closest group of Alamanni gave up their hopeless pounding on the door. They pulled back into the centre of the street. A tall warrior with braids to his shoulders was summoning the others. They came, hurdling their own fallen. All tried, but not all succeeded in dodging the never-ending hail of missiles.

The long-haired leader – miraculously untouched – was shoving them together, making them overlap their shields like tiles. Once the shieldwall was formed, he disappeared into its cover.

As far out into the agora as Ballista could see, the other Alamanni were following this example.

The shieldburg was strong and well sited. Arrows either pinged off the metal bosses, or failed to penetrate the linden boards. To reach the makeshift defence, stones had to be thrown from the roofs, not dropped. The heaviest could not reach. The lighter ones caromed off.

Still, the occasional missile got through, and the noise and level of imminent danger inside the claustrophobic shelter would soon shred the strongest nerves. The Alamanni could not stay huddled there for long. Their obvious recourse was to retreat, holding their formation, through the agora and back to the Little Harbour Gate. But it was a long way, all of it exposed to their enemies. There was no way they could strike back. Nothing undermined morale more than a feeling of helplessness. Ballista doubted they could make it. Even elite regulars would crack under such prolonged strain.

It tempted the gods to celebrate a victory before the field was won. Yet Ballista felt a certain exultation creeping over him. It had been a radical ploy, but it was undeniably going well. Ganymede in the enemy camp, and the six gladiators at the city gate, had done well. Of course, they had been promised the earth. Ganymede would be as rich as some senators in Rome. No doubt the civic council of Syracuse would quibble and wriggle once they were safe again, but Vopiscus had underwritten the payments. Ballista hoped the gladiators had got away. Ganymede, somewhere in the heart of the rebel forces, faced the hardest task. The wealth of Croesus was no use to a dead man.

In the time a man could take a breath and yawn, all the nascent self-satisfaction drained out of Ballista. The nearest shield wall broke apart. Its occupants hurled themselves at the barricade. A final throw of the dice. Their leader must have weighed up the options, and decided they would fight their way out by attacking. If they broke through here, they might yet snatch an improbable victory.

The defending bowmen jostled and impeded the spearmen and swordsmen in their haste to avoid the onrush. Some of the spearmen stepped forward, levelled their weapons over the barricade. But others hung back. The Alamanni did not face an unbroken line of spear points. Already some of them were on top of the low wall of mortared blocks. Their long swords slashed down at the heads and necks of the spearmen.

At the rear of the defenders' formation, the swordsmen were looking over their shoulders; the first one tried to slip away.

Maximus was quicker off the mark than Ballista. The Hibernian intercepted the swordsman, and killed him with an extravagant flourish, designed to impress.

'The next one gets the same.'

The rear rank stood irresolute, torn between fear of the enemy and this no-nosed apparition.

Ballista drew his sword, moved to join them.

'Stand and fight!' Ballista shouted. 'One last effort! Throw them back, and we have won!'

It was going to take more than words. Maximus and Tarchon beside him, Grim and his son behind, he shouldered towards the front.

The leader of the Alamanni was the first over the wall. At the sweep of his blade, the spearmen cowered back. The Alamann leapt down into the cleared space.

Allfather, it is him again.

The *F* branded on his forehead, the long blond braids.

'Here you are, Dernhelm son of Isangrim.'

'A man has to be somewhere.'

They both crouched, poised on the balls of their feet, perfectly oblivious to the storm raging around them.

'Wherever a man goes . . .' Ballista said.

The Alamann completed the saying: '. . . old enemies will find him.'

Their blades shifted, as if of their own volition, like snakes waiting to strike.

'Tomorrow one of us will drink with the Allfather.' The eyes of the Alamann never left the tip of Ballista's sword.

'Give yourself up.'

'And be thrown to the beasts, or nailed to a cross?'

'I swear you will have your life.'

'And my men?'

Ballista was silent. He might secure the life of one man.

'You and me,' the Alamann said. 'Snow blowing from one tree to another.'

'From one tree to another,' Ballista said.

The Alamann thrust to the face. Ballista turned the blow with the boss of his shield, and flicked a low, underhand jab to the thighs. The Alamann swept Ballista's sword wide. They both took a step back, recovering their stance, respecting the other's skill.

A movement in the corner of Ballista's vision. His standard falling. Poor old Grim. The Heathobard was down. His son darting forward, grabbing the shaft with his right hand. The boy had dropped his sword.

Where in Hades are Maximus and Tarchon?

Marcus retreated, fending off a flurry of blows with his shield.

The distraction almost cost Ballista. As he twisted away, the edge of the Alamann's blade scraped across the mail links protecting his chest. His assailant's momentum drove them together. Face to face. The white *F* stark on the tanned forehead. The Alamann's beard scratching Ballista's clean-shaven cheek.

They wrestled, inside each other's blades. Neither could get his weapon to bear. The Alamann's eyes went very wide. His mouth opened in a silent shout.

Maximus spun away. With the grace of a dancer, the Hibernian parried a blow from the man he had been fighting.

The Alamann tottered back. His left leg was laid open, almost severed. He sank to the knee of his good leg. Weapon and shield discarded, he clutched the gaping wound. Blood pumped through his fingers. His dark blue eyes fixed on Ballista's.

'I thought you more of a man,' the Alamann said.

'I still have both legs.'

'True.' A faint smile through the grimace of pain. 'Another time.'

'If the Allfather decides,' Ballista said.

'I am done.' The Alamann lifted his chin, exposed the soft throat beneath his beard. 'Finish it.'

The last straw, as the Christians said, that broke the camel's back. They said something else about camels – something inexplicable about one passing through the eye of a needle. Only their lonely and strange god could explain it.

The death of the chieftain had been the last straw for the Alamanni. All hope vanished, they were running. The majority of them were running. A few groups retreated at a walk, resolute and defiant, huddled together with their shields up – like Socrates after the defeat at Delium. Such courage would not save them, only prolong their suffering. If the townsfolk on the roofs ran out of missiles, they would hurl tiles, prise loose the cornice stones. The Syracusans would not easily be sated with blood.

Christians and a long-dead philosopher – Ballista questioned if he was going down with a fever. More likely he was stunned by the noise, and the wonder of his own survival.

'Some thanks would be polite.'

Ballista stared blankly at the Hibernian.

'For killing the big Alamann.' The tone was teasing.

'Actually,' Marcus said, 'my father killed him.'

They were alive! His son and friend were alive! His mind had been too numbed to think. And there was Tarchon. He drew them to him, hugged them. But poor old Grim. Ballista looked around. The Heathobard was standing there, looking sheepish.

'My lame leg,' Grim said. 'It gave way, dropped the standard.'

They dragged him, too, into their circle. They patted and slapped each other, like puppies, swearing and laughing until the tears coursed down their faces. At an angle, the White Horse standard draped itself over their heads and shoulders.

They were alive! But this was not the time to celebrate. The night was not over. Ollius had most of the gladiators behind the barricade on the other side of the agora. He was an experienced officer, and would know when to unleash them and the picked militiamen on the last of the rout. He would hound the Alamanni through the dark streets to the Little Harbour Gate, snap at their heels until they were driven out of the city, give them no time to rally. Not that the Alamanni would have the heart to regroup. It would be a massacre.

One last thing that Ballista had to do. One last thing that would end the insurrection.

'Time to go,' he said.

They walked back to the horses. Ballista accepted a leg-up. He was exhausted.

At the head of the cavalcade, he rode through quiet streets, untouched by the fighting, down to the gate by the Great Harbour. They rode out into the abandoned district of Neapolis, past the amphitheatre, the Great Altar, the theatre. Clear of the suburbs, they went north-west across the plain. The sky was lightening. Bands of slaves were fleeing the city, some heading inland towards the mountains, others making south for the Elorine Road. They posed no threat. There was no fight in them, if there ever had been. Despite the atrocities, Ballista felt compassion for those furtive, scurrying figures. It was not their fault they were slaves. Their past had been brutal, and now their future was bleak. A few might escape abroad; some might melt back, undetected, into the population of the island, or scrape a living as brigands in the hills. Most would be hunted down. Those summarily executed would be fortunate. The rest were destined for the cross, the arena, or the slow death of the mines.

The heights of Epipolae looked down from the right at the jingling column of horsemen in the half-light. The fifty riders following Ballista's *familia* wore mismatched, elaborate armour. Inlaid helmets, chased breastplates, silver devices nailed on their shields – either antique heirlooms, or made to order. Their wearers, young Syracusans from good families, had money, and they knew no better. Safer to have unadorned armour, a painted shield. A spear point might catch in such fancy metalwork.

They rode beyond the fortress of Euryalus, then circled round, and approached it up the gentle slope of the road. The western gate was open. There were no sentries on the walls. The sky ahead was pink and the clouds gilded. Dawn's fingers were reaching ahead of the sun.

The cattle were gone from inside the gate. The fences of the pens had been trampled. Most of the wagons were still there. Men were looting their cargoes. Those who had not already drunk themselves insensible took to their heels at the sight of the horsemen.

The smaller tents had mainly been flattened, but the big pavilion still stood. Men were dragging out any valuables. Some were so intent, they did not think to run at the approach of the horsemen. Riding in from the west, perhaps the plunderers mistook them for a body of well-mounted insurgents.

'Maximus, you and Tarchon catch some of them, and see if you can find out where Soter has gone.'

The Hibernian tossed his reins to Ballista, dismounted, and stumped off with Tarchon.

Ballista was tired, and eased his back against the rear horns of the saddle. He smiled across at his son. The sun was lifting over the horizon, and the heavens were rafted with purple and gold. It was pleasant enough here, sitting on his horse. To the right, the walls of the keep of the old fortress glowed with the new day. Defying the centuries, they still stood tall. At the very top, a raven stretched its black wings, warming them in the sunshine.

Maximus and Tarchon came back.

'He disappeared after he got word of the defeat. That is all they know. But I found Ganymede.'

Ballista raised his eyebrows.

The Hibernian shook his head.

Where would the slave-king have gone? Ballista gazed round. *Disappeared.* If the wonder-worker was not found, wild rumours would be whispered down the years in the dark of slave-prisons. A tiny glimmer of hope in the blackness of servitude. A beacon to further insurrection.

The raven cawed loudly from the walls.

The slave-king had not gone far.

'Oath-breaker!'

The raven took flight as the figure appeared on the top of the wall. It circled once, then alighted on the man's outstretched left hand.

Ballista reined in. Behind him, he heard Maximus telling the horsemen to surround the keep, make sure there was no way out, and find the stairs up.

'An oath taken under duress is not binding.'

Ballista looked up at the figure: one eye, long white hair and beard, a spear in hand, a hooded cloak over the purple tunic.

'I thought better of you,' Soter said.

'You are not the first to say that, not even the first today.'

'You swore on the life of your son there, that you would give me Syracuse.'

'I can take you there directly.' Without turning his head, Ballista spoke quietly to his son. 'Is there an entrance to the tunnels in the keep?'

'Yes.'

'Take half a dozen men, make sure he does not escape.'

The walls were at least sixty feet high. If there was only one way up, it would be hard to get an armed man out. They needed to exhibit him, dead or alive.

High on the wall, the slave-king never took his gaze from Ballista.

'*There will come a day when sacred Ilion will perish.* Watching Carthage burn, Scipio recited the lines of Homer. Scipio was right. Rome will fall.'

'Not by your hand. Come down, and I will grant you a quick death.'

'It is not in your power to take my life or my freedom. And I can leave an example that nothing can erase.'

With a sweep of his arm, he launched the raven into the air. Then he jumped. For a moment he seemed to hang, the cloak billowing about him, as if he, too, would fly. Then he plummeted head first, hitting the ground with a hideous sound.

The violent movement and sudden noise made Ballista's horse rear. It bored into that of Maximus. They both had to fight to retain their seats. Even back under control, their mounts rolled their eyes and pulled against their bits, sidestepping, alarmed by the smell of blood.

High above, the raven cracked its wings.

In a spreading pool of blood, the face of the crumpled corpse was smashed beyond all recognition.

EPILOGUE

THEY HAD LEFT THE HORSES, and were walking along the upper slopes of Etna. The day was bright, and the mountain quiet. Just a thin rope of smoke rose from the crater to drift away and dissipate in the westerly breeze.

The troopships that had braved the winter sea had docked in Syracuse just three days after the siege had been lifted. The emperor had not waited to march troops from Milan. Instead, the garrison of Rome had been scoured for the expedition. Four thousand men of the Urban Cohorts had tramped down the gangplanks. Five hundred Praetorians, and the same number of the Imperial Horse Guards, had also disembarked, along with the latter's mounts. A day later, still somewhat unsteady and bilious from the voyage, they had fanned out from the city.

Marcus had ridden with the mounted column heading west, led by his father. At the bridge over the Symaethus beyond Hybla, a few hundred slaves had made a stand. They had scattered like chaff before the first charge of the cavalry. The rest of the march had been more like rounding up and butchering cattle. It was surprising with what docility the captives had met their fate. A few crosses had been knocked up as an example, but most had been beheaded. No prisoners had been taken. They would have slowed down the troopers. That could be left to the infantry on the coast roads. They could gather the numbers necessary to constitute a dire warning when they were crucified along the highways, thrown into the arena, or herded into the mines.

At Centuripae – mercifully untouched by the rebellion – they had halted for a day to rest the men and horses. Ballista had sought out Aulus, the potter and market gardener who had offered them hospitality on their desperate odyssey. Aulus had faithfully looked after the possessions entrusted to him by Falx, the fugitive-hunter. Declaring that Falx had turned traitor, and been killed, Ballista had awarded their ownership to their trustworthy steward. Thoughtfully, Ballista had signed a document to that effect, against the remote possibility that anyone should question its legality.

Ballista had sent the main body, under its own officers, ahead to Enna. From there they would advance to Himera on the north coast, then into the west. His father had retained a troop of thirty men, saying that he would take them to sweep for any renegades who had sought sanctuary on the slopes of the volcano. No doubt they would deal with any fugitives they encountered, but Marcus had guessed his father's actual intentions.

Clear of the foothills, Ballista stopped at the same place as before to proceed on foot. He had left Grim with the troopers and the horses. The old Heathobard was too lame for walking the mountain. Marcus knew that it amused his father to leave the proud and elaborately decked out Imperial Horse Guards – soldiers happier on the parade ground than in the field – waiting around under the command of the elderly northern barbarian.

It was just Marcus and his father, along with Tarchon and Maximus, who climbed the big outcrop of black lava, and passed under the cliff from which the deer had fallen.

Marcus was thinking about the girl. Most of his thoughts returned to her that night in the trees, with her tunic hauled up to her armpits. He knew it was wrong. In his mind, he was committing the very act that he had prevented the fugitive-hunter performing in reality. To distract himself from the arousing image, and the moral ambiguities it raised, he talked to his father.

'The revolt is truly over?'

'Apart from the retribution.'

'Do you think the slaves will believe their *Saviour* is really dead?'

The mangled corpse of the slave-king had been dragged down from Euryalus and nailed to a cross in the agora of Syracuse. His face had been unrecognisable.

'Time will tell,' Ballista said. 'It took determination to throw himself head first from that wall.'

'You sound almost like you admire him?'

'No – any fool or madman can show determination.'

'You don't think he believed in the freedom he preached? He never believed that the golden age could return, that Sicily could have been transformed into the Island of the Sun?'

'The motives of any man are unknowable, even to himself. Whatever they were, they were doomed to end in failure.'

'So you never mistook Soter for *your* distant ancestor?'

Following the example of the bodyguards, Marcus had slipped into the habit – a habit quite unacceptable to any stern Roman *pater familias* – of teasing his father.

'If *our* ancestor honoured me with his presence, I believe I would recognise him.' Ballista was straight-faced. 'Besides, the Allfather has *two* tame ravens.'

'Who do you think Soter was?'

'Just what that poor fool Caecilius said at his villa – a Syrian slave called Comazon, with a gift for languages, who had been trained as a magician and actor. Not much difference between those roles and leading men. Your words and gestures manipulate the emotions of your audience.'

'But Soter quoted Aristotle, and knew Roman law.'

'Perhaps before he was enslaved, he was someone else.'

They stopped talking because, just before they reached the tiny settlement, they sensed something was wrong.

The cow and her calf and the goats were not grazing in the meadow. The pigs were not rootling under the trees, and the chickens not pecking in the dirt of the yard. The walls of the two huts and the barn still stood, but they were blackened and scorched, and their thatch was gone.

Marcus tried to emulate the instinctive, almost feral, menace with which his father and the other two prowled through the place.

There were no bodies. That was something.

'They got away,' Marcus said.

'But the life they knew is gone,' his father said.

Ballista sat down on the scarred stump where generations had chopped wood. He looked desolate. Next to him, for once, the irrepressible Hibernian Maximus was quiet. Even Tarchon appeared weighed down with sadness. Both gazed at Ballista with tenderness, as if they had seen him prey to such a mood before.

'Your coming here did not bring this down on them,' the Hibernian said. 'This is not your fault.'

'No, this is not my fault,' Ballista said. 'But this is always the end of war – the suffering of the innocents. This is the true pity of war.'

The others said nothing.

'Nothing more we can do here.' Ballista stood up. 'We had best get back to the horses.'

Marcus took a last look at the torched huts, at the trampled garden and vines.

'Let's go, Marcus,' his father said.

The young man turned, thought before he spoke.

'Marcus is a good name. But Roman children are called by their praenomen. From now, I will answer to Isangrim.'

AFTERWORD

The Roman Empire in AD 265

IN THE YEAR AD 265, THE ROMAN EMPIRE was in the midst of what is now called *The Crisis of the Third Century*. Plagued by political instability, civil wars, and barbarian invasions, central authority was weak. The emperor Gallienus only directly held Italy, Sicily, North Africa and the Balkans. Odenaethus of Palmyra ruled the East, nominally in the name of Gallienus, although the reality of his allegiance was suspect, and he was free to pursue his own policies. In the West, a campaign by Gallienus in AD 265 to recapture Gaul, Spain and Britain from the pretender Postumus ended in failure, with the emperor suffering a serious wound.

Our sources for this period are poor. The best attempt to stitch them together into a coherent narrative is by John Drinkwater in *The Cambridge Ancient History: The Crisis of the Empire, AD 193–337*, volume XII, edited by A. K. Bowman, P. Garnsey and A. Cameron, (Cambridge, 2005), pp. 28–66. Another useful starting place is D. S. Potter, *The Roman Empire at Bay AD 180–395* (London and New York, 2004), pp. 217–262.

Sicily

Sicily: A Short History from the Ancient Greeks to Cosa Nostra by John Julius Norwich (London, 2015) tells a lively story. The best introduction to the Classical period remains *Ancient*

Sicily by M. I. Finley (London, 1968). More recently, *Sicily under the Roman Empire: The archaeology of a Roman province*, 36 BC – AD 535 by R. J. A. Wilson (Warminster, 1990) is indispensable.

Unfortunately, for English-speaking visitors there is nothing more up to date than M. Guido, Sicily: *An Archaeological Guide: the prehistoric and Roman remains and the Greek cities* (London, 1967). For those with Italian, there is *Sicilia: Guide Archaeologiche* by F. Coarelli, and M. Torelli (Rome, 1984).

The Natural History of Sicily

Sicily looked very different in Roman times. The best modern travel books – *In Sicily* by Norman Lewis (London, 2000), and *Midnight in Sicily* by Peter Robb (London, 1998) – blame the deforestation of the island on the Romans. Archaeologists disagree (Finley, op. cit., p.5; Wilson, op. cit., p.6). The forests were cut down between the sixteenth and nineteenth centuries. Up to 40 per cent of Sicily was wooded in Roman times, compared with just 4 per cent now. The great bare slopes of the interior, seen as you drive the *strada della morte*, the E932 from Agrigento to Palermo, would have been thick with trees. Not only was the island better watered, and less eroded with more soil, the woods also would have sheltered large numbers of wild animals and small birds.

Many of the plants now considered distinctive of the Sicilian landscape (see Gavin Maxwell, *God Protect me from my Friends* (London, 1957)) were yet to be introduced. There were no prickly pears or cactuses, no bamboo or elephant grass, and no eucalyptus trees. Behind Palermo, the *Conca d'Oro* was not yet golden with orange groves.

Altogether the countryside might have appeared to us strangely north European, or certainly closer to the sylvan glades of the *Idylls* of Theocritus.

Roman Slavery

There are many modern studies of Roman slavery. Enjoyable ways into the subject are *Slavery in the Roman World* by S. R. Joshel (Cambridge, 2010) and *How to Manage your Slaves* by Marcus Sidonius Falx with Jerry Toner (London, 2014).

Imagining the thought worlds of ancient slaves was made intellectually respectable for scholars by Keith Hopkins, 'Novel evidence for Roman slavery', *Past & Present* 138 (1993), 3–27.

Slave Rebellions under Rome

The slave revolt on Sicily in the AD 260s is only attested in one sentence in a late and incredibly unreliable source. 'There arose in Sicily also a sort of slave-revolt (*etiam in Sicilia quasi quoddam servile bellum exstitit*), for bandits roved about, and were put down only with great difficulty': The Augustan History, *The Two Gallieni* 4.9. Of course, it may never have happened.

Slavery and Rebellion in the Roman World, 140 BC–70 BC by K. R. Bradley (Bloomington, Indianapolis, and London, 1989) was the ground-breaking work which identified the rare interlocking preconditions necessary for large-scale servile insurrection. *Slave Revolts in Antiquity* by T. Urbainczyk (Berkeley and Los Angeles, 2008) broadened the debate, and explored the possibility that some rebels aimed at the abolition of slavery.

Much can be learnt from three other books, each very different, all a pleasure to read. *Spartacus and the Slave Wars: A Brief History with Documents* by B. D. Shaw (Boston and

New York, 2001) gathers the evidence, and puts it in context. *The Spartacus War* by Barry Strauss (New York, 2009) is a model of popular history, underpinned by profound scholarship, and written with the skill of a novelist. *On the Spartacus Road* by Peter Stothard (London, 2010) is a captivating blend of history, travel writing, autobiography and philosophical reflection.

Syracuse

Syracuse was besieged several times in antiquity. Two sieges for which we have extensive material are that by the Athenians in 415–413 BC, and that by the Romans in 213–212 BC. Both are discussed, with full references to the ancient sources, in *The Encyclopedia of Ancient Battles*, edited by Michael Whitby and Harry Sidebottom (Chichester, 2017): the Athenian by Fernando Echeverria (vol. I, pp. 345–365), and the Roman by Eddie Owens (vol. II, pp. 727–735). The siege in *The Burning Road* draws heavily on both. The monument to Callistratus (Ch.18) was invented from an anecdote in Pausanias, VII.16.

Classical Echoes

The Golden Ass of Apuleius is the inspiration for both the description of slaves in the mill in the Preface, and the eunuch priests in Ch.9. The latter also owe a lot to Lucian, *The Syrian Goddess*.

When Marcus recites the *Iliad* in Ch.6, Ballista in Ch.20, and Soter in Ch.23, they do so from the translation of Homer by Richmond Lattimore (1951).

In Ch.7, Ballista and his interlocutor swap lines of Homer's *Odyssey* slightly adapted from the translation of Robert Fagles (1996).

Fittingly, the author of the poem credited to the cousin of Ballista's wife in Ch.11 is unknown. It is found in *The Greek Anthology* (9.499), and the translation is by Peter Jay (1973).

The prodigy of the deformed baby and its interpretations in Ch.11 are adapted from Philostratus, *Life of Apollonius*, 5.11–13.

The rustic utopia of the isolated herdsmen and their families in Ch.13 is inspired by Dio Chrysostom, *Or.7, The Euboean Oration*.

The comparison of slavery among the northern tribes and among the Romans of Crocus in Ch.23 comes from Tacitus, *Germania*, 20: 24–5.

Other Novels

All my novels include a couple of homages to other writers who have inspired me. In *The Burning Road* they are from Jim Crace, *The Pesthouse* (2007), and Cormac McCarthy, *The Road* (2006).

If you enjoyed *The Burning Road*,
why not join the
HARRY SIDEBOTTOM READERS' CLUB?

When you sign up you'll receive an exclusive short story,
THE MARK OF DEATH, plus news about upcoming books
and exclusive behind-the-scenes material. To join, simply visit
bit.ly/HarrySidebottom

Keep reading for a letter from the author . . .

Hello!

Thank you for picking up *The Burning Road*.

The inspiration for this novel, as for several others, was a Classical writer. An obscure ancient Latin biographer of the Roman emperor records a slave revolt on Sicily in the reign of Gallienus (AD 260–268). Sicily is a magical island, which I am fortunate to have frequently visited. I had long wanted to set a novel there. The ancient text gave me the chance to explore both the geography and culture of the island combined with the terrible institution of Roman slavery. A novel is the ideal medium to recreate slavery not only as a lived reality, but also its ways of thinking; the justifications and fears of slave owners, and the thought world of the enslaved. Most importantly of all it also provided an evocative background for a fast paced adventure. Ballista, the barbarian warrior turned Roman general, is shipwrecked into the chaos of a slave uprising. Danger lies in wait round every corner. No one can be trusted. To turn the screw Ballista has to protect his eldest son, an untried teenage boy. Together they must cross the island to safety, facing the many perils of *The Burning Road*.

If you would like to hear more about my books, you can visit **bit.ly/HarrySidebottom** where you can become part of the Harry Sidebottom Readers' Club. It only takes a few moments to sign up, there are no catches or costs.

Bonnier Zaffre will keep your data private and confidential, and it will never be passed on to a third party. We won't spam you with loads of emails, just get in touch now and again with news about my books, and you can unsubscribe any time you want.

And if you would like to get involved in a wider conversation about my books, please do review *The Burning Road* on Amazon, on Goodreads, on any other e-store, on your own blog and social media accounts, or talk about it with friends, family or reader groups! Sharing your thoughts helps other readers, and I always enjoy hearing about what people experience from my writing.

If you have any questions, or would just like to get in touch, please do so via my website – www.harrysidebottom.co.uk – or my Facebook page – www.facebook.com/Harry-Sidebottom-608697059226497

I have never enjoyed researching and writing a novel more than *The Burning Road*. I hope that readers catch that excitement.

Thank you again for reading *The Burning Road*.

All the best,

Harry Sidebottom

ACKNOWLEDGEMENTS

WRITING A NOVEL IS A SOLITARY THING, but, paradoxically, could not be done without others. It gives me pleasure to thank some of those who helped me manage.

Family: Lisa (to whom it is dedicated), my mother Frances, my aunt Terry, and my sons Tom and Jack.

Friends: (in Oxfordshire) Peter and Rachel Cosgrove, Vaughan Jones, Francesco Minto, Maria Stamatopoulou (and everyone at Lincoln College), Jeremy Tinton; (in Suffolk) Fiona Dunne, Sara Fox and Peter Hill, Sandra Haines and Jack Ringer; (in London) James Gill, Kate Parkin, Ben Willis; (in Sicily) Jole de Caro, Sergio Colletta, Tony Zannelli.